Hollywood Prince

NEW YORK TIMES BEST SELLING AUTHOR

KIM KARR

Hollywood Prince
Copyright © 2017 by Kim Karr
ISBN-10: 0-9976194-5-7
ISBN-13: 978-0-9976194-5-4

Cover design by:
Michele Catalano-Creative

Cover model:
Andrew Biernat

Photographer:
Wander Aguiar Photography

Interior design & formatting by:
Christine Borgford, Type A Formatting

Publicity by:
Social Butterfly PR

Hollywood

Prince

*"Never lose hope in love . . .
sometimes you have to kiss a lot of frogs to find a prince."*

~Unknown

PREFACE

The Prince of Tides

Amelia

I'm listening to this song by the Spin Doctors called "Two Princes."

The lyrics are similar to my story. Two princes. One princess. A choice to make. And perhaps even a happily ever after.

Unlike a fairy tale, though, my story doesn't start with "Once upon a time." Oh, how I wish it did. The thing is, a lot has happened in my life that made me who I am. And because of this, I have a lot of issues to resolve before I can get to the end. Yet, rest assured, in its true form—this will be a love story.

It has to be.

Like the song, it's about me and . . .

This one.

And that one.

You'd think choosing between Mr. Right over Mr. Oh-So-Wrong would be easy, but it isn't.

In the light of day, it all seems so clear, but now, in the dark of the night, Mr. Right doesn't seem so right, and Mr. Oh-So-Wrong doesn't seem that wrong.

I met one before the other. Spent more time with one than the other. Now one is ready for the next step, but I'm not sure about the other.

None of that matters.

What matters is in my heart, and I just have to dig deep enough inside to figure out what it is telling me. Move forward or go back. God, I wish I knew.

The doorbell rings.

Rushing over to the door, I swing it open wide, expecting my mother, my father, my best friend—anyone but him.

There he stands with a smile on his face and a bouquet of flowers in his hand. Before I can even take the flowers, I look at the cell clutched tight in my fingers. At the two words I don't know what to do with. They're from him. The other him. The other man, I guess you could say.

This isn't a love triangle; it never was. It's simply about choices.

This one.

Or that one.

Mr. Right, or Mr. Oh-So-Wrong.

With the text still unanswered, I stare into this man's face, and then at my screen.

Who should I choose?

I stand here, reeling, my mind wandering back to how it all began. How I went from searching for the right one to finding two men within twenty-four hours.

Two princes, but only one is meant to be mine.

CHAPTER 1
Blind Date

Amelia

A common misconception is that the *just be me* philosophy works in all situations.

Not true.

Yes, it's wrong to project a false idea of who you are, but a blind date is not the time to let all the skeletons out of the closet. The goal is to present the best version of yourself.

Right?

With that in mind, I stand tall and stare at the golden doors to a club that was once like my oldest brother's second home. Pushing away the memories of him, both good and bad, I suck in a breath and walk inside.

I can do this.

The Griffin is beyond filled to capacity. Wall-to-wall people. Anyone that is anyone in the city is here because this is the place to be. To party. Have fun. Who knows, maybe even hook up with an A-lister looking to have a good time—if that's your thing.

Glass chandeliers sparkle as I make my way through the crowd.

I can't believe I'm doing this.

After my last debacle of a blind date with the creepy guy who wanted to suck my toes, I told myself never again.

And yet, here I am. My stomach a-flutter with nerves and my heart filled with a little more hope than I should have in a situation like this.

Mr. Right has to be out here somewhere.

After all, there is someone for everyone in this world, or that's what I keep telling myself every time Mr. Right turns out to be Mr. Oh-So-Wrong.

It might sound like I'm always looking for a man, but I'm not. It's just at twenty-five I don't want to waste any more time with someone who doesn't get me, or that I don't get. I want to find, and yes I'm going to say it, the one who completes me.

Noisemakers and party hats poke me with each step I take. I glance around, over, and through the people. The velvet benches are occupied by couples shoving their tongues down each other's throats, girls chatting animatedly while smoothing their hair into place, and men high-fiving each other as women walk past them with a suggestive sway to their hips.

I forgot how entertaining places like this can be, and I slow a little to pay more attention.

A woman pushes her breasts into a man's hard chest and looks up at him with fluttering lashes. A guy squeezes a girl's ass, and she whirls around and slaps him in the face. A couple bump and grind like porn stars in a booth.

A tap on my shoulder has me whirling around, wondering if I need to slap someone or rather if my blind date has found me before I could find him.

"Aren't you Brandon Waters little sister?" the stranger asks.

The stranger standing in front of me is a tall guy. Very tall. He has jet-black hair and blue eyes. Just by looking at him I know he's not my date. With his earring, his designer jeans, and his ultra-expensive leather jacket, there's no denying, though, that he must have been one of my older brother's friends. "Yes, I am," I answer.

He sniffs, and his blue eyes start to glaze over as his pupils swallow up their color. A look I know all too well. "I thought so. I wanted to say hi. Brandon and I used to have a great time together. I miss him. He was one of the best guys I ever knew."

I find myself smiling. That was Brandon. Just a giant ball of fun. Everyone loved my oldest brother.

"Sucks about what happened to him," the guy tacks on.

Just like that, my smile fades, and I have to curl my hands into fists to stop them from shaking.

The memory of Brandon's overdose is still so raw, even though it has been almost three years since I found him unconscious on his bed, needle at his side, dressed in his suit as if he'd needed a hit before going to work. I called 911. He was dead before he arrived at the hospital. DOA. Three letters never hurt so much.

That day changed my life.

My brother Camden couldn't forgive him for the longest time, but now seems to have let his anger go.

Me, on the other hand, I can't seem to let anything go. Everything in this city reminds me of him, which is why I can't stop thinking about him and the *if onlys*.

If only I'd gotten there a little earlier.

If only I'd known.

If only he had confided about his addiction to me.

If only.

If only.

If only.

Then again, how had I never seen how bad his addiction was? Too caught up in living my own life, I hadn't paid enough attention. College had meant freedom for me, and freedom had wrung its bell—loud and bold.

Dazed, I force the smile back on my face at the guy standing in front of me. "Yeah, it sucks, that's for sure."

That might have come across snarky. It wasn't meant to. It's just that words meant to ease heartache don't always do it.

"I didn't mean it that way," he responds with a bite of his own in his tone.

Taking hold of his arm, I look into his eyes. "No, I get it. I miss him too."

The guy shakes his head as if I've disappointed him in some small way. Like I'm a bitch who doesn't understand. I get it, okay? I get it.

"Well, anyway, it was good running into you," he tells me uncomfortably, and then walks away, more than likely to join a group of others I am certain also *loved* Brandon.

I watch him for a moment.

Wistful.

Full of memories that I don't want to spill over into tonight.

Brandon's sticky note on my bedroom door that read, "I needed to borrow your laptop. I'll have it back to you first thing in the morning."

The laptop had my paper on it.

I needed it.

The next morning, and surprise, surprise, no Brandon.

My anger.

The phone call I made—how mad I was when he hadn't answered.

The fact that I stormed over to his apartment at nine in the morning, yelling how irresponsible he was as I walked through the door, angrily grabbing my MacBook off his couch, almost leaving, but taking a minute to peek into his bedroom . . . and finding him.

So still.

So cold.

Lifeless.

Sucking in a deep breath, I look around and let it out, along with the memories. The memories of the three Waters children. The ABCs is what we called ourselves. Amelia, Brandon, and Camden.

This was Brandon's favorite club. See, everything in this city has Brandon's imprint on it. He'd been sneaking in since he was seventeen. I wasn't even fourteen the first time I overheard him talking about the place. I used to listen and think about how much fun it would be to go with him.

I asked.

I begged.

He never let me.

In fact, he and Camden never even let me go to a bar. Said they'd tell our father if I did. So I didn't, not until the day I turned twenty-one.

Drinking wasn't the only thing my two older brothers curtailed.

Dating in high school was also a challenge.

Each of them in his own was so protective of me, but the two of them together were enough to send any potential suitors away.

Looking around at this scene, I'm sort of glad they were the way they were.

I kind of miss it.

Shoving aside my sadness, I grab my camera—I use the real thing, not a smart-phone app—and focus on the neon lights before I start to take photos.

Snap.

Click.

Scan.

Behind the lens, I can lose myself. Forget who I am. Forget what happened to Brandon. Forget the fact that Camden left New York. Even push aside who I wish I could be. *In another life*, I tell myself, like I always do.

Shrieking has me lowering my camera and looking around.

I think that might be Justin Bieber over in the corner. Yes, by the horde of girls flocking to him and screaming out his name, it definitely is. They have stars in their eyes and hearts to be broken, and they don't even know it.

It sounds cynical, but it isn't.

Reality is not cynical.

Reality isn't defined as thinking you are going to meet the love of your life in a bar, either.

So what am I doing here, you ask?

I'll tell you—I felt this little thing called hope in my belly and couldn't ignore it. It happened when Carter Kincaid, my best friend, uttered that dreaded phrase: "I have the perfect person to set you up with."

Yes, I rolled my eyes. Like we haven't heard those words a million times. Still, I thought, what if I say no and this one frog finally turns out to be a prince? The guy I'm searching for to spend my life with.

The one.

My unicorn.

The pessimist in me didn't jump at the opportunity. It took some convincing, a little bribery on Carter's part, but finally I relented and said yes.

Clean cut. Wavy brown hair. Nice build. Above average height. That's how my best friend described the guy I am meeting tonight.

Seriously, could the depiction be any more generic?

Eyes searching, I hope to locate Carter and perhaps wring his neck before finding my date, because this is a mob scene that I could have done without. There is no way I'm going to find anyone I know tonight, let alone someone I've never met before.

Click.

Snap.

Scan.

I take a few more photos.

Looking through the shutter of my lens, I search for the up-and-coming Yankees baseball player who is to be my date.

With a description as generic as tall, dark, and handsome, my chances of finding him were close to zero.

Luckily I searched him out on social media, so I have an idea of what he looks like.

Click.

Snap.

Scan.

I'll give myself five minutes to locate him; if I don't find him by then, I'm out of here.

Pushing my way through the crowd, I stop at the staircase and look down. Much to my surprise, I spot the Yankees pitcher in the sea of black tuxes and silver-sequined dresses at the bar. Then again, who wouldn't be able to spot him? His Bahama-blue bow tie is bright enough to light up all of Manhattan.

Totally cute, by the way.

Feeling a little nervous, I let my camera drop and slowly walk toward him.

Wearing a shorter-than-normal dress and a pair of higher-than-usual heels, I attempt to gracefully descend the steps.

Don't trip, don't trip, don't trip.

Carter told his new boyfriend's brother's newer roommate that I'd be the one wearing the pink mod dress with the gold braiding around the neck, a big gold bangle up high above my elbow, and that I'd be further accessorized with a large camera around my neck.

Now, that is a much better description for locating a blind date. And kudos to myself for finding the Twiggy-replicated dress in a vintage store in the Village.

It is fantastic.

Not to my surprise, I catch the soon-to-be star baseball player's eye just as my gold vintage heels hit the marble floor.

It's the camera.

To be expected, he's sitting with his head twisted over his shoulder, looking around. Even after halting his search, he looks uncertain. To assure him it's me, I tap my camera. Right away his face breaks into a grin.

Okay, this is a good sign.

As I get closer, he stands up from the stool and heads in my direction to greet me.

Nice manners.

Big brown eyes focus on me. I smile at him with a nervous, "Landon Reese?" to which he cutely replies, "Guilty."

This is going so well.

"Amelia Waters?" he asks as if still questioning I'm his date for the night.

"Guilty," I repeat with a smirk that makes me feel more than a little spunky right now.

His grin grows wider.

Mesmerized by it, I stare at his handsome face. With his square jaw, chiseled nose, and strands of curly hair that dip over his brows in the sexiest way, I have only one thought—he's no frog.

CHAPTER 2
Say Anything

Amelia

There are three defined phases of a blind date.

The first, and definitely the hardest, being the greeting. The second being the actual date itself. And the third, well, that would be the good-night kiss.

I feel a little warm and giddy inside because Landon and I have successfully made it through the first phase. That is, until he goes in for a hug as I go in for a forearm pat, and his embrace locks my right arm to my chest and presses my camera into my ribs.

Awkward.

Even worse, he smells like Tom Ford, the Tobacco Vanille scent—the very same kind of cologne my father wears. Instead of being left with the heady impression the scent claims to have on women, I feel a little less enthused than I had five seconds ago, and for some reason less excited to be here.

Things aren't going as well as I had originally thought.

"Happy New Year!" he shouts into my ear, still holding onto me.

"Happy New Year," I echo, trying to wiggle out of his big-muscled hold.

Letting go of me, his hand slides down to my ass and his fingers splay wide, like as in they cover an entire cheek.

Whoa!

He is way too aggressive for this stage of our date. He needs to back down. *Way* down.

"Come on, let me get you a drink and then we can dance," he says, already ushering me toward the bar with that large palm of his.

Dance?

I haven't danced since Brandon died. Perhaps I should keep that little fact to myself. Yeah, I probably shouldn't tell him my dead brother danced all the time and dancing will probably remind me of him, and in turn make me sad.

Give this date a chance.

With those dreary thoughts still in my head, I smile at Landon and grab hold of my camera like it's my security blanket, and sidestep the issue. "Sure, a drink sounds great."

Carter insisted I come tonight because he feels that since I was promoted this past summer I'm working too much, and not spending enough time socializing. To sweeten the deal, he asked if I would help him take photos for his stock image library.

My best friend knew I wouldn't turn down the opportunity to snap pictures.

It's scary how well he knows me.

We met our freshman year at NYU in Photography 101, and our passion for taking pictures and everything sixties bonded us from our very first hello.

Back then I was naïve and thought my father would end up letting me pursue the career path I had dreamed of ever since I received my very first camera at age eleven—working for a publication like *Rolling Stone*, *Cosmopolitan*, or even *National Geographic*, photographing people for journalists to tell the subject's story to the public.

Back then I also thought I could go back in time and live in the days when the mashed potato was a dance and not something you ate.

Neither was possible.

Yet, a girl can dream. My maternal grandfather had given me that camera with a note that read, "Don't forget to capture all the moments that really matter." He died a year later. Sadly, though, capturing moments—professionally, anyway—was not in my future because as a Waters, like every Waters before me, I was destined to go Columbia Business School, obtain my MBA, and be trained to one day run The Waters Group.

"What would you like?" Landon asks me when we reach the bar.

I shimmy onto the only open barstool, and by doing so, I effectively force his hand off my ass. "I think I'll have a cosmo."

The tall, hourglass-shaped bartender practically runs toward us and gives the newest Yankees rookie her immediate attention. If you ask me, the busty blonde's smile is in hopes of more than a big tip. "Another gin and tonic?" she purrs.

Landon tosses the overzealous woman the same grin he greeted me with as he leans forward to speak. "Yeah, sounds good, and a cosmo for my lady."

The way he rolls the *l* in *lady* causes me to forget all about the similarities in his greetings between the bartender and myself, and instead causes a shiver to run down my spine. Makes me wonder what else he can do with that tongue.

God, I'm all over the place with my emotions tonight.

Up.

Down.

Next thing I know, they'll be sideways.

In case you can't tell, it's been a while since I've had sex. A year to be exact. Last New Year's Eve, Darren, my boyfriend of an entire month, broke up with me when we ran into his old girlfriend at the party we were at. Turned out, he discovered they were meant to be.

Whatever.

Just another frog turned toad, instead of prince, in a long line of them.

As the bartender starts mixing and pouring, Landon returns his attention my way and then to my lap—more specifically, to the bands of nude satin at the top of my thigh-highs.

You see, my dress rode up a little when I sat, and I have no way of pulling it down without being obvious.

His eyes burn in that direction.

Looks like obvious it has to be. With his eyes still glued to my lap, I shift a little and tug my dress down, or at least I try.

Nothing.

I get a whole lot of nothing.

The dress is simply too short.

What I do get, though, is the wispy lace of my panties rubbing against me. And you guessed it, right there. Not sure I should have worn these skimpy panties at all because now I'm turned on, and not necessarily by my date. I shift one more time to adjust them.

Those big brown eyes are enjoying the lap dance he's getting. Well, not a real lap dance, of course, but my lap is moving back and forth. And yes, I've actually been to a strip club, so I know what I'm talking about.

The sexy lady behind the bar sets our drinks down. "Here you go. Cosmo and gin and tonic with an extra lime."

Landon directs his attention her way.

Saved by the blonde.

Hallelujah.

Quickly, I lean forward and reach for my drink and then, I un-characteristically down the entire thing.

So very unladylike.

My mother would be appalled, if we were actually on speaking terms and she had a say in the matter, but we haven't gotten along well since she left my father for a younger man.

Moving on, after the talk about my brother with that perfect stranger and my erratic nerves, I really need the alcohol to help calm me.

A little surprised that I drained my glass so quickly, Landon stares at me with his glass midair as if he was about to make a toast.

Oops.

"Sorry, I was thirsty," I lie.

By nature I'm not a liar. Not at all. But this little white one is in the best interest of not airing all my dirty laundry.

So incredibly cute, all he does is laugh.

And just like that, I've decided I like him.

The bartender sighs and without prompting, mixes me another. Make that two more. Wednesday night or not, it's New Year's Eve, so why not?

Scooting to the edge of my seat, I rearrange myself one more time in the process. Mission accomplished. For now, anyway. Or at least until I have to move again.

"Anything else?" the bartender asks.

Landon's attention goes to that sugary-sweet voice once again and as he tells her no, he quickly pays for our drinks. Then, turning a little, he faces me and cocks a hip against the bar. "So, Amelia . . ." He lets my name hang.

Unable to cross my legs for fear of another wardrobe malfunction, I slowly twist my stool in his direction. "Landon." I smile, filling the silence. "I hear you're new to the city."

"Yeah, I am. Really new. In fact, I moved here from Atlanta the day after Christmas."

"Don't you have to head back south for spring training?"

He nods. "Tampa. I thought I'd make the move while I had at

least a month of less intense training. As a rookie, my time isn't really mine." He says the last part with a smile, like he loves not having any time. Loves his job. It's such a turn-on.

I lift my glass. "Well, Landon, welcome to New York. What do you think so far?"

He clinks his gin and tonic against my cosmo and his brown-eyed gaze roams over every inch of me. "Unfortunately, I haven't seen much of the city yet. I've been pre-training all week. Maybe you could show me around before I have to leave for Florida?"

With more than a sip of my fruity concoction, I nod and smile. "Yes, sure, I'd love to."

Okay, great. We are on track.

Landon's slow grin warms me and the feeling goes straight between my thighs.

That upward tilt of his mouth has me staring at his lips. Wondering what they taste like. How they would feel on other parts of my body.

"So, the test is over?"

It stays fixed even as I ask, "What?" over the rim of my cosmo.

"The toad test."

As what he is saying clicks, I fight to keep my smile in place, but can't hold back my horror, and my jaw drops.

"Since you already agreed to a second date, I have to assume I passed," he laughs, turning to one side to show off his profile, then to the other side to show off some more, until finally he looks at me again.

Trying not to spit out my drink because crimson has already coated me from the top of my head to the tip of my toes, somehow I manage to choke out my response. "Actually, it's a frog."

He snaps his fingers and points at me. "Right, the frog turns into a toad if you kick him aside. Kind of like Cinderella's carriage turns into a pumpkin."

I pick my jaw up off the ground. "Carter told you about my theory?"

The guy next to Landon vacates his stool and Landon takes a seat, swallows a sip of his drink, and then looks at me. "Actually, Carter told his boyfriend, who told his brother, who told me."

Laughter spills from my mouth, and a joke is the only response to that total and complete embarrassing information leak. "That's a mouthful. Why don't you try to say that ten times fast?"

Landon is good-looking and I can't help but stare at his mouth as he sucks on an ice cube, chews it, and then clears his throat. "Here goes nothing," he says. "Carter told his boyfriend, who told his brother, who told me you've gone out with a lot of frogs and they all turned out to be toads." He pauses and holds up a finger. "Carter told his . . ."

I grab his finger and push it down. "Kidding. I was just kidding."

Landon swivels his stool to fix me with an intense gaze. "I could totally do it, you know."

Okay, he's funny, and I like him.

"Hey, love! There you are."

Before I can answer Landon with a flirty, "I'm sure you *can* do it. In fact, I'm sure you can do anything you put your mind to," that very familiar British accent has me twisting my stool.

Dead meat. Carter is such dead meat.

Just at the exact moment I turn around and realize the tops of my stockings are once again showing, Carter decides to snap my picture with his top-of-the-line Nikon. The flash blinds me and I lose my balance while trying to pull my dress down. Before I can stop myself, I'm sliding right off the stool.

Falling.

Falling.

Falling, right onto the floor.

This isn't really happening.

"Are you okay?" Both Carter and Landon ask in unison.

Blowing the hair from my eyes, I look at them in utter embarrassment.

Seriously, what could possibly be worse than this?

Ever the gentleman that he is, Carter outstretches his arm. But Landon has his hands under my ass—of course he does—and is hoisting me onto my wobbly heels before I can grab for Carter's hand.

Now standing upright, I pull my dress to cover up the naughty parts that anyone else sitting down there might have seen.

Luckily, I was the only one on the floor.

Squaring my shoulders, I stare at the two of them, who have moved past my mishap and are introducing themselves to each other.

Hello. Hello. What about me?

Landon is holding out his hand toward Carter. "I've heard a lot about you."

Carter reciprocates. "Not all bad, I hope."

My little incident is long forgotten.

Okay, this is good.

Embarrassment over.

Landon shakes his head. "No, man, not at all."

Oh no. Carter is not getting off that easy. I kick him.

"Ouch."

"Oops," I say and take a sip of my drink.

With a careful nod, he looks at me. "What was that for?"

Ignoring his question, I smile and say, "Right before you showed up, Carter and I were discussing the fact that you have a big mouth."

"Me?" he asks innocently, and slaps his hand to his chest for added effect.

"Yes, you," I tell him and leave it at that.

We will talk later. He and I will definitely be having a chat about what he is and is not allowed to repeat to his new boy-friend. Especially the *friends trump lovers* rule that he should already know.

"So," Landon says to him, "You're here to take pictures tonight?"

"Yeah, party scenes make for great stock images."

"I bet they do." Landon smiles.

"Well, listen, I have to run. I just wanted to say hi," Carter says.

"How about a drink first?" Landon offers.

Dismissing the idea, Carter raises his camera. "Working tonight, I can't, but you two have fun."

Practically forgetting I am supposed to be helping him, I raise my camera. "I got some good shots on the street before I arrived and some inside here earlier. I'll email you everything tomorrow."

"Bloody awesome," he says removing my camera from my neck.

"Hey, what are you doing?"

"Taking this. I'll drop it off at your flat. Don't worry, love."

My head tilts to the side in confusion.

"I already snapped more than enough. I'm quitting soon and meeting Eli at his place."

Accepting that my working for him was simply a guise to get me out, and that now my work is over, I raise a brow. "For a midnight kiss, perhaps?"

Carter gets embarrassed easily talking about anything sexual in front of strangers. It's the British in him. The façade that he is all buttoned up is hard to take. He is anything but. I mean, he leaves the porn channels on all day long. Since I know this, I can't help myself. "Maybe even a little New Year's Eve shag?"

Carter and Eli have been dating for two weeks and have yet to do the deed. Carter isn't normally like me. Which is to say, he doesn't wait to have sex. He doesn't abide by the three-date rule, like I do, or any rules for that matter. However, with Eli he hasn't made his move. I think he's waiting for the moment to be perfect.

How romantic.

Carter narrows his stare at me. "You never know what the night will bring."

I smile at him and kiss him on the cheek, then whisper, "Yes, you never know."

Carter smiles. "I'll call you later."

"You better."

He then gives Landon a nod. "Treat my girl right," he says before leaving the two of us alone again.

"He seems like a great guy," Landon comments when Carter is out of sight.

"Yeah, he is. The best," I say, and take my seat at the bar.

Landon sits too, and leans in close.

Close enough that instead of his cologne, I can smell the gin he's been drinking and also catch a whiff of the soap he uses. Fresh and clean. Irish Spring I'd bet. When I ignore any lingering tobacco-scented cologne, he smells like a whole lot of yum. Out of nowhere, I have this urge to lick him.

It's the alcohol.

"So, Amelia," he says, and once again leaves the word hanging.

Smiling at his nervousness, I stare at him and I swear I feel my clit pulse so frantically that I have to squeeze my thighs together. "So, Landon," I lamely respond.

His tongue slides along his bottom lip, leaving it glistening. "Tell me your favorite things to do in the city."

I cross my legs, knowing exactly what I'm doing, and start talking about the Met, Central Park, and all the hidden places I escape to and photograph.

His eyes are once again glued to my lap and they widen more and more with every word I say.

Just like that, we are in phase two of our blind date, and in the words of my best friend . . . it is going bloody well.

Or as my brother Camden would say . . . fanfuckingtastic.

CHAPTER 3

Mean Girls

Amelia

Traveling back to the gilded age at The Griffin is a long-reigning favorite pastime of New York City's nightlife elite. The supercharged and hyper-swanky atmosphere is favored by the city's jet-set crowd, Wall Street wolves, top fashion models, and entertainment moguls. And of course, their sons and daughters, too.

Four drinks, and more than an hour and a half later, I find myself about to do something with Landon I haven't done in a while.

Dance.

My anxiety increases tenfold as Landon makes his way through the crowd and leads me up the stairs.

Back on the main level, the crowd is jammed elbow to elbow. The dance floor is all the way at the back of the club and it might take a while to get there.

Which good, because I could use the time to gather my courage.

Passing the built-in benches wedged against the wall, I find myself searching the faces of those sitting there. Most I don't recognize. And though some of them are people I know, from where

I'm not exactly certain.

I think one of them is a famous DJ who spins records, or whatever it is DJs do these days. Oh, and I think that is Ed Westwick sitting in the corner. I met him once when he was filming *Gossip Girl* outside my school. Oh, oh, I think that is Jensen Ackles on the dance floor. Although I wouldn't swear that it is. I really don't care for supernatural television shows. I prefer comedies to drama because I like to laugh. Hate reality TV. And love to watch old *Batman* reruns.

Now movies and Hollywood film actors, they're a different story. I love watching movies of all kinds, from romantic comedies to scary thrillers. I don't discriminate, but the sixties, sex-kitten kind are my favorites.

Suddenly, Landon's cologne seems to have grown stronger. The smell of tobacco almost suffocating me, I have to hold my breath.

When my gaze lands on a familiar female face, I forget all about the scent in the air. She's no celebrity or mogul, but wolf—that title fits her perfectly. Although I prefer to use the term *ice queen* when it comes to her. My workmate, who also happens to be my brother Camden's ex-girlfriend, is sitting with her back pressed against the velvet cushion, and some guy who I can't see at all has his face buried in her neck.

I never liked Vanessa.

Ever.

I avoided her when she was with my brother, and now I avoid her in the office at all possible costs. Luckily, The Waters Group is big and we rarely run into each other.

How Vanessa managed to win over Camden's heart and befriend Brandon, too, is still a mystery to me. I never understood it.

Still don't.

Thank God, Camden finally came to his senses and ended his

relationship with her. Something big went down, though, because he not only broke up with her, but also took off for California at the same time. Incompatibility is what he claimed as the reason for their breakup. I know there was more to it but didn't push him to tell me. He was upset enough. Besides, it wasn't any of my business anyway.

And with the fucked-up condition of our fractured family, I didn't blame him for moving across the country. I've thought about it many times myself. Just never got the courage to leave my father here alone.

Those vibrant green eyes of hers lock on mine. Vanessa is beautiful. Tall and thin, with long, dark hair and a confidence about her that brings men to their knees.

Seriously, I don't get it. I mean as soon as she opens her mouth, that snotty personality has to snap men out of her hypnotic spell.

Yet it doesn't.

Like I said, I don't get it.

The club is lit in lines of silver and gold. Confetti is being thrown everywhere. I think the room might be spinning. No, that's my head. Needing to catch my breath, I tap Landon on the shoulder. When he turns around, I tell him I have to use the ladies' room. Leading me there, he stops at the end of the hallway and leans against the wall. I give him a smile and a peck on the cheek, and then make my way toward my destination.

Seeing Vanessa with another guy is opening up the closet full of memories I want to keep shut. Reminding me of my reality.

That Camden is gone.

That Brandon is dead.

That my parents are divorced.

That I hardly speak to my mother.

And that I really don't like my job. The fact is that took the job working for my father because I don't want to disappoint him, not because I want to be there. I had to do it, though. My father had already lost so much, there was no way I was about to let him down and do something other than work for The Waters Group.

Inside the glitzy walls of the restroom, I take one breath, two, three, and four. After having calmed myself, I splash water on my cheeks, my throat, the insides of my wrists.

Rolling on some lip gloss and powdering my nose doesn't change much. I'm one hot mess. Trying to fix my hair, which at this point in the night is completely unfixable, also doesn't change much.

Frizz is in style, or so I've heard anyway.

I fuss for a few seconds with the part that is far over to the right and tuck some of my shoulder-length hair behind my ears. I've thought about cutting my hair even shorter, like Twiggy once did, but with the amount of volume and natural curl I have, I might look more like a chia pet than a girl.

Giving up on my appearance, I place my palms flat upon the vanity and look at my flushed reflection in the mirror.

This is the face of a woman who is lost. Looking for something at every turn that she very well may never find.

Do happy endings even exist?

Glancing at myself again, I catch sight of that one place that once held a strand of turquoise hair. It was my long forgotten quest to be who I wanted to be.

Sad. Really freaking sad.

I've always been of the school of thought that resolutions are not special. If you are the kind of person who waits for a new calendar year to make changes to your life, then that's unfortunate. After all, the reason you always give up on said resolution is directly correlated to the fact that you made one in the first place. If you want to go to the gym more, or be more confident and speak up at work more often, or travel more, just start doing it now. I think my point is that New Year's resolutions don't mean crap because it's the doing that matters, not the making.

And yet, I find myself about to make one.

I look into my own eyes, the pupils dilated so wide the black almost overtakes the normal gray. My tongue sneaks out to lick my lips and then I find my mouth moving on its own, silently making my resolution: *This year I vow to figure out what makes me happy. What I want out of life. And to live my life the way I want to live it.*

Another glance in the mirror, and I feel better already.

After I use the facilities, I approach the vanity again, this time to wash my hands, before I return to my date and see what the night brings.

"Bad hair day?"

Just as I'm pumping soap into my palms, the hairs on my neck stand up. The haughty tone is a dead giveaway as to who has joined me in the restroom. I don't even have to turn around.

Sashaying next to me, Vanessa sets her red crystal clutch on the counter and opens it up.

Already washing my hands, I try to hurry.

"You know, my stylist offers a treatment to help control curly hair," she continues as if we are actually having a conversation about my hair.

With daggers in my eyes, I turn in her direction. "I like my hair the way it is, thank you very much."

Grabbing her lipstick, she applies the red like she's the devil herself. "I'm trying to be nice, Amelia. It's an olive branch."

Rinsing the soap from my skin, I turn the water off and twist toward her. "An olive branch?" I laugh. "What on earth for?"

Running her fingers through her dark hair, she looks at me in the mirror. "You are so clueless."

"What the hell are you talking about?"

She shakes her head and snaps her clutch closed. "Nothing."

The towels are next to me and I grab one. "No, Vanessa, don't say *nothing*. Why don't you tell me what's on your mind?"

Those Louboutin pumps, which she is never without, slap against the marble floor as she moves for the door.

Normally, I'd let it go. Confrontation is not my thing. Not tonight. I could blame it on the alcohol or the skeletons this place has brought out of the closet, but the plain truth is I just don't like her. "Come on, Vanessa, talk to me. Wait. I know why you're leaving. After all this time, you're still upset about the way my brother dumped you, aren't you?"

She whirls around with the eeriest of smiles on her face. "No, Amelia, I wasn't leaving because of Camden. I was leaving so I wouldn't tell you the truth about your family."

With narrowed eyes, I practically dare her to continue. "Truth? What truth could you possibly know?" I laugh.

She takes a step toward me. "The truth that your father had been cheating on your mother since the day they married. Or the fact that your mother finally left your father because—"

I cut her off. There's a good chance I'm in an alternate universe right now. "Liar!" I shout. "My father never cheated on my mother. In case you are unaware, she left him . . . for another man. You're just upset over the fact that my brother didn't want you anymore, and I was happy about it."

She shakes her head calmly. "You are so delusional, Amelia. It was I who didn't want him anymore."

I give her a haughty laugh, similar to one of her own.

Her smile grows wicked. "Poor little Amelia. You have always been so clueless."

Outrage burns in my blood. "You're the delusional one. And now you're making things up to get under my skin."

Vanessa is suddenly in front of me, frowning. "That's just it, I'm not. You're the one who has always lived in your own world. Up high in your tower. You're the one who all the Waters men consider to be a princess. Poor little Amelia, so fragile she might break."

"That's not true," I say in a flat voice because if I really think about it, that might just be true.

"Open your eyes for once, Amelia. See what you're missing. Your life isn't the picture your family has painted for you. I promise."

Emotion rises in my belly. There's something not untrue about what she is saying. I blink away tears and swallow them as I try to sort through her lies.

Standing taller than me, she glares down. "Haven't you ever wondered why your parents broke up so soon after Brandon's death? I mean they'd been together for so many years, so why then? Why, when the family was already so fractured?"

There's a pause as if it is my turn to speak. I don't. I have wondered that, but I know why—my mother strayed from their relationship. Found another man.

"It's because your mother blamed your father for Brandon's death. She might have lived with your father's philandering for all those years, but Brandon, that was too much."

"What the hell are you talking about?"

There's a wicked gleam in her eyes. "Your father was the one who introduced Brandon to this scene. Got him in the clubs. Hooked him up with the ladies, and I guess in a roundabout way, the drugs. Of course he never thought Brandon would take it as far as he did."

My vision is swimming and all I can do is shake my head no.

"Come on, little A, you can't be *that* naïve."

"Don't call me that."

"Right. The ABCs. That term of affection was only meant for the three of you. Your little club. Amelia, Brandon, and Camden. But I guess that's all gone."

"Stop it!" I shout.

She shakes her head no. "There's one more thing you should know."

I want to cover my ears.

"Haven't you wondered what could have been so bad between us that Camden felt he had to leave New York?"

Clutching the edge of the vanity, I'm finally able to speak reasonably. "I know what was so bad—the thought of seeing *you* every day."

She laughs. "No, not me, but your father, yes. You see, he caught your father and me together—fucking on the dining room table at Thanksgiving."

"Liar!" I scream.

The cold-hearted bitch laughs. "But I'm not."

"You are."

"Then tell me—haven't you ever wondered why we don't see each other at work?"

I stare at her.

"It's because your father has asked me to avoid you. He doesn't want you to know about us. He doesn't want you to know about a lot of things. But protecting you from the truth was Camden and Brandon's job, not mine."

My mind drifts to the man I saw her with less than five minutes ago. The salt-and-pepper hair of the man kissing her. The fact that I thought Landon's cologne got stronger for that one moment I was passing by her. Was that man my father? Or just someone who looked like him? Oh, God, I'm going to be sick. I run into the bathroom stall and slam the door closed.

"Happy New Year, Amelia," Vanessa coos, and as I drop to my knees on the floor, I hear the door shut behind her.

My heart is pounding.

My head is spinning.

Outrage burns hot and heavy in my blood.

Liar. She is such a liar.

Isn't she?

Pulling my shit together, I rush to go after her. To see for myself that the man she is with tonight is not my father.

Right at the end of the hallway is my worst nightmare. A man I can't see with his arms outstretched as Vanessa falls into his embrace and kisses him right on the mouth.

Bitch.

Skank.

Whore.

I suck in a huge breath, trying to ease the tightness compressing my chest.

This isn't real.

I'm imagining it.

It's not him.

He looks taller than my father. Slimmer. And much more casually dressed than my father ever would be.

To be certain it's not him, I decide to take a step forward. Another. One more.

Suddenly, a large torso blurs my line of sight. *Move it, buddy,* I think. I have to be certain, and besides, I have a lot more names to call her. Trying to push the big body out of my way, I don't succeed. When he doesn't move, I look up and see who it is.

"Are you okay?" Landon asks, staring at me with concern in his chocolate-brown eyes.

On tiptoes, I look over his shoulder. They are gone. And I'm left wondering if it was my father. If her words are true. Something tells me they are, and the thought is too much to bear.

"Are you okay?" Landon asks again.

No, I'm not okay. My world is crumbling around me in the most unexpected way. Yet, I keep that fact to myself and instead say, "Yes, I'm fine."

Just as he takes my hand to lead me back into the club the crowd starts to shout, "Five, four, three, two, one. Happy New Year!"

With that I stop and push Landon up against the wall and then throw my arms around his neck so I can kiss him right on the mouth.

Confetti streams through the air. Noisemakers are loud in my ears. And people are still screaming Happy New Year.

Landon's lips are soft and warm and when he pushes me against the wall, his eagerness has my heart beating faster. Our teeth bump and our tongues clash as our mouths move fast, and faster still.

Certain that if we weren't in a public place his hand would be under the hem of the dress, I feel a jolt of excitement at the thought of him diving between my legs.

Delirious, or maybe drunk, or maybe just needing a distraction, I kiss him for a long time before I pull away and look up at him, wondering if he is the one.

Breathing hard, Landon presses his forehead to mine, wordless.

With what has to be the cheesiest line in the book, I murmur, "Why don't we get out of here and make our own fireworks."

And just like that I have officially obliterated the last two stages of a blind date, and all my rules, too.

Fuck it.

Who needs rules?

All they seem to do is break you.

With that cold, hard truth, I pull back and look into his eyes. Yes, I might be about to turn this night into more of a one-night stand than an everlasting love affair, but I don't care right now.

Hey, love everlasting might be way overrated, anyway.

CHAPTER 4

Roman Holiday

Amelia

Pajama bottoms are so 2009.

Wearing nothing more than a T-shirt and the wisp of lace I dare to call panties, I roll over and squint as the sunlight streams through my bedroom window.

Landon is beside me with a cup of coffee in one hand and a plane ticket to California in the other. "Time to rise and shine, sleeping beauty. You have an hour before you have to be at the airport."

Sitting up, I rub the sleep from my eyes and try to remember what happened last night, and how the hell I decided to fly out to see my brother.

Oh, yes, right. Me being me, I started crying before Landon and I even got in the cab. And before we even made it to my apartment in the Village, I had told him everything.

Even though he had his hands all over me at the club last night, once I had broken down, he turned into a perfect gentleman. The whole damsel-in-distress thing does it to men. Kills the desire, that is.

Anyway, he listened to me.

Talked to me.

Even gave me the quarter I used to decide what to do.

Alcohol raging in my blood, I resorted to the age-old way of deciding what to do. Heads, I was going to California to talk to my brother. In person. Find out what the hell was going on. Tails, I would stay in New York and call him. Once I'd sobered up, of course.

As crazy as it sounds, I left my fate in the hands of that coin. Tossed it high in the air, caught it, and covered it with my other hand. Then slowly I lifted my palm. Heads it was. And as fast as I tossed the coin, I bought my ticket.

Landon didn't make a move on me, but he did sleep beside me. Such a change from earlier that night when he was all hands and mouth. Then again, letting your skeletons out of the closet is like pouring ice water over someone else's libido.

I told you so.

Yet, as I sit here right now, in a flimsy T-shirt and no panties to speak of, his gaze roams hungrily, and I have to say, I like it.

With a secret smile, I take the cup from his hands and sip the hot liquid, and then I groan.

"Head hurt?" he asks.

I nod. Normally, I'm not much of a drinker, although after last night, I'm not sure he'd believe me.

In the blink of an eye, he's handing me a glass of water from my bedside table and a couple of aspirin. "Here, I thought you might need these."

"Thank you," I say, and look at him. And think how gorgeous he is. How hot he is. How perfect he is.

Wow!

How cruel life can be?

I finally find someone who might have turned out to be my prince, and I'm not sticking around to find out.

I can't.

Now isn't the right time for my happy ending. There is a lot about my life I have to figure out. Starting with what the hell has my family been keeping from me?

I never thought of myself as naïve—boy, was I wrong. I feel like I've been living in an alternate universe. Perhaps a delusional one.

Tossing back the pills, I drink the water and grab my old camera. After snapping Landon's photo, I look at him and smile. "You're definitely not a toad."

Landon moves a little closer, caging me in. "If you didn't have to leave right now, I'd have you on your back, showing you just how much of a toad I'm not."

The camera falls beside me, and I find myself breathing heavily. "Can you hold that thought?"

"I'm not sure," he breathes.

It happens all at once, so smoothly, how he pulls me close to him, like he is going to kiss me again. But at the last second, I turn my face, unable to allow things to move any faster when I'm leaving. "We shouldn't," I whisper.

Landon smiles and everything inside me melts. Then he pulls me closer anyway and kisses my neck. Loving the way his no longer clean-shaven face rubs against me, I thread my fingers through his hair and give in to this one small moment of intimacy. "I feel like you're saying goodbye," he says between kisses against my throat.

I toss my head. "Not goodbye, really."

He pauses his kisses, and his breath is hot on my cheek. "For some reason I feel like you're never coming back to the city."

"Oh, I'll be back."

His mouth slides up, and he kisses me on the forehead. "I'll call you because I like you, and I want to see where this goes, but I have to tell you I'm not so sure you'll be back."

And it's then I think, with the feel of this man on my skin, this man who I really want to get to know, this man who might be my Mr. Right, that neither am I.

Neither am I.

CHAPTER 5

When Harry Met Sally

Brooklyn

I'm easily seduced—by places, that is, not women.

Backgrounds draw my attention. Growing up as Hollywood royalty, I have to admit it's in my blood. I'm always looking for the perfect location to set a movie. I film different settings to look at later. Search for inspiration I don't even know I'm looking for. Find the perfect this or that to fit in with my story.

Lucky for me, California is one of the best states for riding a motorcycle. With its thousands of miles of scenic routes, elevation changes, and twisty roads, to me it is one of the best places in the world to ride.

I rode over Tioga Pass on my BMW Roadster a couple of years ago and fell in love with Yosemite. So much so I stayed extra days to film the still waters, and I ended up writing a bit, too.

Sonora Pass is another favorite place of mine. Snow-covered mountain peaks, meadows, waterfalls, and a whole lot of nature make for an interesting ride. Also, the roads are steep and narrow with some sudden drop-offs, which keeps the ride fun and exciting.

Need that little rush every now and then.

Today I celebrated the New Year with a cruise along the Pacific Coast Highway in the rain, enjoying its tight little slick curves and the danger of it all.

Nice thing about places, as opposed to women, is that I can like more than one of them at the same time and not be accused of philandering.

The memory of what happened last night hits me like a slap in the face.

Went to the Montage for a party. Ran into a chick I've known for years, started talking about old times, and after midnight we decided to make the party private. It was then this other chick showed up that I'd taken out last week, and before I knew it they were both accusing me of being a cheater.

A cheater?

Fuck, no.

I don't even think I knew either of their last names.

Pissed as hell, I crashed by the pool—alone.

Who needs that shit?

Women.

Sometimes I just don't get them.

The possessiveness.

The black-and-whiteness of relationships.

It boggles my mind.

Then again, maybe, just maybe, the problem is me, not them.

To be blunt, women are a giant pain in the ass. Always looking for something from me I can't give them. And that's the problem right there: they are interested in Brooklyn James the ex–television star, the Hollywood Prince, not the real me.

You see, almost eight years ago I was famous. Pretty fucking famous. As the star of the MTV reality show *Chasing the Sun*, I was a teen who loved to surf, and had a team of execs who wanted to film me doing it.

Cool—right?

Not so much.

For years a crew of cameras followed me everywhere. And I mean *everywhere*, as I made my way around the California surfing circuit, navigating not only the waves, but life, too.

Unsupervised, my life was full of things not every teen would be allowed to experience—women, waves, and wild turns, all the time. Whenever I wanted any of them, it wasn't a problem.

The show was doing well, but I quit after I went off to college at UCLA. I'd had enough of the lack of privacy. You might not think so, but it can drive a person crazy.

So yeah, at the young age of eighteen, my television career was over. And shit, I was more than ready for it.

Yet all these years later women still keep thinking a camera is going to pop out of the shadows and they are going to be famous, like the chicks it happened to back in the day. Every time with every chick is like they're auditioning for my next new show.

Last night was no different.

Same old shit. Different day.

And to boot, they have this whole possessiveness thing going on.

I just don't get it.

The rain continues to fall, and I pull over to flip open the shield on my helmet. Moving once again, the cool air blasts my face as I ride faster.

Weaving in and out of traffic, I lean left, lean right, swerve over a hill, around the bend, and then before I know it, it's dusk and I'm slowing to take the turn onto my street.

After I graduated college, I told myself I'd take a year to get my shit together and figure out what I wanted to do with my life.

Needing to get out of LA, I left and came to Laguna Beach. I couldn't remain in my famous mother's shadow or try to clean up the darkness my father's bad reputation had cast on me any longer.

That was almost three years ago and I'm still here, and although I know what I want to do with my life, I'm still trying to figure out how to do it—from Laguna Beach.

Staying here has kept my mind free. Still, I know if I want to take my screenwriting career all the way, I should move to LA.

Yet moving back to the same old scene I grew up in scares the living shit out of me. Losing yourself in the fame, fortune, and women is just too easy.

I saw it happen to my old man, who before I was born was an A-list actor. Witnessed firsthand how his need to be on top destroyed his life. Took him apart piece by piece until there was nothing left but a washed-up hack. I won't let it happen to me.

Acting, though, would be an easy out. But after seeing what happened to my father I'm glad it isn't my gig.

I studied film because I want to create movies, not star in them. Two years ago I started to write my first screenplay, so I felt vindicated for a while that I still wasn't settled in my career—that I still wasn't sure what direction my life would take.

I finally showed *Fangirl* to my mother on Christmas Day. Emma Fairchild is a very independent woman. Broadway star turned film actress turned director, she's never been able to stay married for longer than two years. But let me tell you, she knows her shit in Hollywood. To be honest, she's a powerhouse. Everyone wants her attention. She's gold, considered Hollywood royalty since the day I was born.

So when she said my screenplay was good but it lacked real emotion, I felt a little crushed.

Okay, more than a little.

In her defense, she wasn't totally heartless; she gave me some ideas on how to improve it.

I trashed it the next day. *It was shit.*

Thank fuck I have my lifeguard job to help relieve the draw on my royalties from the syndication of *Chasing the Sun*, or I'd be in some serious financial trouble until I get my other manuscript polished and ready to show people.

If that doesn't happen fast, though, I might be taking the network up on their offer for a little reunion show, and won't that just rain down all kinds of chaos on my life?

Fuck me.

Riding slowly, I pass the house I rented when I first moved to Laguna years ago. Back then I lived with Camden Waters. He is my brother's—well, half-brother's—best friend, and mine too, I suppose.

At the time, Maggie May lived alone next door, until her best friend moved in with her. A woman Cam was instantly smitten with and couldn't get out of his head. Then one day he told me he was in love and asked if I minded moving next door, so that Makayla could move in with him.

Asshole.

Not really. I love the guy like a brother, and honestly Maggie's house was nicer anyway. So it all worked out.

No longer my place, I push on to the next beach bungalow. The one I now live in—alone, most of the time, anyway.

The place isn't mine. Like my last place, I rent. It still belongs to Maggie, who just so happened to marry my brother. I knew her first, but there was never anything romantic between us. I met her lifeguarding, and she, like Cam, and unlike me, grew out of that job and went on to bigger and better things.

Just a year ago, she met my brother. She and Keen are so much alike it's no wonder they hit it off. Anyway, last year Maggie moved out and moved to West Hollywood with my brother, where they live with their two-month-old son, my nephew, Presley. The cute little family comes down on weekends, so Maggie's room has stayed intact, and because of this, my rent is cheap.

Yes, I'm surrounded by love, and sometimes it's too much. Sometimes I have to disappear to get away from it all.

Lost in my own mind, my head snaps just as I pass Cam and Makayla's place. There is a sack or blob or something of the sort on the front porch and it catches my attention.

Slightly concerned, I stop, remove my helmet, plant my boots on the ground, and push backward.

Fairly certain now that it is a person, I park my bike in the drive and open the gate. The rain is still coming down, but even through it, I can see the figure on the front porch is a woman with a mass of curls covering her face. For some reason she is slumped against Cam's front door with a winter coat wrapped around her and an older-looking camera hanging from her neck.

Paparazzi?

Taking the two steps up, I glance around. Looks like whoever she is, she's been here for a while. On one side of her are bite-sized bags of empty peanuts surrounded by a half dozen small vodka bottles, like the ones you get on an airplane. On the other side of her is a suitcase.

Ruling out paparazzi—they'd stay alert—my next thought is that this is possibly a homeless person seeking refuge from the rain on Cam and Makayla's porch.

My eyes wash over her.

I'd say homeless is out as well. Then again, the cleanness of her vintage-style coat should have given that away at first glance.

In what has to be the dickiest of all dick moves, I take advantage of her eyes being closed and lower my gaze, taking her body in. She's wearing a T-shirt with a peace sign on it and black yoga pants that cover shapely legs with a pair of what look like go-go boots on her feet. And her eyelashes—her lashes are so long, unlike any I've seen that weren't fake. A throwback from the groovy chicks of the sixties in a way, and I say that meaning in the most attractive way.

Lowering onto my haunches, I push her hair from her face and speak softly. "Hey, are you looking for someone?"

Rather than answer me, she slumps some more and is now practically lying on the porch, her mass of out-of-control curls once again covering her face.

Not wanting to startle her, I carefully try once again to push the hair from her line of sight. "Are you looking for someone?" I repeat.

Her eyes open and she sits straight up and then points her finger at me. "I know who you are," she slurs.

Great.

Another fan.

Another campout.

And here I thought those were over.

Wrong house, girlie, I think. Then I think, *No, this is great. Leave her here.* Cam and Makalya went with Maggie, Keen, and Presley to Mexico for the weekend. That means no one is home. I laugh to myself. She'll be waiting for the ex–television star Brooklyn James, who no longer lives here, for a long time.

On my heels, I'm about to take the two steps down and slither onto my bike to roll it out of sight next door, when she says, "You're the pool guy, right?"

Pausing with one foot on the first step, this time I can't contain my laugh. "Ummm . . . no, I'm not the pool guy. In fact, there is no pool at this house."

She laughs, and a small hiccup leaves her full lips. "Wait, wait, wait. I know who you are."

Here it comes—*Brooklyn James, the famous surfer, the MTV star, Hollywood's Prince. Can I have your autograph? Or better yet—wanna fuck?*

The porch creaks behind me. "Securty. Secrety. Secutiyity."

For some crazy reason, I have to laugh over my shoulder. "Security?"

Another creak. "Yes, that."

Unfazed in the slightest, I'm more bemused than concerned

that she is walking toward me.

"I probably set the alarm off trying to break in," she slurs.

Surprised by the quick closeness of her voice, I whirl around.

I should call the police.

I don't.

Her coat might still be on the ground, but her hot little body is only inches from mine. And this time when I look at her, I take her in fully. Mounds of curly light-brown hair. Petite. Perky little tits. Extremely toned limbs. Somewhat athletic in nature, but way more hot chick. As soon as my stare meets her gray one, my body gives a little jerk of excitement.

Chill, boy, chill.

Stranger danger.

Stalker alert.

And all that kind of shit.

Yet, I can't wipe the smile from my face because she is fucking adorable.

This girl is standing, or maybe I should say swaying, and she has her hands outreached like I might handcuff her. Kind of wish I had a pair of cuffs on me, because screw adorable, she's fucking gorgeous. A proverbial ten and a half, and I never rate any chick over an eight.

I tilt my head in a coy gesture, more than interested in playing along with her. Even if she is drunk, she's funny as hell. "Guess again."

She makes a face as if thinking really hard. "Gardner?" *Hiccup. Hiccup.*

Really enjoying this, I shake my head and make a buzzer sound. "In the rain? No. Want to try again?"

Those eyes sparkle with good humor, and this time she takes me in from head to toe.

I can feel her stare all the way to my cock. As soon as this girl sobers up, I'm so doing her tonight.

With her bottom lip between her teeth, she hiccups, "Another frog?"

"A what?" I ask, with a raise of a brow.

"I'd say my Prince Charring, Charming, but as of last night I've given up on furry tails, no, not bunnies, fairy tales, for a while."

Puckering my brows, this time I don't laugh. There's something sad in her voice and for the moment, I'm at a loss for words.

Trying to remain standing straight, she blows the hair from her face. "Who are you?"

"You tell me."

That's when she takes a step back as if suddenly she's worried about who I am. "It wubee just my luck that Jack the RRRipper decided to make a stop at my bruther's house tonight."

Her words are slurred, but I get the gist of what she is saying. Brother?

Fuck.

Fuck.

Fuckity fuck.

Surprised. Shocked. Stunned. I look at her. Her eyes. Her gray eyes. Then I see it. The resemblance is right there. *How could I have missed it?*

All of a sudden, I can so clearly picture the photo Cam has of her with their brother on the wall inside. I can also remember the one and only time I met her. I was ten and my mother sent me to visit my brother Keen in New York City. His father got called away on business and Keen ended up taking me to Cam's house for the weekend.

This is Amelia Waters.

The girl with all the dolls who made me play house with her, or Cinderella, or some fairy-tale crap like that, and then forced me to marry her. She was my first kiss, if you could call it that at ten. The girl I've laughed with on the phone more than a few times over the past two years.

The girl with the gray stare.

That stare that is slaying me right now.

The girl . . . who isn't really a girl. Not anymore.

"You're Amelia?" I finally manage to say.

She snaps her fingers and points at me. "Bingo."

All I can do is stare.

Leaning against the house for support, she lifts her finger a little higher. "And you are?"

Somehow I manage to utter my name. "Brooklyn James."

"Oh my God, Brooklyn!" she screeches and throws her arms around me. "You are my Prince Charming."

Pressed against her, I feel that familiar tension erupt within me.

Lust.

Desire.

That kind of primal need to fuck right here and now.

What the hell?

Asshole, she's off-limits. She's Cam's sister.

Right, I think, but I am not in the least bit convinced. Or my cock isn't, anyway; it's long and hard and throbbing in my pants.

And that's when I know it's time to get my head on straight. Carefully peeling her off me, I look at her. "What are you doing here?"

She stares at me for the longest time. Eyes moving from the top of my head to the tip of my toes.

Fuck, I think she just licked her lips like I might be dinner.

I clear my throat as a reminder that I asked her a question.

Again, she tries to steady herself and then she says, "I found some things out last night that were very disrobing, I mean, undressing, no I mean—" She continues to stammer.

Finally, I speak up. "Disturbing. I think you mean disturbing."

"Yes, that's what I said, disrobing. Anyway, like I was saying before you interrupted me, I'm here to talk to my brother and get to the bottom of it."

Unsure what to say to that, I stupidly ask, "Does he know you're coming?" I know he doesn't. He'd never leave her on his front porch in the rain.

Color appears high in her cheeks as if she's angry. "No, I told you I just found this stuff out."

Casting my gaze anywhere but at her because I think I might laugh at the little firecracker, I blurt out, "Cam is gone until Sunday."

Still angered, she points to the driveway. "But his car is here?"

There's doubt in her voice, like she's uncertain I'm being truthful. "That's not Cam's Jeep. It's Makayla's."

Pivoting on her toes like a ballerina, she points to my driveway. "Then that one is his."

I try not to laugh. I wonder if we're going to go duck, duck, goose, down the entire street. "That's not even a Jeep, it's a BMW, and it's Maggie's. She and Keen drove down from West Hollywood and left it."

Very gracefully, especially in her condition, she whirls around, and by the look on her face I think she finally believes me, but I'm not certain about it.

"Cam drove to Mexico," I tell her to prove my point.

Barely able to stand straight after her pirouetting stunt, she looks around before her eyes focus on a black bag near her suitcase. "Then I'll call him and tell him I'm here, and see when he can come home."

I stare at her. Her head is still moving with that shake of a no, but now her body is swaying. Worried she might fall, I step closer to catch her if I have to.

Somehow she manages to get to her bag, but when she bends down, she instantly stands up. "Wow, why are you making the porch spin?" she asks.

She's funnier than I remember. The serious girl who bossed me around has a silly side, or perhaps it's the booze. I slip my hand in my pocket and remove my phone. "Here, use mine."

Her hands bring it closer and then push it farther away. "What kind of phone is this?"

"Ummm . . . an iPhone."

"It's not in English," she says in frustration.

My snicker is hard to contain. Still, I somehow manage. I think she'd be pissed if I laughed right now. Closer and closer I move and flip it around—she had it upside down. Then I place my hands over hers to find Cam's contact and tap it.

Ring.

Ring.

Ring.

Then an answer. "You've reached Cam. Leave a message."

Beep.

She stares at it as if in shock and disconnects the call. "He's not answering. He always answers when I call."

Tucking my phone in my pocket before she drops it, I feel kind of bad for her. "He's in some remote location in Mexico with really shitty cell service and I'm sure the weather isn't helping. I have the phone number of the resort over at my place. You can call and leave a message for him at the desk."

Before I can catch her, she's sliding down the side of the house in utter defeat. I wish I had paid attention now when Cam tried to tell me where he hid the spare key after he had the security system upgraded, and what the new pass code to it is.

Next thing I know she's crying. *Crying.* Like waterfalls-of-tears crying. "Now, I'm homeless."

I bend and tip her chin toward me. "Hey, it's fine. You can stay with me."

She looks up and smiles. "You sure?"

"Yeah, of course."

All the color is now gone from her face. "See, you really are a prince."

Hardly.

If only she knew the thoughts running through my mind right now, none of them princely like at all.

"Vlka," she mutters.

"What?"

"Vokla," she says, this time licking those full lips again.

Shaking my head, I say, "Come on," and offer my hand. The last thing she needs is another drink. "I'll get your things after I get you over to my place."

"You're so nice," she slurs as she grasps onto my fingers and squeezes really tight.

She's light and I easily bring her to her feet, even with the Chinese finger torture she's giving me.

Before I know it, she's leaning against me again. I know that I shouldn't get aroused by this; trust me, I do. My cock, on the other hand—he has lessons to learn about friends' sisters because he's standing up for attention.

Sniff.

Sniff.

Sniff.

What in the hell?

Amelia is drawing air in through her nose while her head is buried in my neck.

"Are you sniffing me?" I ask her.

Not in the least bit fazed, she answers, "Yes, and you smell so good."

Yeah, my cock does a leap with the prospect of what that means.

Down, boy.

Not happening.

"Nothing like my father," she adds.

Okay, I'm so ignoring that comment.

Even though it kills me to untangle myself from her, I do. "Let's get you in bed," I tell her.

She purrs.

Actually purrs. Like she's excited about the idea. Does she think I'm joining her? I think she does.

Okay, maybe I will.

Twist my arm.

No! I have to squash that thought right now and it's so goddamn hard, but she's my best friend's little sister, and let's face it—Cam would fucking kill me if I touched her.

With my head on straight, I'm determined to get her in bed. I mean *to* bed. And not my bed.

I take a step.

Then another.

Things are going so well . . . until we get to the stairs and she looks at me like she's seeing stars, and passes out. Cold.

Great.

Just great.

Catching her, I toss her over my shoulder and try not to think about how soft the skin is on her back where her shirt has lifted. Or how shapely her legs are dangling in front of my chest. Or about the fact that judging from the low rise of her yoga pants, I don't think she's wearing any panties.

No panties.

Just kill me now.

CHAPTER 6

The Hangover

Amelia

Of all the miseries inflicted on humankind, some are so minor and yet, while they last, so very painful.

My head is pounding.

My stomach is rolling.

My eyelids can barely stay open.

How is it that after all these centuries a true remedy for a hangover has yet to be discovered?

Glancing around, I take in my surroundings. Bright, colorful tapestries and bold prints are everywhere. Different-sized paper lanterns hang from the ceiling above the bed. A crib is in one corner and a baby swing in the other. Piles of blankets and baby clothes are stacked on one of the chairs. And photos of a happy couple and their little baby cover the dresser. This room is filled with love from top to bottom.

I'm in my brother's girlfriend's best friend's room. Maggie May Masters used to live here, and by the looks if it, she comes back often. I've been here, but not since Maggie married and had a child. She was wild and single the last time I visited, which makes me realize just how long it has been.

Still, I'm thankful for where I am. At least this house is next door to *he who shall not be named right now*'s house.

I cover my eyes. Oh God, I can't believe my brother is MIA.

Good thing I met Maggie two Thanksgivings ago when I came to visit *the keeper of secrets himself*. So I'm not sleeping in a total stranger's bed.

Makayla, his girlfriend, had just moved in with him at the time—my secret-keeping brother, that is—and Brooklyn had just moved out. Brooklyn wasn't around, but Maggie, who is Makayla's best friend, and I had hit it off wonderfully. She is a lot of fun. And of course I fell in love with Makayla immediately. How could I not—I could see how much my brother loved her. Honestly, she couldn't be more perfect for *the evil one*. Even if I am mad at my brother right now, I am really happy for him. He deserves happiness.

A beeping noise has me trying to lift my head. My phone is on the night table and after two tries, I'm finally able to grab it. My father has called five times. Wonder if the bitchy witch Vanessa told him about seeing me? I can't imagine she did. I know I have to deal with my father, but I can't right now. Thumbing down, I read Carter's five text messages.

> *Carter: Are you there yet? Call me.*

> *Carter: Mia Girl, I'm waiting for your call.*

> *Carter: That's it. You are officially no longer my best friend.*

> *Carter: Okay, so I was hasty. Your status remains intact. Now call me.*

> *Carter: Amelia, I'm worried. Call me.*

Feeling bad I didn't call him last night, I shoot him a quick text.

> *Me: I'm here. Don't worry about me. I'll be in touch soon.*

And then I send a text to my mother, who I know I have a lot of making up to do with, but the way I'm feeling right now, that, too, will need to be postponed.

> Me: Hey Mom, I want you to know I decided to take a last-minute trip to see Cam. I'll call soon. And Mom, I love you.

I love you—three words I haven't spoken to her in a very long time. Like I said, if what Vanessa told me is true, and I think it is, I have a lot of making up to do.

One more text to Cam telling him to call me, and after I set my phone down, I decide it's time to get up.

Stumbling out of bed, I feel a slight draft. Looking down at myself, the first thing I notice is that I'm wearing a man's T-shirt—no, not just any man's T-shirt; it's the same black T-shirt Brooklyn was wearing last night under that fine leather jacket of his. I know this because it reads *Voodoo*. Last night I kept thinking it read *Vodka*, and all I wanted to do was lick him, and his brooding stare.

The second thing I notice is that I have no pants on, which means I'm bare down there. Having stripped my panties off mid-air yesterday because they were uncomfortable, I now can't believe I ever did such a thing.

Inside the bathroom, I use my finger to brush my teeth, search for some aspirin, find it, take it, and then look at myself.

That's one hot mess looking back at me.

Unable to stand this feeling, I decide I should resort to drastic measures to cure this hangover.

Let's see.

There's burned toast. Hate that.

Greasy food. Don't think I can stomach that.

A Bloody Mary. No way. No more vodka.

Carter swears by the harrowing concoction called "The Bull's-Eye." Which is raw egg mixed into a glass of OJ. I can't even. Just the thought gets to me. In fact, I think I just threw up a little in my mouth.

There has to be a better way to silence the house DJ playing in my skull.

I got it.

Extreme temperature change.

Opening the bathroom door, I'm back in Maggie's room. Somehow I manage to still the room long enough to make it over to the French doors that lead outside. I fling them open and stand there in the cool temperature, waiting to feel better.

Waiting.

Waiting.

Nothing.

No change.

Okay, I really need to amp up this cure.

Glancing around, I catch sight of my camera. That makes me smile. I brought my old one because Carter took my newer one on New Year's Eve. It's my most favorite one anyway. Maybe because of the happy memories it evokes, maybe because I want a piece of my past that makes sense—who knows.

Continuing to look around the room, I locate my suitcase lying on the floor. It takes more than five minutes to ward off the nausea while trying to find what I'm looking for, if I even brought it. I packed in a rush and just threw things in.

Ah-ha! Found it.

No, never mind. That is a bra.

Tossing it aside, I continue looking.

Hair tie. That is helpful.

Rifling through some more things, I find nothing.

Okay, so I have no bikini top or bottoms. And no underwear, either. *Great.* Doesn't matter. I find the panties I stashed away in my purse on the plane and slide them up my thighs.

Don't judge.

They are practically clean. I mean, I wore them for like a whole two hours.

Yes, I'm so convincing myself of this.

Whatever.

Here goes nothing.

CHAPTER 7

Splendor in the Grass

Brooklyn

Holiday weekends suck.

When you have to work, that is.

Even in the winter months, if I'm not painting or doing paperwork, I'm patrolling, which is my job today.

Shit, I think it is time for me to quit and start writing full-time because I really don't want to be out here.

The back-to-back storms blamed on El Niño are nothing to be happy about, although I can't say right now I'm that upset about them. With over two inches of rain yesterday and another three expected today, the National Weather Service is working on issuing a flash-flood warning for Southern California. And the only light at the end of the tunnel of this crazy weather is that it has warranted closing the beach.

Thank fuck.

It means I get to go home.

Although I'm certain Amelia will be passed out for many more hours, I'd still like to be around in case she wakes up. And not because I want to see that hot little body of hers or watch the way she puckers those sexy lips. No, that's not why. In fact, I don't know why. It's just that I feel like she needs someone to fuck—I mean someone to talk to her.

Yeah, talk to her, not fuck her.

Typical of storms like the ones we've been battered with the past couple of days, the clouds are darkening quickly and the wind is picking up speed. The waves are calmer than usual, but out in the distance I can see the whitecaps. A sign of what's to come. The rough waters are headed this way, and fast.

Chasing the last of the beachcombers away, I stick the "Public Beach Closed" sign in the sand and give one last look around. A couple of kids are being ushered up the pathway to the public parking lot by their parents and an old man is searching for loose change with his metal detector; otherwise, the beach is clear.

With a twist of the lock to the tower, I consider the run-swim-run workout I had planned to get myself home, but figure I should skip the swim part since I'd be breaking the beach rules I just posted.

Having jogged here, though, I have no choice but to huff it the two miles home. Staying as far from the shoreline as possible, I lunge forward, but don't rush. When the white clouds disappear, I decide to pick up my pace.

Light drops of rain slide down my face just as I hit the one-mile mark. That's when I start to run hard and fast. It's cool, though. Sprinting barefoot in the wet sand has to be one of the best workouts. Second mile goes fast and soon I'm approaching my place. Just in time, too, because the rain is starting to pick up.

I shoot a wave to Ryan Gerhardt. He's the famous mystery novelist who lives in the large, ultramodern beach house next door to me with his wife, Pam. Standing on his deck with his Yorkies, Romeo and Juliet, he's staring out into the water with such a concerned look on his face that he doesn't even notice me.

My head quickly does a 180 so I can see exactly what, or rather who, has his rapt attention.

It's Amelia—in my black T-shirt, thigh-deep in the surf, standing unmoving. Her long hair is knotted up in a twist on top of her head and her hands are skimming along the surface of the water as if it is the most natural thing in the world to take a dip in the middle of a fucking storm.

There is something sad about her, though, which makes my heart twist. She's staring vacantly out at the horizon. I watch for a beat, and then two, as she stands immobile.

What the hell is she doing?

She raises her hand to shade her eyes, and looks out into the Pacific Ocean as if the increasing wave heights and the rain are of absolutely no concern whatsoever.

They should be.

When she takes another step, farther out, I snap into lifeguard mode.

She shouldn't be out there. The current is crazy strong and in an instant could ripple and carry her away with it.

"Amelia!" I yell with a frantic tone in my voice.

The waves are crashing, the seagulls above are squawking, and the dogs are barking, and I'm not sure if she can't hear me or is simply in her own zone.

Dropping my phone in the sand, I take off toward the water at a dead run.

Just before I hit the shoreline, she squeezes her nose with her fingers and plummets below the surface.

Is she out of her mind?

Like a bat out of hell, I dive into the fucking 50-degree water and swim as fast as I can the fifteen feet or so to where she disappeared.

The water is murky, but I catch sight of her and take hold of her around her chest, immediately jetting us both up to the surface.

True to California weather, the storm is starting to rampage.

Lightning illuminates the sky in the distance. Thunder, far away but coming closer, rumbles and roars loud and fierce. The ocean is getting rougher, choppier. The sky is suddenly grayer. Soon it will turn black.

Amelia is shouting, but I don't stop to figure out what. I'm determined to get us safely on the shore.

Soon we're knee deep in the surf and she stands on her own and shouts, "Are you crazy?"

Me?

Am *I* crazy?

Is she for real?

The storm has now reared up in full force, and again I have no time to answer her absurd question. The rain is coming down in fat, stinging splatters. Sand is flying all around the shore. We need to get inside. I grab her hand and yank her along with me. Luckily for her, she follows, or else it would be over-the-shoulder time—again.

"Do you need help?" Ryan yells from afar.

I look up and he is now below his deck and standing beyond the gate to his pool, raindrops striking the top of his head, his arms, and his silk shirt.

I wave over to him. "We're fine, but thanks."

Ryan nods, yet remains in place as if not willing to move until he is assured the storm isn't going to carry us away. He and his wife lost their son a few years ago when his boat got lost in an unexpected storm.

Taking the last step out of the ocean, I look at Amelia, who has stopped to search the beach for something. "Let's get inside!" I yell over the wind, pointing to the house.

"I left my camera and my phone wrapped in my towel on the sand!" she shouts.

I look away for one minute to where I dropped my phone. *Fuck*, that area is now covered with both water and sand. Looks like I lost another phone. That's three in the past six months. Turning, I see Amelia is beginning to drift out into the ocean because of the strong current. "Forget it. It's long gone!" I shout.

Squinting her eyes, she continues to search the beach for it. "No, I can find them. I have to find them. They're somewhere on the beach," she says and starts walking, in the opposite direction of the house, and she's still in the water, too.

Lightning strikes overhead and the thunder roars. "Amelia! They're gone!" I shout. "Get out of the water, *now*."

Adhering to my command, she hurries out of the surf, but wanders toward Ryan's house instead of toward me.

"Amelia!" I shout again over the rain and thunder.

Finally, she stops, and for a moment I think she is going to follow me, but instead of heading home, she looks out at the ocean.

Catching up to her, I take hold of her arm and look out as well, only to see a piece of yellow terry cloth flying away, almost like a flag. It's one of Maggie's towels. Amelia stands there watching it, unmoving, as the storm batters fiercely against us. Looks like it's shoulder time after all. Jetting in front of her, I bend and grab her legs and toss her sexy little body over my shoulder.

Unlike last night, this time she's not very pliable and stiffening her body, she tries to kick and punch her way free. I can't hear her ranting over the sound of the wind, which might be a good thing.

Tiny fists pummel my back. It doesn't really hurt.

Ouch, fuck. That one hurt. A kick right in the balls.

Ignoring the bodily harm she's causing me, I run to Maggie's door and thank you very much, it's unlocked. As soon as I'm inside, I toss Amelia on the bed and turn to close the door.

Whipping around, I'm about to unleash my wrath upon Cam's little sister when all I see is a tiny piece of fabric covering what I shouldn't even be looking at.

My heart is pounding even harder.

My pulse, too.

Raising my gaze, I see her looking at me with those gray eyes, so much like the storm clouds outside that I can't manage to get my pissed-off button to work right.

Stalking past her, I try to ignore her heavy breathing and grab two towels from Maggie's bathroom. Striding back, I remain a good distance from her while I hand her one. "Here, you're shivering."

Standing up, she takes it and wraps it around herself. "I was trying to cure my hangover," she tells me, her teeth chattering like Mexican jumping beans.

Water drips all over the wood floor as I stand here trying to process what the hell she said. "You were what?"

Letting her hair loose, she pats her head with the edge of the white terry-cloth towel, revealing her curvy body once again.

I avert my gaze, but find myself stealing a peek. Just a small glimpse at the tiny nipples protruding through the fabric of my T-shirt, and then lower to those shapely legs.

While towel-drying her hair, she tries to explain herself. "Extreme temperature change is supposed to cure a hangover, so I thought if I took a dip, it might cure mine."

Lightning from outside lights up the room, and it's then I notice the power must be out because the room is extremely dark. At first it arouses me. Causes my cock to stir even more. Then another flash finally refocuses my attention. The storm is bad. Really bad. Ignoring the power outage inconvenience for now, I fight the fury starting to bubble in my veins. "Did it?" I ask harshly.

Amelia laughs a little. "Yes, I think it did."

In an attempt to tame my rising anger, I run a hand through my wet hair. "Good, I'm glad," I manage through gritted teeth.

As if knowing I'm upset at her actions, she attempts to explain. "The storm came up fast—I wasn't expecting it."

That's when I lose my cool. "You could have gotten killed out there. If you weren't Cam's little sister, I swear to God I'd take you over my knee right now and spank your little ass until it turns beet red for not listening to me when I told you to get inside."

Those gray eyes widen to saucer-like size and her chest rises and falls even faster than about a minute ago. I can't tell if what I just said scared the mother-fucking shit out of her or turned her on beyond belief. "What did you say?" she asks bitterly.

Okay, so I may not be reading her right. "You heard me."

We seem to be staring each other down, and then she tucks a piece of hair behind her ear and clears her throat. "I'm sorry," she manages.

Teetering on the edge of feeling a little bad for acting like an ass and telling her she should be sorry, I find myself clearing my own throat. "Don't do it again. I'm a lifeguard, but if you had gotten taken away by the current, I'm not sure I could have saved you."

She blinks, then narrows those come-to-me eyes at me. "I meant, I'm sorry, I don't think I heard you correctly."

I narrow my eyes at her. "Oh, you heard me correctly."

We come to an impasse, so to say, both staring the other down.

Cam's little sister or not, I give it to her straight. "You could have hurt yourself, and I'd prefer you not do it on my watch."

"Your watch?" she sneers.

Okay, so I might have taken it a bit far. "Look, all I'm saying is I'd prefer nothing happened to you."

At that, she takes a deep breath and then blows it out. "You're right. I am sorry. I wanted to find my camera and phone, really just my camera. I didn't realize how bad it had gotten out there," she says, and then out of nowhere her eyes well up with water and tears start streaming down her cheeks.

Oh, fuck.

Feeling sympathetic now, I take a step closer and place my hands on her shoulders. "It's okay. You can get another."

Taking in a full breath, she lets it out. "That's just it, I can't.

My grandfather gave me that one before he died," she says with an obvious attempt to stifle her tears.

Before I can say anything else, a flash of lightning and an almost instantaneous crash of thunder makes her jump. She slips a little, but I am there, with a hand having shifted to her elbow to catch her. With my hold, and her small hands on my forearms, she doesn't fall.

We are touching like a game of Twister—my left hand to her left shoulder, her right hand to my right arm, my right hand to her right elbow.

Should we spin again and see what else we can connect?

Another rumble follows another flash. Suddenly, it's even darker inside. Although it is still early in the morning, outside it is getting very dark, very quickly.

Her body is trembling, and somehow we seem to be pulled closer together. A little too close.

My balls might still be shriveled up from the cold, but my cock has been recovering rather quickly. He doesn't seem to understand the forbidden circumstances surrounding this closeness because he's beginning to do more than the little wakey, wakey of minutes ago.

The lights flicker on and jolt me out of my lustful haze.

No.

No.

No.

That is not the way I should be thinking . . . at all.

Pulling back, I try not to stare at her, not to look at her, not even to breathe on her. "I'll look for it when the storm clears."

"You will?" she asks in surprise.

"Yeah, sure, who knows—maybe the sand covered it. For now, though, why don't you get changed and I'll do the same."

I mean if she wants to get changed now, with me in the room and the lights back on, I'm cool with that, too.

No wait, no I'm not.

Cam would fucking cut my balls off if he knew I saw her in her panties, her very skimpy panties at that. Who knows what he'd do if he found out I saw her naked.

Better not to find out.

The question is—better for whom?

CHAPTER 8
Silver Linings Playbook

Amelia

As a former Goody Two-shoes, I remember the awkwardness of high school well.

I was a good girl with good grades, who was constantly paralyzed with fear over everything. Smoking a cigarette under the bleachers—what if my brother Cam saw me? Leaving campus to grab lunch with my friends—what if we got caught and the headmaster called my father? Kiss a boy in public—what if my brother Brandon knocked his teeth out?

As crazy as it sounds, I didn't realize my peers were even having sex until one day someone (*gasp!*) dropped a condom.

I'm not lying. In fact, my high school yearbook quote should have been, "I can't. I'll get in trouble," instead of the lame, "There is a princess inside each of us."

Seriously, the only edge I lived on was the edge of my classroom desk, front row and center, carefully taking notes on stuff that wasn't going to ever come up again in my whole damn life. But I did it just in case it would be on the next quiz.

I had to get those grades.

Then I went to college.

And slowly, almost painfully, things began to change—*I* began to change.

Experiment.

Figure out what I like, what I don't.

Lose my virginity.

Even kiss a girl, and no, I did not like it.

I did, however, find things I was passionate about, and somehow that allowed me to stop worrying so much about what I should be doing and do more of what I wanted to do.

Even then, though, I never stopped worrying about what my father would say, how he would react, what he would think if he knew.

So I hid most of my life from him.

My boyfriends.

My crazy clothes.

My hopes and dreams.

You see, the problem with being a former Goody Two-shoes is that you never quite leave that persistent little ghost of yourself behind, no matter how supposedly chill your adult self is.

Now, my brothers, they were never afraid to go after what they wanted, the wrath of my father be damned. They lived their lives freely. No, perhaps *freer* is a better term; they still walked the edge of the Waters line—until the day there was no more line.

A year after Brandon died, Cam took off, and all that was left was me. And me, I became the good little princess once again, and did what was expected—went to work for my father.

Well, I'm done with what's expected.

I'm done with good.

In fact, I'm more than done.

Stepping out into the hallway, a chill catches me and I can't believe how cold it is here in California.

On the plus side—my hangover is cured. Looks like some myths aren't just myths after all.

Dressed in yoga pants and a tank top—and no underwear, damn it—I head toward the small galley kitchen. Maggie's house might not be big, but it is really nice. Dark hardwood floors, ivory-colored walls, top-of-the-line appliances, and granite countertops surround me. There's even a wine chiller, although there are more water bottles than wine bottles in it.

Helping myself to one, I screw the cap off and down at least half of the water. Food is going to be next, although I'm in a strange predicament—no car, no phone, and no idea where anything is in Laguna Beach. I do remember that the village area is walking distance from here.

With my head turned toward the window, I blow a piece of hair out of my face and contemplate going out in the rain. In an effort to try to recall how to navigate around, I run right into a bare chest.

My water bottle hits the floor and bounces. It makes me scream. Loudly.

I glance up.

Brooklyn James smiles at me with those smoldering eyes that always make him look like he is brooding.

But oh, that grin, and those dimples, they are panty melting.

Overcome by a strange urge to run my fingertips along the curve of his lips and force the corners up into a real smile, I have to drop my gaze to stop from doing just that.

When I do, my eyes land right on his midsection. And, *oh*, those abs. They are ripped muscles that form a perfect six-pack.

Does he know what he does to women? I have to say he does. From the little I've overheard from Cam, he's a womanizer, a playboy, a manwhore.

"Hey," I say, my gaze steady on all that lean muscle. "You're not dressed yet?"

That was just dumb.

Looking at me, he tips my chin up, and then he blinks, his grin growing more sinful as he takes a step back and crosses his arms over his very fine, very naked stomach. "Getting there. Just grabbing a shirt from the laundry room."

Caught in his sex appeal, I find myself once again staring up into his smoldering blue eyes and at the same time, getting wet.

Normally, men don't evoke that kind of illicit reaction from me. Perhaps this one has because he has saved me—twice—but a knight in shining armor Brooklyn James is not. Like I said, I've heard the groupie stories, know all about his reputation, not so much from my brother as from Maggie and Makayla. They had all but confirmed his player status ways when I visited two years ago. I doubt he's changed.

The boy I'd once forced to pretend to be my husband is anything but husband material. He's a bad boy with a bad reputation—he drinks, he smokes, he parties, and he fucks. A lot.

The kind of man my father would not approve of.

Ding! Ding! Ding!

My once Prince Charming is not so squeaky clean and it just so happens this princess is looking to dirty her tiara.

Brooklyn casts a glance at the water bottle at his bare toes, then at my face, then down a bit. With his bad-boy grin still in place, he bends to pick the bottle up, but those blue eyes remain glued to my chest. Handing the bottle to me, he says, "Don't get too used to having me at your feet."

My stomach flutters with an odd excitement. "Oh, come on. When we were ten, you bowed to me and called me a princess. This is nothing," I respond with a smile.

As if bothered by our closeness, he eases past me and opens the refrigerator. "That's because you scared me back then, and I'd have done anything you wanted."

I laugh and take a few steps to lean against the row of cabinets. "How in the world did I scare you?"

Setting some containers on the counter between us, he closes the refrigerator door with his foot and looks across the island. "I thought you'd tell your father on me, and he was one person I didn't want to piss off."

"My father," I whisper under my breath.

"Sore subject?"

The laughter that escapes my throat has a grim tone. "Brooklyn?" I ask.

He nods.

"How much do you know about my family?"

"Is that a trick question?"

This time I genuinely laugh. "No. I'm curious. What has Cam told you about our father?"

Brooklyn clears his throat and shifts from foot to foot, and then without answering, he starts to open one of the little white boxes. "I hope you like leftover Chinese. Besides PB&J or tofu, it's all I have. As soon as the rain lets up, I'll make a run to the grocery store."

Gulping the last of my water, I set the empty bottle on the counter and rub my stomach with my hands. "I think I'd eat anything right about now, except maybe the tofu."

Brooklyn laughs. I kind of love the way his face lights up when he does. "That would be Maggie's, not mine. Keen eats it too, pussy that he is—he eats what she likes to make her happy."

My elbows land on the counter and I set my chin on my hands. "That's so sweet of him," I say with a slight giggle bubbling out of my throat. "Boy! I guess he has really changed. The Keen I knew growing up was anything but accommodating, especially when it came to women."

Brooklyn moves on to the remaining container. "Yeah, I guess you could say he changed, and so did Maggie. I've never seen either of them happier. Hey, whatever works, right?"

I nod and try to ignore the touch of sadness that suddenly seems to fill me up. "Yes, I guess sometimes it really is as simple as finding the right one."

There's contemplation in his eyes as he gathers the food in his arms.

"By the way," I say, "I don't think I've told you this yet, but thanks for letting me stay here. I hope it's not too big of an inconvenience."

Easing around, he pops the food in the microwave and looks over his shoulder at me. "It's no problem. I had little planned this weekend except work."

The doubtful look I give him isn't meant to be seen, but he catches sight of it as he whirls around.

He shrugs. "Okay, so I have a little engagement party thingy for one of my friends on Saturday night, but I'll be happy to blow it off," he tells me.

"No, you can't do that; wedding events are always so entertaining."

Leaning against the counter, he smirks at me. "In what world do you live in?"

I take a seat at the breakfast bar, and excitement flares to life with each word I speak. "I'm serious; I've been to at least twelve weddings in the past three years."

He shakes his head. "That sucks for you."

I ease back on the stool. "No, it doesn't. I was there to assist the photographer, but even so, not a single one was boring. You have to think of yourself as a wedding crasher—you know, like Vince and Owen—and that you're just there for the food and drinks, and to watch the dynamics, of course."

"What do you mean, 'the dynamics'?"

Excitement bubbles up as I speak. "Things like the fact that the dresses are always ugly, the groomsmen are typically mismatched with the bridesmaids on purpose, and either the groom or the bride is always jittery. And then there's who is sneaking off with whom."

He raises a brow. "Go on."

"Well, someone is always hooking up, and as long as it isn't the bride or the groom with someone else, things usually go on without a hitch, but later in the night there are always catty arguments. I don't know; I like to sit and watch. I mean, not in a bad way. You can't change it, but you can observe it. Learn from it, even."

This time his grin is devilish. "Amelia Waters, you are so coming with me."

"No, I can't do that. It's not like I'd be working the event."

"You can come—my invite says plus one."

I contemplate the offer. "Hmmm . . . well, it could be fun. Who is the happy couple?"

"A buddy of mine, Chase Parker, and his fiancée, Gigi Bennett."

My excitement returns. "Oh, I've heard of Gigi—she's on some television show, isn't she?"

He nods. "Yeah, the show is called *Where's My Latte?*"

I point my finger at him. "That's right! It's about a woman and her assistant in Hollywood. I've watched it a few times; it's pretty funny."

Brooklyn claps his hands together as if equally excited. "It's settled, then—you are so coming with me."

"Okay, but only if you insist," I mock protest, a little more eager to be a part of the Hollywood scene than I would have thought.

"You're not going to get stars in your eyes, are you?"

I shake my head. "You don't know me well enough, Brooklyn. I am anything but a fangirl."

That triggers something, and he seems to lose himself in his thoughts.

Uncertain as to why, I shift uncomfortably. "Just for the record, crasher is still the better way to go."

Snapping out of it, he laughs and says, "We can always pretend."

Pretend. I've been doing it so long, what's a little longer? Now I find myself the one lost in my thoughts.

The microwave dings and with another laugh, he strides over to remove the containers. Setting them on the island, he grabs two plates, four chopsticks, and two bottles of water. Looking at me, he bows. "Your meal is served, Princess Amelia."

The laughter that escapes my throat and the snort that leaves my nose is anything but ladylike. "I did make you say that, didn't I?"

He nods. "You sure did. Except I believe I was serving soda and Doritos. Cool Ranch Doritos, to be exact."

"Doritos—I haven't had those in years," I say a little dreamily.

"Is that right?" he says, rounding the island and disappearing into the small laundry room around the corner, I guess to put a shirt on.

Damn.

Leaving me alone, I find myself wishing I could just stare at his abs all day, but quickly dispel that thought and return my attention to the Doritos. "Is it weird that I can still remember how they taste?"

There's no answer, but I can hear him in the room. I look up and see him watching me. Black T-shirt on. Eyes bluer than blue. Worn denim jeans that look like they were made for him.

"What?" I ask, starting to lick my lips, and not at the thought of eating a Dorito, either.

He blinks. "Nothing. Just remembering too."

Right then thunder roars from outside and the power goes out again with a last-minute beep from the microwave. I look out the window and see lightning flashing in the dark sky. "The storm is bad," I say dumbly.

Duh.

Obviously it is.

Brooklyn strides toward me and sits beside me. "It's supposed to be this way for the next two days. I heard it's worse farther south."

"Like in Mexico?" I ask.

"Yeah, the mudslides are going to make it hard for them to get back."

"I hope they'll be okay."

Brooklyn laughs. "Cam drove and he's a New Yorker. The one thing he can do is drive."

"So true. Cam can maneuver through a traffic jam like no one else."

Brooklyn nods. "I've seen it, but don't forget he has Presley in the car, so my guess is my brother will have outlawed the crazy driving for Cam on this trip."

I smile, thinking of those cute little baby pictures I saw on Maggie's dresser. "Yes, I'm sure you're right, and for good reason."

With a nod, he picks up two containers. "Moo shu pork or sweet-and-sour chicken?"

"I think I'll have the chicken. No, the pork. No, no, the chicken," I answer indecisively.

His dazzling grin is as bright as he is charming.

"How about we split them both?"

I pick up my chopsticks. "Bring it on."

He laughs and then dishes out the food. I find myself wondering what the small bit of laughter was for. Once we both start eating, he says, "You're not like the girls around here."

I swallow a bite of deliciousness. "What do you mean?"

He finishes chewing. "You're just so real."

I dig into the pork and laugh. "Oh, I'm real alright. I turn up drunk on my brother's front porch and then almost drown trying to get rid of my hangover. You can't get any realer than that."

He laughs too.

Then there's a heartbeat of silence.

"You asked me about your father before," he states after taking a sip of water.

I grab a piece of chicken between my chopsticks. "Yeah, I did. That was an unfair question. It's just I found out some things about him the other night that . . . well, to be honest . . . kind of crumbled my world."

Brooklyn sets his chopsticks down and sits back in his chair. "Who told you?"

Not surprised that he knows, I answer truthfully. "Vanessa. I saw her out on New Year's Eve. That's why I'm here—to talk to Cam and make sure it's all true before I confront my father."

As if nervous, Brooklyn rubs his hands on his pants.

I have to say, I don't know him well, but I can tell he knows. And if he knows . . . that must make it true.

My heart stops.

My life is a lie.

I've lived in a bubble and now it's popped. Like with a big bang. Trying to ease the uncomfortable feeling in the air, I give him an out. "Well, you don't have to say anything. I get that you don't want to betray Cam's trust."

Brooklyn takes a sip of his water.

After shoving another forkful of food in my mouth, I turn to him. "Do you have any weed?"

He practically spits his water out and then starts to pound his chest to stop from choking. Once he recovers, he turns to me. "Did you just ask me for pot?"

"Yes, but think of it as for medicinal purposes."

Standing up, he rounds the island and cracks the fridge. "Sorry—even if I had anything, which I don't, there is no way I'm getting high with Cam's little sister. That is not happening."

Frustrated, I sigh. "FYI," I point between the two of us, "we're the same age."

Grabbing two beers, he sets one on the counter and opens the other. "Yeah, but you're still Cam's little sister."

"And you're Keen's little brother. What does it matter?"

"It matters."

"Tell me why?"

"Because you're a girl."

I raise my brows. "And you're a boy."

He huffs in frustration. "It's an unspoken rule."

My eyes narrow. "What is?"

He shrugs.

"Tell me!"

"Come on, Amelia, everyone knows you are, well, good."

Beyond annoyed, I point to him. "And that's the problem right there."

Opening the top, he slides one of the beers across the counter. "What exactly about that is a problem?"

"I've always had to be good. I'm sick of it. What if I don't want to be good anymore? What if I just want to be bad?"

Tipping his bottle, he takes a sip of his beer. I never noticed how sexy a man could look when swallowing. "Aren't you a little old for rebellion?" he asks.

I shrug without answering.

As if testing my resolve toward rebellion, he pushes the bottle in front of me my way.

I glance at the clock on the wall, which from the second hand moving I can tell is battery operated. "It's not even noon."

Brooklyn shifts his gaze toward the clock and gives me a little shrug. "It's five o'clock somewhere."

I laugh. He's right. Staring at the bottle, and then at him, I finally decide to answer him. "Yes, I'm sure I am a little too old to rebel, but that doesn't change how I feel." Lifting the bottle, I tip my beer in his direction. "Drinking before noon—that has to count as bad, right?"

He raises both of his brows. "You, Amelia Waters, are certifiably insane."

Taking a sip, I look at him and think, *Boy, he is good-looking.*

Not my normal type. Not the kind of guy I could see myself with long term. Too wild. Too unsettled. Too rough around the edges. Too much sex appeal. Not Mr. Right by any means.

Still, does going after *the one* even matter anymore?

After another sip and another glance, I remember to respond to his comment. "No, I'm not."

But that doesn't mean I don't want to be.

Insane has a good ring to it . . . *don't you think?*

CHAPTER 9
Betty Blue

Brooklyn

It's four o'clock in the afternoon, but looking outside, you'd think it was midnight.

The power is still out and the storm has only let up slightly. I started a fire to get the chill out of the air. Even still, it is cold enough that I had to grab a hoodie.

Amelia added a layer or two as well. I have to admit, I kind of liked looking at her tiny nipples as they popped out from her tank top before she added more clothing. In fact, I was becoming a little obsessed by them. Wondering how pink they are, how soft, if they would turn to hard peaks with my tongue lapping around them.

Yeah, yeah, I know—I shouldn't be looking at them or thinking that way. Cam would take my manhood. And yet still, I pictured them until I bit the inside of my cheek so hard, I drew blood. That's when I finally stopped. I already scolded myself, trust me.

The room's hazy glow makes it hard not to think that way. Amelia found some candles in Maggie's room and she's placed them around us for light. Good thing, because the only flashlight in the house has no batteries in it. Go figure.

Just as the final chords of the theme music for *Jaws* fade away, I shut the lid to my laptop that serves as a great divide between Amelia and me and stand up to stretch. "I can't believe you've never seen that movie."

She's staring at me, watching me.

Is she checking me out?

"I don't think I'll ever go in the ocean again," she proclaims.

Okay, so not checking me out, but instead, she's in what I like to call *Jaws* shock. It's hard to argue with the original. The sequels don't come close. Shit, if it wasn't for *Jaws*, the idea of a great white shark attack probably wouldn't cross your mind at the beach—they're so very uncommon. Yet more than a few decades after the movie's debut, everyone's eyes are still peeled for a fin on the horizon.

Or mine are, anyway.

Blinking out of my own *Jaws* shock, I laugh. "Sure you will. That's the thing. We all do. But next time, you'll be looking around—I guarantee it."

She narrows her eyes at me. "That's just mean."

"What is?" I laugh.

"You're trying to make me paranoid."

"No, I'm not."

She glares at me.

I pinch my fingers together. "Okay, maybe just a little, but it will keep you from going out too far and drowning."

That glare turns into a leer. "That's enough. I told you, I was trying to cure my hangover, and it worked."

"Yeah, yeah, I know. I just don't like the fact that something could have happened to you on my watch."

"Your watch?"

"You know what I mean. Cam would fucking kill me if a hair on your head was harmed and you know it."

Amelia gives me a sad smile and then stands. "I am not your responsibility. In fact, I'm not anyone's. I am an adult and can take care of myself."

"Yeah, tell that to your brother."

"I plan to," she says, and then lifts her arms over her head in a stretch that lifts her sweater just enough that I can see her belly button. Images of flicking my tongue in and out of it flash through my mind. Drawing my gaze up her body, my eyes travel to the slight curve of her hips, to the waistband of her yoga pants, to her perky little breasts, to her long neck, to her mouth, to those lips, and picture what she might be able to do with them. How she could wrap them around my cock, lick me with that pink tongue of hers, and suck me with that luscious mouth. Make me come with her name on my lips.

Shit, I shouldn't be having those thoughts about her—at all.

"Let's watch *The Deep* next," she proclaims.

"Yeah, sure, anything," I say, preoccupied with watching the way she moves. Then it registers. "Wait. What?"

"*The Deep*. I love that movie."

I have to maintain eye contact to avoid looking at her hot little body. "Isn't that about the Bermuda Triangle?" I ask.

She nods, and with a smile says, "Don't tell me there's a movie out there you've never seen?"

So yeah, I might have told her while we were finishing the leftover Chinese that I've seen every water movie ever made. And it's true. There are only a few I haven't seen. "That is not a choice, just so you know."

Something devilish gleams in her eyes. "We are so watching that next."

I tuck my hands in my pockets. "Nope, can't do it."

She walks my way and stops right in front of me. "Are you scared of a little black magic?"

"No, I'm not *afraid*," I say incredulously, "but Wicca, voodoo,

Santería, black magic—whatever you want to call it, that stuff creeps me out."

"Are you superstitious?"

"No," I say with conviction.

"Yes, you are. I bet you don't walk under ladders, believe in beginner's luck, you probably pick up every penny you find, despise black cats, and believe luck comes in threes."

I tip my head to the side and want to scratch it. She's good. "Well, I don't like cats at all, the color doesn't matter, and who walks under ladders? Everyone knows it's bad luck."

Amelia doubles over in laughter.

"Hey now, everyone has their thing."

She looks up and once she sees my face, she stands straight and draws in a breath. "You won't share your weed with me, so you can at least watch my movie of choice."

"For the last time, I don't have any weed."

She casts me a doubtful look.

I raise my palms. "I don't. I don't do that shit anymore." I don't. Don't smoke cigarettes anymore, either. And besides, even if I did have any, there is no way in hell I would be getting high with Amelia.

She's still staring at me with expectation in her gaze.

"Okay," I concede, "I'll watch the movie as soon as I make a run to the grocery store for some dinner."

Amelia's eyes light up. "You ride a motorcycle, don't you?"

"Yeah, why?"

"I'm coming with you."

I look out at the rain, and then back at her. "You want to ride on the back of my bike in the rain?"

"Yes, I do."

No chick I know would get her hair wet.

She smiles as if she just won a prize.

I narrow my gaze at her. "I'm not taking my bike, I'm taking the Cruiser."

"Oh, come on."

"We're in the middle of a storm, Amelia. What's this about?"

She shrugs. "Nothing. Never mind."

I raise a brow. "Talk to me."

With a sigh, she looks at me. "When I was a teenager, my father strictly forbade me from doing anything like that. He had me so ingrained with his expectations that even when I wasn't under his thumb anymore, I never wanted to disappoint him. There are so many things I've never done that I want to do, and that's one of them."

"Later, when the rain stops," I tell her, and I'm already picturing her arms wrapped around me. Her beautiful tits pressed up against my back. Her breath hot in my ear.

"Really?" she asks excitedly.

I snap out of my daydream, because really, there's a sadness about Amelia's quest that shouldn't breed sexuality.

And believe it or not, I get it.

In fact, I more than get it.

I understand it.

I feel like I've walked in shoes like hers, under my mother and father's shadows, and that's why I ended up here in Laguna trying to figure myself out.

Yet, I can't help but get the feeling that I need to put a wall up or I might end up being one of those things she's never done . . . and just wants to try.

Because she's good and she wants a little bad.

But just a little.

Not too much.

There was a time that would have been just my thing.

But I'm not sure I'm up for that kind of ride anymore.

Not anymore.

CHAPTER 10

500 Days of Summer

Amelia

Princess Amelia.

The memory of Sir Towhead addressing me as such makes me smile even in my dreams.

Sir Towhead.

I pop up in my bed, having just remembered that was what I called Brooklyn that day we played together.

My brother Brandon always called him a towhead because his hair was so blond when he was younger. When he came to our house that day, I adopted the name and knighted him so. You see, it was my brother Cam who forced me to play with Brooklyn. He said we were the same age and it only made sense. I didn't really want to, so I acted bossy. I wondered why he did everything I told him to do.

Fear of my father.

I should have known.

I fall back onto my pillow.

Trying to get comfortable, I have the strangest feeling in my belly as I lie on Maggie and Keen's bed, and I have no idea why. I'm not hung over. I'm not hungry. Maybe too many Doritos before bed.

Who knows?

In the state I woke up in yesterday, I should have slept soundly all night and a good portion of the morning, too. Perhaps I should have gone to bed earlier, not as late as I did. Somehow, though, *The Deep* led to Brooklyn making me watch *Creature from the Black Lagoon* because I hadn't seen it before. Or perhaps he had to cover up the Haitian black magic with a big green creature.

The thought makes me laugh.

When that movie ended, Brooklyn asked me a very important question. "Would you rather get taken out in a few big chomps by a shark or in tons of vicious nibbles by a piranha?"

Rather thought provoking. Wouldn't you say?

When I couldn't answer, he made me watch *Piranha*. After that, the answer was clear. Hands down, I'd take the sharks any day of the week. That's how much the *Piranha* movie freaked me out.

For some reason I'm lying here and forcing myself to stop thinking about Brooklyn, when it's Landon I should be thinking about. Yet, if he really is my unicorn, my prince, I wonder why I haven't thought once about him until now. From what I know of him in the short time we spent together, he is perfect for me in every way. If I had my phone, I'd send him a text. Ask him what Brooklyn asked me—piranha or shark? I wonder which he'd choose.

The wind is howling as my thoughts start to wander again. Something has me jerking my head toward the beach. The French doors are rattling as if someone is attempting to get in. Trying to remain calm, I turn the bedside lamp on, but nothing. The power has gone on and off all night. Looks like it's off again. It has to be close to six in the morning because there is the faintest amount of dawn light coming through the windows.

With the flashlight Brooklyn bought at the grocery store last night, I hop out of bed and navigate to the stairs that lead to his room.

Maybe he could check it out for me?

Once upstairs, I hear something else—nothing scary this time, but something that sounds an awful lot like a groan.

I'm not certain.

Immediately, I turn the flashlight off.

The door is slightly ajar.

I know he's alone, or I'd think—well, you know what I'd think.

The thought of what is going on between the sheets makes my pulse start to race with an odd excitement. Listening for more sounds, I hold off on knocking, my heart beating faster and faster with each passing second. Then I hear it again.

Peering inside the room, it's dark except for the faint light of the sunrise through his partially opened blinds. Brooklyn is on his bed, sheet just below his waist, his hand right where I thought it might be.

I should turn around and leave.

I don't.

I can't.

I mean his hand is on his cock. And, well, I want mine there, but since I can't very well walk in and ask to join him, to help him jerk off, I settle for watching.

I hold my breath as his hand moves beneath the sheet. He goes up and down his cock in long, strong pulls and pushes. And then he kicks the sheet away and arches his back. One hand going to his balls, the other gripping the tip of his cock loosely so he can thrust up into it.

So turned on, I slap my hand over my mouth to stop my moan.

I have never actually seen a man pleasure himself before in person, and this is beyond what I ever thought it would be. Sure, I've seen it happen in the porn movies that Carter watches, but in those, the guy is always yanking his cock so hard, it looks painful.

That is not what I'm watching now.

This is so much more erotic.

Slower.

More intense.

I want to touch myself. To rub my fingers over my clit in small circles in tandem with the rise and fall of his hips, but I don't.

All of a sudden, Brooklyn's fist pumps faster, and his hips rise and fall to meet every quick stroke, which in turn causes my heart to beat at an alarmingly high rate. Now I want to finger myself and press my thumb against my clit with enough pressure to make myself come.

Another groan, and this time I see his mouth open and his face contort in pleasure.

I think he's coming.

And I think I might be too.

Suddenly my clit starts to throb and I'm aware of how very wet I am.

He stills.

My legs are wobbly.

And then there is nothing but silence.

I want more, so I strain my eyes to see if he'll do it again.

Oh my God, I'm a peeping Tom. A perverted peeping Tom. This is bad. Really bad. And yet for some reason, that makes me smile.

I'm so going to hell.

Turned on in a way I never knew I could be, I find myself squeezing my thighs together, and then I feel another slight tremor in my sex.

I look down.

Had I come twice?

No.

No way.

Not like this.

Not standing up and watching a boy I hardly know jerk off and thinking of touching myself.

Refocusing my attention through his door, I catch a glimpse of his very fine naked ass as he strides into his bathroom.

Okay.

Okay.

Okay.

Time for me to leave. Yet my brain is still focused on those tremors that have left my nerve endings feeling tingly.

Staring into the empty room, I know I should go. I make myself take a step back, then another. I flick the flashlight back on when I reach the dark staircase and try to decide if I want to turn around or go down the steps backward to avoid making any noise.

His footsteps on the hardwood floor send me staring wide-eyed into the darkness, and then the squeak of his door hinges makes my heart stop.

Immediately, I turn the flashlight off.

A square of sunlight appears, and it's right then that the door swings open.

Closing my eyes tight, I stifle and slow my breathing.

"Amelia?" Brooklyn asks.

I freeze like a deer in headlights. Busted. I'm so busted. Wonder if I still have time to run back to my room? No, I absolutely do not. Perhaps I should pretend I'm sleepwalking? Maybe. No, that will never work.

"Amelia?" he asks again.

I look across the small space toward him and turn the flashlight back on, accidently shining it right in his face. "Hey," I try to say calmly. Acting as if I'm just reaching the top step. Acting as if the whisper of a thrill in my voice is not from the fact that I caught him masturbating, but rather excitement from reaching the top after my climb up the narrow steps.

Thank God, he's dressed. Somehow, some way, in the midst of my insanity, he pulled on a pair of track pants. He raises his hand to shield his eyes from the bright light. "What are you doing up here?"

I deflect the flashlight to the side wall. "I . . . I . . . I ummm . . . I thought I heard someone trying to open Maggie's door. But now that I'm up here telling you about it, it sounds absurd."

Much to my surprise, he strides toward me as if to act on my ludicrous concern. "Stay up here."

Panic grips me. "Wait!"

Brooklyn stares me directly in the eyes. "I'll be fine," he says with that sinful bad-boy thing he has going on. His total *I don't give a fuck* attitude resonating with each step he takes.

"You can't go there alone."

Turning, he goes back in his room and comes out with a baseball bat. There is a raw edge in his gaze that sends shivers up my spine.

I stare at the bat.

The wood slaps against his palm. "A present from Maggie to Keen, some kind of inside joke, but hey, a Louisville Slugger nonetheless. I confiscated it when they moved out."

"Maybe we should call the police?"

He's shirtless, and all I can see is the silhouette of his rock-hard abs as he threads the bat through one arm, across his back, and under the other arm. "No phones, remember, but seriously, don't worry; it's probably one of Maggie's old boyfriends. I'll go tell the guy Maggie's married now, and her husband will gladly cut his balls off if he finds him anywhere near her."

I give him a questioning look.

His sexy bare feet take a step toward me. "She has a few stray former boyfriends who come calling once in a while. It's nothing new. I think I've had to get rid of at least three since she moved out."

"Oh." My hand flies to my fast-beating heart. "So someone is really out there?"

Brooklyn is beside me now with the bat in a new position at his side, and suddenly everything about him gets serious. "Possibly. Good thing he didn't get in."

All I can do is stare, wordless, maybe looking a little scared, although I try not to.

Perhaps sensing my anxiety, he seems to let whatever issues go that are troubling him, and the corners of his mouth quirks upward. "He would have had a real surprise when you scratched his eyes out."

I suppose he has a right to make that comment. Self-defense classes were something I'd attended regularly while going to college. My father had insisted on them when I insisted on living in Greenwich Village. Although I hated them, I went, always the dutiful daughter. To help ease the tension of those classes, I attended yoga sessions even more frequently. I guess you could say I kept fit for my own sanity.

The stairs creak as he takes them two at a time, and I watch the muscles of his back bunch.

Even though he told me to stay put, I follow him slowly through the house and to the door that leads to Maggie's room. And then even slower still inside the bedroom, where I find him standing in the open doorway overlooking the beach with no one in sight.

"It looks like I was wrong and no one was there?" I say.

Brooklyn whirls around, and it's in the brighter light of the bedroom that I feel his stare like a fire burning out of control. "I told you to stay upstairs."

Very aware that I am wearing only a T-shirt, I find myself

uncomfortably tugging at its hem. "I wanted to make sure you were okay."

His nostrils flare. "Jesus Christ, Amelia, do you ever listen to anything anyone tells you to do?"

My breath stutters raggedly over my lips as I try to find equal ground. "I'm a grown woman who is capable of making my own decisions, Brooklyn, so I'd appreciate it if you stopped treating me like a child."

Stop treating me like Cam's little sister is what I want to say. Yet I don't. I don't want to bring my brother's name into the conversation. This is between Brooklyn and me, and it is a matter of wills.

Slamming the door closed, he locks it with a jerk and struts toward me. "I'm going for a run and then I have a few errands to take care of. The keys to Maggie's car are on the kitchen table and there's a spare key to the house hidden under the pot on the patio. Do you think you can handle the rest of the morning without supervision?"

Annoyed, I find my brows furrowing and my lips pursing just like that child I told him I wasn't, and if that doesn't make my blood boil. "Fuck you, Brooklyn James."

The way he strides past me without a second glance tells me what I should have already known . . . in his eyes I will always be Cam's pain-in-the-ass little sister.

And nothing more.

So much for getting the bad boy.

CHAPTER 11

Edward Scissorhands

Brooklyn

R iding a motorcycle is like dancing sitting down.

Squeeze. Tap. Release. Twist. Left hand. Right hand. Feet in place.

Blazing along the road, everything unfolds in perfect sequence and rhythm. Like always when I ride, I let my mind go free.

And as soon as I do, it goes right where I know it shouldn't.

To her and her sexy little body, to those feline eyes, and to that pouty little mouth. Thrashing the throttle, I try to erase the image of her. No matter how hard I try, every time I twist the hot rubber of the handle, I imagine her soft skin under my palms, the taste of her pussy on my tongue, the feel of her fingers pulling my hair.

Yes, fuck me. I am so fucked right now.

Squeezing my knees tighter against the sleek black gas tank, I tuck my head so low out of the wind that it's almost between my legs. And that's when I picture her between my legs, her mouth wrapped around my cock, her tongue licking at my balls, her moans hot and heavy for where I can take her.

"Fuckkkkk!" I mutter low under my breath. I shouldn't have

lashed out at her, but I had no choice. The way she was looking at me with those sultry gray eyes, I had to get the hell away from her.

I had to, before I took her and fucked her hard and fast amid the sea of sexual tension that surrounded us right there in my brother's bedroom. And I know she would have let me; I could see it in her gaze. She was craving that bad.

My bad.

And I wanted to give it.

I really fucking wanted to give it.

Toeing it to fourth gear, I yank the throttle and fly down the road as a rush of guilt rattles me. I left her alone all morning and afternoon, and I really need to get the hell home.

The day flew by.

After getting a new phone, I called Cam, left him a message, and spent the rest of the day riding up to LA and back in the fucking rain. Just me and my head. And you see where that got me.

Now I find myself slaloming through traffic at ninety miles an hour, until at five o'clock I'm pulling off US 1 and onto my street and then finally up my driveway.

As soon as I open the front door, the house smells of microwave popcorn and I can't hide my smirk. I swear she eats junk food as often as I do.

"Amelia," I call.

Nothing.

I glance around, but she is nowhere in sight. I stride down the hallway. Maggie's door is open, but Amelia is not in there.

I search the rest of the house and nothing.

When I head up to my room, that's when I see the light on at the top of the stairs. Taking the steps two at a time, I hustle up only to come to a dead stop in my doorway.

Amelia is on her stomach on my bed in some kind of hot little number. Her knees are bent and her feet moving back and forth.

Her hand casually reached into the popcorn bowl beside her, reading my manuscript.

My manuscript.

The one I threw away!

Unable to control myself, I stalk over to the bed and snatch the bound pages. "What the hell are you doing?"

She casts me a look of utter annoyance. "Hey, hi to you, too. And give that back right now. I want to finish reading it."

The words *Fangirl by Brooklyn James* are across the front, so there is no chance she doesn't know what she is reading. "No, it's shit. I threw it in the trash, and that's exactly where it is going back."

She pops off the bed and in her bare feet, starts chasing me across my room. "It's not shit," she says, or something like that.

Christ, I can't even think. I have a hard-on immediately. She's wearing a very short green dress, and I mean *very* short. Her hair and makeup are all done up. She is the spitting image of Ann-Margret when she starred alongside Elvis Presley in *Viva Las Vegas.*

And trust me, I've seen that movie plenty of times.

My brother Keen has a thing for Elvis. Hell, his kid is named after him. Presley, not Elvis, but if Keen had his choice, I think it might just have been Elvis instead.

Anyway, Amelia is a fucking knockout.

Plucking the manuscript from my hands, she resumes her position on my bed, but this time picks up the pen beside her and goes back to making notes as if I'd never taken the manuscript away.

I'm speechless. "What . . . Why . . . Why are you dressed like that?"

She looks up with the pen in her hand. "The engagement party, remember? I went out and bought something to wear this afternoon. I assume that is okay with you?"

Totally and completely forgot about that little ditty. Blinking, I have nothing on my tongue but a "Yeah, sure," even though I am completely aware she's being a smart-ass.

With a stroke of the pen, she draws a line on the page and glances up. "Don't you have to get ready?"

A frown mars my face. "Yeah, sure," slips out of my mouth again, but this time I'm able to add, "What are you doing up here anyway?"

Writing something in the margin, she answers without looking up. "Your neighbor, Ryan Gerhardt, came by with my camera and phone. His wife had rescued them when it started to rain, and he hadn't realized it. He said he came by yesterday afternoon, but we weren't here. Turns out he was the one at the door this morning." Now she looks up with those pouty lips and my mind instantly goes to wanting my lips right on them. "Anyway," she says, waving the pen in the air, "my phone was dead and I didn't have a charger, so I came up to look for one." She redirects her attention back to the page. "I didn't think you'd mind, and that's when I found your manuscript."

Well, that answered that question.

Slowly, I walk toward her, trying to dispel my dirty thoughts of what I want to do with her on my bed right this minute. How I want to flip her over and run my hands under the hem of her dress and then slip my fingers into her panties and make her scream my name.

"Brooklyn?"

The pen is now between her teeth and she's looking up at me with those sultry movie-star eyes.

With my chin, I indicate the page she has marked up. "What is all that?"

She pats the bed, and then takes the pen from between those lips of hers to point to a line on the page. "This is my suggestion on how Kate should react when Kellan doesn't show up to pick her up from work like he promised because he was out surfing and lost track of time."

Curious, I pick up the manuscript. "You don't want her to call him and leave him a message asking him where he is?"

Her head moves back and forth. "No! That's not what a girl would do. Not right away, anyway."

I tap my chin in thought. "Why not? *I* would."

There's a click of her tongue and then the pen is pointing at me. "Exactly, that's what a *guy* would do, not a girl. Kate would wait, and wait, and wait, and get angrier and angrier with Kellan by the minute, no matter how nice she is. Then she'd leave, go home, maybe text a girlfriend, and think about him until he finally calls her. And if he doesn't call her after another hour or two, then she'd call him."

I scratch my head. "Why wait to call him like it's an afterthought?"

"Because he was an asshole who blew her off for something more fun, and he doesn't deserve to know that she's been waiting for him."

"No, that's not why he was late. He just got caught up in the moment."

"Well, Kate doesn't know that."

"But he tells her that later."

Amelia shrugs. "It was still wrong. Kate has been thinking about him for hours while he hasn't given her a second thought until he's off that board. Now he has to prove that he wants to get caught up in her."

"Really?"

She nods. "Absolutely. However, their relationship is new at this point, so both will be cautious. He can't overdo his apology or he'll lose that bad-boy edge of his, but he still has to be sincere."

I smirk at that. Do women even get that we don't go out there and try to be this version or that version of bad?

"And," she goes on, "Kate can't be too bitchy or too mad or she'll lose him. It's a fine line."

All I can do is shake my head. "Women are complex."

"We are. It's the whole *I said no, but I really mean yes, and you should know that* syndrome."

Perhaps that is what my mother meant when she told me *Fangirl* lacked real emotion. Maybe she wanted to tell me that I don't understand women. Then again, that would have evoked the fail flag on her part, and although she has made more of an effort to be part of my life over the past couple of years, it doesn't make up for the years we lived in the same house and she was never around. Not even close.

Everyone thought being Hollywood royalty was so glamorous. Well, it wasn't. The Queen was never home, and the King was normally drinking himself into a stupor in some bar. That left me, the Prince, to fend for myself.

I hate thinking about those days.

I blink it all away and focus on Amelia.

More than intrigued, I sit beside her and flip through the manuscript. If I could think of her as a friend, then surely I wouldn't have issues with my cock going to full attention every time I see her.

Yes, friends.

Cam's little sister and I can be friends.

Now that is doable.

I hope, anyway, but fuck, she smells so good.

I have to remember that she is Cam's little sister, and he would fucking kill me if I touched her.

Clapping my hands together, I'm determined to try my hardest to stay on the friend train. "What else did you make notes on?"

She glances over her shoulder to my nightstand and at the clock. "Do we have enough time?"

I nod. "I can get ready fast and we don't have to be there until seven thirty."

"Okay." She takes in a deep breath. "You won't get mad?"

"I won't get mad."

"Well then, I'm not done, but so far I think Kellan's character is far superior to Kate's."

"And you don't like that?"

She shakes her head. "Not at all. I think the viewer should struggle more with which one of them is in the right or wrong. Bottom line, Kate needs to be more endearing."

I jerk my chin toward the manuscript that I spent the last two years writing and haphazardly tossed away because of negative feedback. "In what way?"

Amelia sits up and crosses her legs, tucking the fabric of her dress over her thighs so that her panties won't show. "Can I be honest?"

"Are you ever anything but?"

She shrugs, and the way her shoulders lift I can't help but stare at her breasts. They look like a nice handful. "You make her out to be kind of stalker-like, and I don't think Kellan is looking for that. He wants real love, a real girl, and I think you need to turn Kate into that girl. She needs to be Cinderella and he's her Prince Charming. It will add to the heartfelt feeling you are going for if you do that."

I nod, taking in her criticism and actually feeling good about it. Like I can do this. Make this better.

Her large gold hoop earrings swing back and forth as she makes another note in the margin. "Maybe you could give Kate a sad backstory."

"Like?"

She smiles as if she already had that covered. "Perhaps her mother died tragically and her father turned into an alcoholic because he misses her so much. Kate's younger brother could be sixteen instead of six, and wild, and he needs to be taken care of."

"And Kellan could take him under his wing?" I throw out there.

"Yes, something like that. Something that allows the viewer to understand that Kate is a strong woman with determination and drive."

I find myself blinking at that. At how on-the-mark she is. And for the first time, I begin to wonder if I haven't been paralleling my own life without even realizing it. "Go on," I tell her. "What else?"

"Well, I also think . . ."

For the next sixty minutes, Amelia proceeds to tell me what she thinks I should do to make Kate more of a star. And I listen, without any distractions or thoughts of us, and how we could wax poetic, because this, this right here, is important.

No, it's more than important . . .

It's my fucking life.

CHAPTER 12

Blue Valentine

Amelia

By the time I turned eleven, I'd been married a dozen times. I'd wed each of my four best friends, three dogs from the neighborhood, two stray cats, and my two very unwilling brothers. Cam was much more unwilling than the always fun Brandon. The last of my husbands was Brooklyn James, and he married me under total and complete protestations.

All of the weddings had been planned and ranged from simple to elaborate—elopements, garden affairs, and yes, even a royal gala, which was the one to Brooklyn.

My nanny always officiated and started out with "Dearly beloved."

I loved that.

Amid Barbie dolls and stuffed animals, I wore the same white designer dress that my mother never knew was missing from her closet. With a veil made from a white pillowcase, I clutched dandelions and wild violets that I picked in Central Park, and said "I do."

After the ceremonies, I always took pictures to capture the special moments, and then we ate cupcakes and drank lemonade.

My grandfather attended a few of my weddings, and he used his camera, the one he eventually gave to me, and pretended to be the photographer. He was always so much fun. And like him, I love taking photos of moments that are happy, ones that will last forever after.

Who knows, maybe they are the only thing that really ever does.

The little zing in my heart as I watch the people around me smile and laugh makes me wish I were the one capturing the moments that would last forever right now.

Snap.

Click.

As the professional photographer circles around the room, taking photos of the newly engaged couple and their guests, I watch, perhaps a little wistfully, and smile as he asks them to pose for the camera.

Snap.

Click.

Full of envy that is anything but welcome, I take a sip of my white wine and can't help but look over my shoulder to escape the atmosphere, if only for a few seconds.

The Cliff is an amazing place. The interior is like a cream-colored box of luxury, yet not overstated in the least—with exactly the right amount of sparkle to add a touch of magic to it. Outside is the real gem, though. Just like its name, the restaurant sits high on top of a cliff and overlooks the Pacific Ocean. The deck is huge and provides a view to die for. Tonight, however, we are stuck inside due to the continuing poor weather conditions.

After having met nearly everyone and eaten our way through the cheese-and-cracker trays, hors d'oeuvre table, and filet station, I insisted on people-watching while Brooklyn made the rounds one more time.

Perhaps slightly buzzed, I stare out the giant window and

reflect upon the beauty it allows to be seen so clearly. The rain is still falling, and I watch as it hits the ocean like sheets of glass. As the endless drops fall, my mind wanders again to the tall, black hat Brooklyn wore on our fake wedding day and the face of disgust he made when I kissed him.

Or at least I think I was the one who leaned in first to touch our lips together. Honestly, I can't remember. The kiss was light, of course, just a peck, and nothing sexual in nature. Yet, it was my first kiss, and he was my last husband, the wedding game having grown old by the time I reached eleven and was ready to move on to movie stars and teen idols.

Laughter jolts me out of my childhood dreams, and it's a sound I've become attuned to in the strangest way.

My once-upon-a-time husband has been charming his way around the room. Chatting animatedly with the bridal party, he is making all the women laugh, and on occasion blush. It's the way he looks at you, the way he eases close, the way his breath blows across your cheek.

Flirty by nature, I don't even know if he realizes what those dimples do to the women he talks to.

Body language is a strong aphrodisiac, and he has it in spades.

I press my lips to the rim of my wineglass, warming it, and look up to find him striding toward me. When he gives me that flirty grin, I'm not immune to it either, and suddenly I'm somewhere else entirely. A place where my phone has stopped its incessant buzzing and my life isn't a shattered mess.

Here.

With him.

Brooklyn has a bottle of Guinness in his hand. He's been holding it for as long as I've been watching him, but I haven't seen him take a drink from it even once. "Hey," he says, low and slow. The sound of his voice just another reason my brother calls him the pantydropper.

"Hey," I say, "did you meet the girl you'll be matched with in the wedding?" I sip more wine and stare at him, waiting for him to point her out.

"Yeah, I did. She had to work late and she just got here."

"Well, who is she?" I ask over the rim of my glass when he doesn't elaborate.

Brooklyn bobs his head over toward the dessert table, which is completely filled with decadent-looking pastries. "She's Gigi's cousin. The one in the white blouse and black skirt."

Eyeing her, then him, I give him a bland but sweet smile, and inside I'm doing a little happy dance. Glasses. Hair pulled up perfectly tight. Little makeup. Flat shoes. "She might be one of those crazy librarian types with an insane sex life that she covers up by appearing to be all buttoned up, like Batgirl on *Batman*."

Slipping a hand in his pocket, he grins. "She's an accountant, so I doubt that."

"Oh," is all I can say.

He shrugs as if it doesn't matter. "Tell me again what am I looking for?" he says with that deep voice of his directly into my ear.

This, at least, makes me laugh, and then my breath catches in the craziest way when I shift a little to answer. It's because of how he is standing. He has one arm against the glass. The crease in his pants perfect, his broad shoulders strong, and his lean waist more emphasized in his dress slacks than the board shorts I've seen him wearing. Once I gather my wits, I answer in a flirty tone that is not much different from his own. "The obvious hidden among the unobvious."

"Right," he smirks, as if it all makes sense, and then for the first time tonight, he tips his bottle back and eyes the crowd with those blue brooding irises of his. "I'm on it, the obvious among the unobvious. How hard can that be?"

I laugh and finish off my wine. We took an Uber car here.

Brooklyn knew with all of his friends from his old television series, *Chasing the Sun*, in the same room, he'd definitely be drinking, and I didn't offer to be the designated driver because I knew I wanted to drink.

It must be that with his social obligations completed, he's ready to people-watch and let loose. I eye the crowd too, and begin this little game with the grown-up spin on the marriage game from years ago.

His eyes shift from right to left, looking around the room, and then over to me. I can tell he needs me to elaborate. "Okay, so," I say, "you're looking for who is coupling up without anyone noticing. Who is flirting with whom. Sneaking glances when they think no one is looking or stealing touches on the sly," I go on as a waiter refills my wineglass.

In my pointed-toe gold kitten heels, meant to match the thin gold belt around my waist, Brooklyn stands a whole head taller than I do. He's long, lean, and extremely attractive, and I find myself stealing glances at him more than I am at the dessert table. Perhaps I'm the one he should be watching. When he takes another sip from his bottle, I find myself wondering what he tastes like, and thinking it might be better than a chocolate éclair.

Except there's one small problem with that thought.

Something happened in Brooklyn's room today that I'm not sure I like. Somehow, I went from the forbidden-sister zone to the friend zone. Sure, I like that his moody hostility seems to have evaporated, but I hate that the sexual tension that lingered in the air seems to have gone with it.

Now we're buddies, looking around the elegantly decorated room with crystal champagne flutes and bottles of wine practically floating in the air, and playing a game. Like friends. And just friends.

Taking my attention off my own woes, I resume the game and ignore my vibrating phone. My father has been calling, my mother, and Landon, too. Just not Cam.

Landon and I talked to each other most of the afternoon.

He is nice.

Really nice.

Really, really nice.

And yes, somehow during our two-hour phone conversation earlier today, my Mr. Maybe-Right proved he is Mr. Right material. And the only thing I had to say to myself when we hung up was *yes, he is so nice.*

How anticlimactic.

Exasperated with myself, I blow the hair from my eyes and find the soon-to-be-wedded couple, who are working the room—on opposite sides. This intrigues me enough to pay attention to them. Although I don't mention it to Brooklyn, I watch, taking another slow sip of my wine.

Chase Parker starred right beside Brooklyn James on *Chasing the Sun*. Not only did they surf together, but they also grew up in Beverly Hills together, attended the same private high school together, and both have parents in the business.

I did a little social media snooping this afternoon while on the phone with my Mr. Right.

Chase, unlike Brooklyn, has been trying his hand at acting. He's landed some small parts here and there, but nothing noteworthy or earthshaking. He did, however, meet Gigi when he played Gigi's boss's boyfriend on *Where's My Latte?*

Gigi, on the other hand, is the talk of the town as the feisty assistant to the established actress who seems to be the force behind her boss's rejuvenated rise to fame.

Chase may not be an A-list actor yet, but he is most definitely movie-star material, with his Rock Hudson–turns–bad-boy good looks. He, like Brooklyn, is tall and lean. He has a wide mouth with full lips. Dark, laughing eyes. Smooth, perfectly shaped ears, one of which boasts a diamond stud. And, unlike Brooklyn, he has dark hair that is shaved close to his scalp.

Chase catches Gigi's stare from across the room and his lips curve into a slow, sexy smile. In a way a bride-to-be should not act, she looks away, but a few moments later she looks back at him. He waggles his eyebrows at her and blows her a kiss. Instead of catching it, she rolls her eyes at him.

Not that I profess to be Dr. Love or anything, but something isn't right.

Laughing good-naturedly, Chase crosses the room toward her, sitting in the chair beside her. He pulls her onto his lap and appears to be punishing her with his lips.

Gigi, though, doesn't get all hot and bothered by his affections; instead, she ducks her head away from his tickling mouth and elbows him until he lets her slide from his lap to the seat beside him.

"What are you so intrigued with?" Brooklyn's voice is so deep that it sounds like thunder, even though he's whispering.

Hesitantly, I lift my glass toward the happy couple. "Them."

"What about Chase and Gigi?"

I draw in a breath.

"Tell me," he commands, and my pulse races a little, as it always does, when the alpha in him emerges.

"It's just I don't think she's as into him as he is her."

Brooklyn frowns. "What makes you say that? They're so much in love that they don't want to wait to get married."

"Really?"

He nods. "They're tying the knot in two weeks at some undisclosed remote location that we all will be helicoptered to in order to avoid the press."

"Or gain its attention," I mutter under my breath, and then I raise a brow. "What's the rush?"

Brooklyn eyes me and then gives me a shrug. Such a guy thing not to question the whole rush-to-the-altar reasoning. "I guess they want to be together. I don't know. It's not something I thought to ask."

"Appearances? Awards season?" Words I should keep to myself.

His frown deepens. "You think?"

"Maybe? I don't know. I mean I've only been watching them for a few minutes—what do I know."

"But what do you think?"

I speak honestly. "That something isn't right, on her part."

Brooklyn finishes the bottle that moments ago was full. "For his sake, I hope she's just uncomfortable with PDA because Chase is a really great guy, and I'd hate to see him get burned."

Seeing the unhappy twist of Brooklyn's lips, I point to the dessert table. "What do you say we get something to eat?"

He quirks a brow, and goose bumps dapple my skin. "You've been eyeing it for a while now; I wondered how long it would take you to cave."

"Shut up! You've been eyeing it too," I tell him. And then I take his hand to lead him toward the sweetness, abandoning the game that somehow turned sour. The sparks I feel upon contact cause me to misstep, but I quickly recover.

And as we walk toward the pastries, I wonder the same thing as him . . . how long it will take him to cave . . .

It's just that my thoughts aren't about the food.

CHAPTER 13

Four Weddings and a Funeral

Brooklyn

Wedding rules of conduct are interesting things.

The bridesmaids are all pissed that their dresses are ugly, but don't want to say anything to offend the bride. The groomsmen are worried that their assigned bridesmaid is going to be uglier than fuck, so they don't want to ask who they are paired with. The bride is worried that her day won't be perfect, and acts like a bitch. And the groom just wants to move on to the honeymoon so he can fuck his new wife, who has cut him off until after the big day.

Me, I'm worried about the bachelor party. Can't send my man Chase off into ball-and-chain territory without a proper send-off. I discussed this with the guys and although we didn't nail a date, I'm certain the big night will take place soon.

The engagement party ended rather early, with so much wedding confusion that no one could take the discussions any longer. Now Amelia and I are standing outside under the awning, waiting for our car to arrive. At least there is only a light rain.

Jingling the change in my pocket, I allow my gaze to slide back to her, and realize my resistance to her feminine wiles is slipping.

It has been.

With each passing tick of the clock and every sip of alcohol, I tried hard to remain in the friend zone I had created in my room.

Amelia just has a way about her, though.

It has become clear that she's treated like the princess of her family not because she's a girl, but because she has a magic about her that draws people in, makes them want to please her.

Mesmerizing is the word.

And I saw her do it all night without even knowing she was. The way the waiters refilled her glass before it was even empty. The way the men offered her whatever she needed without hesitation. Even the women were complimenting her on her look—on her dress, her shoes, and her cat eyes.

Like her glittery eyeliner, she just sparkles.

I lean a little closer and run my finger over her lips. "Just brownie crumbs," I laugh.

She reaches with her hand and our fingers touch, right on her lips.

I clear my throat and shift from foot to foot in the cold. "They're all gone. I hope you weren't saving them for later."

The glow of the dim lights overhead highlight her gorgeous features. "No," she laughs, "I think there are some Doritos left if I get hungry."

Like a moth drawn to the flame, I find myself moving closer to her. "Sorry, I ate them all, but I hid a bag of Sour Patch Kids behind the Ritz crackers if you get desperate."

Her flirtatious behavior is escalating, or maybe it's mine. "I'll keep that in mind."

Self-loathing fills me. Cam would want me to look out for her, not try to get inside her. How can I keep ignoring that one simple fact?

"Hey, James, there you are!"

I turn to see Rick, one of the groomsmen, walking toward me.

"Tonight's the night, man."

I look at him in confusion.

"Tonight. Is. The. Night."

The message is now clear. "You want to have the bachelor party tonight?"

"Hell, yeah. Now come on—we have a couple of cars waiting around at the back entrance to take us to the Venetian. Gigi would flip if she knew, so keep it on the DL."

Amelia steps out of my shadow, and Rick grimaces.

"This is Cam's little sister. She won't say anything, man—chill," I tell him.

Her hand is on my shoulder. "Go ahead, Brooklyn," Amelia says. "I'll be fine."

I'm buzzed, but still I'm shaking my head. The Venetian Gentlemen's Club is in Anaheim, and me going north while she goes south just doesn't jive. "Nah, you guys go," I tell Rick.

"Pussy," he mutters.

"Shaming me isn't going to work. You've met Cam, and you know he'd kick my ass if I let his little sister go back to my house alone in the rain."

Amelia makes a small noise of disgust. I don't dare look at her.

"Then bring her along."

"I can't do that."

"Sure you can. In fact, Gigi will be much cooler with this whole thing if she finds out some chick came along to keep Chase in line."

"I'll go," Amelia says, "as long as it's cool with Chase."

"He won't mind," Rick says.

My neck flips back and forth between the two of them. "Are you sure?" Amelia asks.

Rick is overeager and I'm biting back the urge to punch him.

"Yes. Absolutely. Chase is not planning to do anything. Trust me. He's way too in love with Gigi to risk anything. He's only going along with this for us guys."

I blink at Amelia. "I'm not taking you to a strip club."

"Why not?" she pouts. "It's not like I haven't seen tits and ass before. And besides, I've been inside a strip club more than once."

I narrow my eyes at her.

"I have."

Rick starts walking backward, giving us some privacy. "That's enough, Amelia," I say through gritted teeth.

A set of headlights pulls up the circular driveway, and she leans close and whispers into my ear where and why she's been to a strip club.

Our car pulls up and the guy rolls his window down. "You Brooklyn James?"

"Yeah, just a sec," I tell him, raising a finger and looking at her. Is she playing me? I have no fucking idea. Either way, I give Rick a slight wave of my hand. "Have fun, buddy. I'll catch you all the next time."

Rick is still walking backward. "P-uu-ss-yy," he calls.

I shake my head. "Fuck you, dude."

"I'm going with you," Amelia calls to Rick.

Rick motions to her. "Come on, sweetheart, the cars are waiting."

My eyes dart to Amelia. "Get in this car. We're going home."

Before I can blink, she's striding toward Rick. "You can go home; I'm going to the strip club."

I want to scream so loud right now, but instead I reach in my pocket and hand the driver a twenty through the open window. "Looks like we got another ride," I tell him, "but thanks anyway."

Hustling, I catch up with Amelia and grab her arm, yanking her toward me. "What the hell are you doing?"

For an endless moment, our eyes lock. Her gray ones more

like glittering, shimmering pools of something that looks an awful like trouble. Mine so full of confusion, torn between right and wrong, I find myself having to step back.

Finally, she answers me. "What does it look like I'm doing? Going along so you don't miss out."

"I won't be missing out on anything. Now, let's go catch another ride."

"No. Not going to work. I'm still going with Rick."

"Shit," I swear under my breath.

"It will be fun," she says, walking faster to catch up with Rick, and then she turns around and adds, "I promise."

I've heard that before.

CHAPTER 14
Moulin Rouge

Amelia

The kind of girl a guy is looking for in a strip club is their unicorn.

I get that.

She doesn't exist in real life. Actually, she doesn't exist in the club once the lights are turned on, either.

It's all an illusion of sexiness.

A fantasy.

I know this because like I had told Brooklyn at The Cliff, I've been in a strip club more than once looking for my brother Brandon. Whenever he didn't show up to family functions because he couldn't handle the stress he felt in the presence of our father, I knew he would be at Sapphire.

One day in the very early hours of the morning of a very long night, he had confessed this to me.

I never told Cam I knew where he was. I would simply say I was going looking for Brandon, and in turn, Cam would go looking, too.

It was wrong to allow him to waste his time, but Cam would never let me set foot in there, and I knew Brandon would be more likely to come home with me than with Cam.

Brandon never wanted Cam to see him any way but as a real Waters, a credit to the family.

I not only knew this, I understood it.

Understood *him*.

For the first time in a long time, when I think of Brandon, I don't feel any lingering sadness. Any lingering guilt. Any lingering anything.

Maybe it's being out of the city.

Maybe it's time passing.

Maybe it's my situation.

Or maybe it's the feeling that I'm free of something I didn't even know was shackling me—that unwanted tie to my father. Whatever the reason, I'm holding onto this feeling, and doing my best to not let the past bring me down.

The car pulls up to the strip club, and I blink away the memories. Brooklyn is sitting next to me, so close that our thighs are touching, and for once he hasn't moved away.

Feeling the strangest flutter of excitement, I lean forward to look through the front window at the building. It is huge and there doesn't appear to be anything else around us. This place is pretty much in the middle of nowhere.

When I sit back, I look over at Brooklyn, who is strumming his fingers nervously on his pants. "Relax, will you?"

He shakes his head. "Your brother is going to fucking kill me."

I lean a little closer and kiss his cheek. "Then we won't tell my brother."

His intake of breath can't be denied. "That's probably not the best idea either," he mumbles.

Struck by just how worried he is, I reconsider my earlier decision. "I'll do whatever you want," I whisper, hating that his night will be ruined because he's worried about his friendship with my brother. "Do you want me to go home? I will."

Again, he shakes his head no.

"Do you want to have the driver take us both home? That's fine too—whatever you want."

This time he gives me no response.

For me, at least, in the darkness, everything seems so much easier, simpler. I shouldn't have put him in this situation. I should have known better.

There's a weighted silence between us. As the other guys talk shit, Brooklyn really seems to contemplate the situation I've put him in.

Then, when the door opens, and he steps out and he holds out his hand for me to join him, I know he's decided that we will both stay.

Still, I don't move right away.

"Come on, it will be fun," he prompts with a rueful laugh, and I know he's mocking me, but I don't care, and feeling free, I finally step out.

Following me, the other guys get out of the car we all drove in, but the car with Chase has yet to arrive. There is no rain here, just a dampness left clinging to the air. Together we huddle under one of the streetlights near the entrance walkway to wait.

I listen to Rick, who is the loudest, as he spouts off about how he likes coming here but prefers full nudity. He goes on to say he doesn't understand why strip clubs with full nudity don't allow alcohol.

Seriously, now, that isn't too hard to figure out. If the men get carried away, the amount of bouncer coverage needed would be too expensive.

Unimpressed with the others' responses, I tune the conversation out. Brooklyn isn't talking; instead he's looking at me. The weight of his gaze so heavy, I have to turn away.

Taking a closer look at the building, I have to say it looks an awful lot like the Roman Coliseum. The bricks look old. There are columns to support an archway at the entrance. Statues of life-size lions are on either side of it, and benches, too, for sitting.

Snap.

Click.

In my head, I take a photo to remember it by since I don't have my camera with me. I could use my phone camera, but I'm not sure the guys would think that is cool. In fact, I know they wouldn't.

Headlights sweep the space in which we are standing and Chase's car pulls up. Once the four men get out, it is clear that unlike the men in our car, this group drank the entire trip here.

The men are swaying and laughing, and I begin to wonder if I made a mistake thinking it was okay that I come here. Somehow, being part of a big group of carousing guys watching topless girls in thongs dance seems very different from me tagging along so Brooklyn wouldn't miss this outing with his friends.

"Come on, let's go inside!" Rick shouts.

Everyone follows, Brooklyn close to my side. I'm unsure if I imagine his hand on the small of my back and don't want to look behind in case I'm wrong, or maybe in case I'm right.

Suddenly, my stomach starts jumping nervously, and I stumble a bit when the door opens, caught off guard more than anything.

Music and light spills out, along with a bunch of rowdy guys holding one of their buddies up as they walk toward the parking lot.

"That's going to be you, Chase, my man," Rick croons, pointing to the guy with his head down and drool on his chin.

"You okay?" Brooklyn's warm breath is in my ear, and I'm now certain his hand is on my back, almost possessively.

A thrill runs through me.

Looks like I'm out of the friend zone.

Just as we cross the threshold from outside to inside, feeling nervous, I glance up to see his blue eyes peering at me, and I instantly feel a little better with him by my side. "Yes, sure."

"Welcome to The Venetian Gentlemen's Club," says a rather gruff voice from behind the counter. The voice belongs to a buff man with a goatee wearing a black shirt and a red-striped tie.

The heavy thumping bass is enough to pound the pulse in my wrists and throat. The song "Birthday Cake" is playing.

From the song to the lighting to the antechamber-like entrance, the air is nothing short of provocative.

Rick leans over the counter and talks to the host or bouncer, or whatever he is. All I can hear are the words *private hostesses* among a mouthful of others. The guy nods, smiles, takes whatever money Rick slips his way, and then talks into the microphone around his ear.

Our party consists of eight guys and me. Clearly the man behind the counter is not surprised to see me, as he doesn't hesitate one bit when stamping my hand with the word *Elite* and slipping me a small packet, about the size of a condom foil pack, marked *Stamp Remover.*

Ahhh . . . for those who don't want anyone to know where they have been.

The host hands Rick stacks of dollar bills, and Rick hands them out, giving me a wink when he places a stack in my hands.

Admittedly, my reluctance has returned; still, there is no backing out. Within seconds, we are moving through the antechamber and into the club, where everyone looks around, including me.

Sapphire was much more elegant. More upscale, I'd say. They had a champagne lounge and everything was blue, except the floors, which were brown and white and art deco in style. This place is no dive, just not as nicely decorated or laid out, and much more crowded.

Flashing lasers bisect the different stages in purples, pinks, greens, and blues. There are two floors with an elevator. The main floor has a large stage in the center with VIP rooms surrounding it—for private dances, would be my guess. There is also a full bar, and smaller stages are scattered here and there, with large, comfortable leather sofas just beyond them for viewing. I heard the guys talking on the ride over that the Elite VIP rooms are on the top floor.

At Sapphire, I know for a fact, the Elite packages cost a minimum of $150,000, and included an overnight suite and transportation from any location in the United States. What else was included, I never asked Brandon. I didn't want to know. Anyway, I am not entirely certain Elite doesn't mean something else here, but I'm certain I am about to find out soon.

The main stage appears to be where all the action is. It is filled with poles set around the perimeter—how many I'm not sure, but there appear to be around a dozen. There are chairs positioned below each pole for the men to sit, and there are also three unoccupied, taller poles, clustered together in the middle of it all.

Cages are also set around the room here and there. In them, practically nude girls are dancing, bending over, giving even more of a show than the girls at the poles, as they are wearing even less bottom coverage. However, there is no seating around the cages. The men are standing and slipping money in through the bars.

I also notice that unlike at Sapphire, no pasties are worn here. Breasts are fully bared and come in all shapes and sizes.

Mere seconds later, an exotic-looking girl with a completely sheer top and the biggest grapefruit-like breasts I've ever seen walks up to us. In addition to her see-through blouse, she is dressed in fishnets and is wearing short shorts. She has a bottle of chilled Grey Goose in each hand, and when she greets Rick, she lifts both bottles. Obviously knowing what to do, he tilts his head and opens his mouth wide. As she pours vodka down his throat, some splashes onto her top and her nipples peak into steel points.

I'm not going to lie—I'm a little turned on. I'm not into women, but the whole sex vibe in here is already getting to me.

Soon the greeting moves to the rest of us, and I assume the stripper is saving Chase for last on purpose.

"Hi, hon," she says to me, and immediately Brooklyn moves even closer, his hand on my back replaced by his front—his entire front. "I'm Venus. Are you two together?" she asks, glancing from me to him.

Just as I am about to say no, he blurts out, "Yes."

This girl is my age, Brooklyn's age, and drop-dead gorgeous, with the longest dark hair and deepest, reddest lips.

Just as she did with the rest of the guys we are here with, she raises the bottles, but this time she aligns one over my mouth and one over Brooklyn's very pretty mouth.

His hand goes to my hip as he moves to the side.

Electric.

Sparks of energy swirl around us.

Hot.

Hungry.

For a long moment, I can't move—the possibilities of what might lie ahead somehow palpable, and I don't mean between Venus and me, either.

Venus flutters her eyelashes. "Ready, hon?"

Snapping out of it, I tip my head and let the cool liquid hit the back of my throat. When I lower my chin, the room seems to spin a little, and not from the Goose. I think it might be because now Brooklyn moved even closer, leaving not even an inch of space between us. His hard body pressed almost snug against me that for a moment, I have the most absurd thought that we are two puzzle pieces come together.

Venus doesn't stick around like she did with the other men, but that might be because neither Brooklyn nor I are looking at her; we are looking at each other.

He licks his lips.

I lick mine.

"You okay?" he breathes hot and heavy in my ear.

The slight buzz of alcohol has me grinning over my shoulder at him. "Better than okay."

The blur of Chase being dragged away sparks my curiosity. Venus has him by the collar of his white shirt. It's then I notice that he and all the guys except Brooklyn have ditched their ties and jackets.

"She's yours, buddy," Rick shouts to Chase.

Perplexed, I look at Brooklyn. "What does that mean?"

He dips his chin. When he does, his constant five-o'clock shadow is so close to my ear that I can practically feel the delicious prickle of it. "With the Elite package, a girl is assigned to each party member. She was assigned to him."

Not a girl—a stripper. I swallow, not entirely certain what that means for me. I really don't want my own girl.

"We're together," he adds, as if reading my mind.

I blink. "Oh." And I don't ask what that means either, because I'm not sure I want to know right now. The thought of another woman's hands on him makes me see green. I should have thought this out more before jumping in headfirst.

Clapping redirects my focus. Venus is climbing up on a small stage in the corner near the entrance, and in turn, we all follow. This stage isn't like the others. It has a chair on it. Just a single chair, and the lights show off the dancer, making her and him the only attraction. Under the lights, I can see that Venus is athletic looking, and that her perfectly round breasts sit up high on her chest.

She also has perfectly sized pink nipples, like so pink I'm pretty certain she must have some kind of makeup on them.

As she points to the chair, the lights dim and she makes Chase sit before she turns toward us, putting her ass to his face. It's not large and not small, just a perfect shape that looks great on her body.

The music changes and it's her cue to start moving. First thing she does is sit down on him. With her ass in his lap, she slowly presses it into his groin, and I gasp. Everyone has their eyes glued to the stage, and I turn to Brooklyn, who is also watching, and whisper, "What is going on? I've never seen something like this before."

His hot breath is in my ear. "Us guys have this tradition for the groom to get his first lap dance in front of everyone."

"Oh," I say again, and try not to laugh. They obviously want to put the groom-to-be on the spot.

I mean, come on, there is no way Chase can't be getting hard. Especially when she slowly leans back with her shoulders into his chest and wraps her left arm around his neck. This gives him the perfect view of her supple breasts. And with each move, she is still pulsing her ass on his lap—on his cock, to be more exact.

I swallow the noise my throat tries to make, and I'm frozen. Can't move. They aren't naked, but I swear it's like watching two people have sex in the flesh, not on screen like one of Carter's porn flicks, and definitely not two men.

This is hot.

Erotic.

Provocative.

I become hypnotized by what is taking place up onstage. If that makes me a pervert, so be it, but practically watching porn in the flesh is mesmerizing.

The chorus changes and Venus stands up to turn around. Now she is facing Chase, and from our side view, I can see the sweet, subtle grin she gives him. Slowly she straddles his lap, one knee on each side of him.

Venus leans forward, and at the same time, Brooklyn shifts a little, moving more beside me than behind me. I wonder if he is getting hard. I want to look. I don't. It would be way too obvious.

Right before her perfect breasts meet Chase's face, he moves back. Venus doesn't seem to like that, so she grabs his face and presses it into her breasts. As if that isn't enough, now she's spreading her fingers and squeezing her breasts around his face, all the while grinding on his lap.

I laugh to myself, picturing him motorboating between those giant grapefruits. At this point, I truly think the only way this can end well is with her dry-humping him fast enough to make him come in his pants.

And I have to tell you, the thought both repulses and fascinates me at the same time. Not sure if lines are being crossed or not, I honestly do not give a crap.

Still, I consider looking away. This seems so private, and yet we're in a club, and it is anything but private. When I do finally decide to glance away, Brooklyn's eyes are on me, not them, and his lips are parted, his breathing forced.

He's turned on. And that face is so completely gorgeous it makes me realize how wet I am.

Closer.

He moves closer.

I part my lips.

Close my eyes.

Ready myself for the touch of his lips to mine.

Just then the song ends and lights on the stage turn from spot to full-blown white. When I open my eyes, Brooklyn isn't leaning toward me any longer, and I don't know if I imagined the idea that he was going to kiss me.

Still, I'm breathless and embarrassed, and yes, turned on. Unable to let him see any of that, I set my gaze on Chase and watch as Venus stands up, smiling at him, bowing at us.

It was a show.

And now it's over.

Another sultry song starts to thump through the bass, but it isn't nearly as erotic as the last.

Before I can even snap out of my daze over whether Brooklyn was going to kiss me or not, he's got my hand and he's leading me away from the group.

"Hey, James," Rick shouts over the start of the next song.

Brooklyn turns.

"We're upstairs," Rick says, pointing.

Brooklyn gives him a nod confirming he's aware, but doesn't go anywhere near the stairs or the elevator. Instead, he leads me over to one of the small leather sofas in the middle of the club that has a perfect view of the main stage. As we walk, his thumb passes back and forth over my skin, and it makes me shiver.

I know I said I wanted him, yet I know he is so not what I need. Landon is what I need—he is a man looking for a relationship. Brooklyn isn't, or I don't think so. Yet that doesn't matter right now because he is so what I am craving.

A look over my shoulder alerts me to the fact that a topless woman with red hair is following us. She isn't as attractive as Venus, but still she is beautiful, with all her pale skin and the largest breasts I've ever seen uncovered. Like most of the girls working here, she has bottles of alcohol strapped around her on belts. Hers, though, aren't whiskey or tequila—they are Grey Goose.

Instantly, I make the connection.

She's *ours*, for the night.

"Hi," she offers cheerily as we sit, a small gap of space between Brooklyn and me that I'm not certain is intentional or unintentional.

"Hi," Brooklyn says. "How are you?"

"Oh, I can't complain. I'm Lana. Can I start you off with a drink?"

Again, we both tilt our heads, and again one spill from a bottle goes down my throat, and another down Brooklyn's. This time the portion is larger, and I tip my head before she is done, spilling the liquor down my front.

"I'm so sorry," she says, attempting to wipe it up with her hands.

"It's fine," I respond, a little more sultry than my voice normally sounds.

"You sure, hon'?"

I nod, brushing the remaining liquid off, and notice Brooklyn looking anywhere rather than at her breasts.

"Okay then, with that out of the way, do you want a lap dance?" she asks.

When I don't respond, her head shifts to Brooklyn, and then back. Brooklyn looks at me too, and then as if reading my mind, he says, "Maybe later, okay, Lana?"

"Sure thing," she says with a wink. "Maybe after the show."

He nods and slips her a twenty, although I notice he doesn't tuck it into her G-string, but rather hands it to her.

She takes it and offers another drink, which we both gladly accept.

Once she leaves, Brooklyn leans a little closer. "We're leaving after the show."

The alcohol is hitting me, and my inhibitions are low, just not low enough to agree to a lap dance, not yet anyway. "I might not be ready."

His fingers rap-a-tap to the beat. "I think you're ready now."

That last dollop of vodka begins to work its magic, and I run my finger around his pretty mouth, the touch electric. "Lighten up, Brooklyn. I'm buzzed, not drunk, and just because I wasn't ready for a lap dance doesn't mean I'm not having fun. I am."

Suddenly, the lights turn colors, and the beat to another Rihanna song fills the room. This one is "Skin." It's louder than before, and as soon as my gaze hits the stage, I know why.

It's showtime.

I sit a little taller and clap my hands together, waiting with anticipation.

And then the spotlight hits the center of the stage and three girls come out with different variations of little black dresses and the highest spike heels. Each takes one of the poles. The other girls around the perimeter of the stage don't stop dancing, though; instead, they keep on dancing provocatively to the beat.

It soon becomes clear; these girls in the center are the show. And when they start to move, all eyes are on them. Like a cheerleader routine, they move in the same pattern. First, they turn away from us and bend at the waist with butts out so we can all see their lacy thongs, and possibly a hint more. And then they are doing some kind of split, turning and twisting so they are now facing us. Next, they stand tall with their breasts out and take a step over to their pole, where they proceed to shimmy up and down. Twirling, spinning, moving. Doing splits and bends, and climbing down and back up the pole, they give us a show almost equivalent to Cirque du Soleil.

Then, the routine changes, and the girl in the middle remains in place up high on the pole, hanging there by using only her thighs.

She's in fantastic shape.

The other two are standing in place, moving their arms and bodies to the beat in sync. Soon the girl on the pole comes down and the three of them pick up their routine once again.

Now, on the ground, they unzip their dresses and stand in lacy black bras and garters. Soon they are bare except for a faint piece of fabric that covers their pussies, their garter belts, and shoes.

Now I can feel Brooklyn's thigh against mine. Somehow, he shifted closer, or I did. I take a long, shallow breath and have this crazy urge to squeeze my own nipples.

Insane.

The three women move to the beat, bending and turning to face us in a way that allows a tiny glance of the puckered skin of their asses and their pussies. Men start hooting and hollering.

Dollar bills are being tossed everywhere. I consider tossing some, but don't. Instead, I keep watching as a piece of material is ripped away to reveal even skimpier thongs. One of the girls is bare down there, I can tell. The other two have slight hair, as it shows through the sides of the material of their tiny thongs.

The girl who is bare has blond hair and she looks like a Barbie doll. She's the only one I'm watching now as she arches her back and the tips of her long hair brush the floor. I press my thighs together against the ache of arousal as I watch the girl I'm not interested in, instead of the man I am. I'm not sure what I'll do if I see the need in his eyes again.

A thick wave of desire prickles my skin, and I swear I feel Brooklyn's fingertips now strumming against my bare thigh.

When I look down, I'm uncertain. His hand is on his own thigh, close to mine. Was it on mine? And then I dare look up. I know I shouldn't. And his eyes aren't on the stage, but rather on me. I lick Grey Goose from my upper lip, and imagine it as the taste of him.

Overcome with so much arousal, my clit is hard and begging for more than the press of my panties against it. I can't take it. I can't take the way he is looking at me. I have to turn to watch the show. More crumpled dollar bills are being tossed, and now there are loud catcalls coming from all around.

The strippers' bare breasts bounce as they grasp the poles and writhe against them. And they move gracefully around the poles, giving us a truly artful show before the song ends. The lights dim on the three center poles, letting us all know the show is over.

The next song begins, and the three girls head into the audience to collect their dollars. When the Barbie-doll-looking one approaches us, Brooklyn tucks some money into her garter, and it surprises me. Then he crooks his finger and she leans close to him so he can whisper in her ear.

Before I know what is happening, she takes me by the hand

and I find myself rising to my feet, not sure why. Freeing myself of her hold, I look over my shoulder to Brooklyn, nervous, very nervous, and I notice he is already standing beside me.

"Hi, Amelia, my name is Sparkles. Follow me."

Before I can protest, she grabs my hand, and Brooklyn's too, and leads us through the club to one of the doors with the three letters *VIP* etched in the smoky glass, making the room almost like a tease. You think you can see inside it, yet you can't.

With each step closer the three of us get, the more my stomach jumps.

Sure, I've been in a VIP room before . . .

But never like this.

CHAPTER 15

Vertigo

Brooklyn

Men go to strip clubs for many reasons.

They go to see boobs, and in some cases, pussy. They go to hear the classics, like C+C Music Factory and Crazy Town. They go to spend their money on expensive, watered-down drinks, and get lap dances that are high school in nature, with their dry humps being a giant, never-ending tease.

And they go to celebrate or commiserate the passing of bachelordom. Personally, the latter is the only reason I've ever gone. And I'd never admit this to anyone, but I've never said yes to a lap dance.

Come on, did you see Chase's face? His, like all men's faces during lap dances, was the portrait of welcomed yet unwelcomed want—why the hell would I sign up for that?

Strippers tease. Fuck, their dances are called stripteases. The last thing I want in my life is a tease. Still, I make the best of the fantasy of it all, and happily tip the ladies with the bouncing ta-tas.

Amethyst, Cherry, or Candy, or whatever stage names they have given themselves, have never interested me. At least with all of my fangirls, we actually get to fuck. With strippers, you leave with the same bunch of men you came with, and go home alone—to jerk off.

No, thank you.

Yet, watching Amelia, watching the way her body reacted to the show, the feral vibe in the air, has made this scene all fresh and new.

The vodka has liberated my views, downplaying how truly wrong it is to fuck my friend's sister. Not saying I plan to do that, but watching her is so fucking hot.

Remember, too, everything everyone does has a reason.

Amelia wanted to come here to have fun and be wild—I know this. I can read her pretty well. And since we're here, I intend to make sure this little outing is just that.

The etched glass door swings open, and never having been inside one of these small rooms, I take a quick glance around. The walls are painted purple and the room is lit by black lights. The white leather bench glows fluorescent, and when the stripper turns, her eyes shift from Amelia to me. "Come on, don't be shy." She beckons to us.

There are tables on either side of the seating area with ice buckets and more liquor bottles. Amelia is hesitant. I lean in close enough to brush my lips across her temple, yet I don't; instead, I whisper, "Sit down, Amelia."

She does. I grab a bottle and take a long pull on it before I sit beside her, this time making certain to leave no space between us. Inhibitions low, I allow my attraction toward her to take the lead, and am willing to see where it takes me, takes us.

There's a stereo set up in the corner, and the stripper is over there.

"What's her name again?" I ask Amelia quietly.

Big, wide eyes look over at me. "Glitter, I think."

With a laugh, I shake my head. "I don't think that's it."

She shrugs, and her smile alone intoxicates me. With the

bottle still in my hand, I consider offering it to her, but I think she's had enough, so instead I set it back in the ice bucket.

"What do you want to listen to?" the stripper asks from the corner, looking at me.

"You pick," I tell Amelia.

She shrugs. "I'm not sure. Maybe something old?"

That makes the stripper's face light up. "How about nice?"

Amelia doesn't seem to care, so I answer, "Sure."

"And rough." The stripper winks.

Uncertain how Amelia will react to the stripper's sense of humor, I'm happy to see she shrugs the comment off with a haughty laugh.

Just then, the room fills with Tina Turner's version of the classic "Proud Mary," and Amelia throws her hands together in excitement. "I love this song."

Heat sweeps up and down my body in waves as I watch her move—Amelia, that is, not the stripper. In this moment, I wonder if it would be rude if I asked the stripper to leave and ask Amelia to pop my cherry on the lap dance front.

Already knowing it wouldn't be allowed, I sit back and watch as the stripper approaches Amelia. I already told her this was solely for Amelia, so she knows I'm off limits.

She starts slow, circling the bench, swaying her hips, leaning down from behind us to blow glitter all around.

"Like magic," Amelia remarks.

"They don't call me Sparkles for nothing." The stripper laughs.

Tiny speckles of gold and silver land on Amelia's face, and she smiles, her grin bright white in the black light.

Sparkles turns the corner near Amelia and tips her chin up. "You a virgin, baby?"

"No!" Amelia exclaims, sounding more nervous than ever.

My mouth finds her ear, and she smells so good, I have to take a breath before speaking. "She means for lap dances, not sex."

This makes Amelia laugh too, and flush as well. "Yes."

Sparkles' smile is wide. "I'll be nice, but not so easy on you," she says, in a Tina Turner–like voice.

At least this time she didn't say *rough*, because to be honest, I didn't care for that bit of humor.

Amelia grabs my hand when Sparkles hovers over her lap, and I don't shrug away. Instead, I hold onto it, the feel of her small hand in mine is so good, I almost think it belongs there.

The lights dance along to the beat, and so does Sparkles. Amelia, though, looks over at me, and I catch her gaze, allowing the atmosphere to pierce me in ways I know I shouldn't.

Breathing heavy, hands clasped, thighs touching, the woman dancing seems to fade away, and it's just Amelia and me. Mouths parted, eyes locked, lust swirling around us. By the very last chorus of the song, I finally allow myself to admit—I am going to fuck her.

By the time the song ends, I have to say, Sparkles took it easy on Amelia. Not really touching her, but moving around her, making her know this is about her, and her experience. Nothing else.

As soon as Sparkles walks over to shut the music off. Amelia lets go of my hand and stands. I look up at her. She is flushed, and otherwise unreadable.

"Hey," Sparkles calls from the door.

So lost in Amelia, I didn't even realize she'd moved from the corner. I stand up and look over to her.

"Thanks!" she says, opening the door. "Come see me anytime. Since you already paid, you have three minutes. See you out there."

She's gone, we're alone, and the door is open.

My lips curve into a smile, and I find myself inching closer to Amelia. "We have three minutes."

Her gaze flicks over me. "I think more like two and a half now."

Glitter is in the air, and it lands on the two of us. This makes me smile even more because she looks almost enchanting.

Hungry for her, I reach for her and grab her by the waist. I am already opening my mouth when she angles her head. And then I'm moving closer, clutching her hips, pulling her to me, feeling the touch of her beneath my fingertips. Finally, after what seems like a lifetime, our lips touch and I'm kissing her. Moving forward with something I know better than to do, and yet, with her soft, warm, lips on mine, I can't seem to care.

She lets out a gasp, a moan, and I'm lost. *Fuck me.* This is so much better than all those years ago.

She's delicious.

Perfect.

I'm so fucked.

My hands slide around to her ass, and I push her body into mine. At the same time, her shaking fingers run up my shirt, clawing at my skin, and then pressing into my chest when our bodies mold into one.

The way her body reacts to mine makes it impossible to keep the tempo between our mouths slow, and I can't stop myself from kissing her hard. Then harder still.

And for the remaining two minutes, it's just the two of us, spinning in the magic of the room . . . in the magic of our first kiss.

"Let's get out of here," I find myself saying, as I pull away more than breathless, and more than aware we've been here way past the time allotted.

And that's all that needs to be said to start a chain of events I hope to God doesn't break me . . . or her.

CHAPTER 16
Some Like It Hot

Amelia

The act of hailing a cab with a whistle in New York City might not be in any danger of ever becoming obsolete. However, I have to wonder, with the growing success of Uber, if taxi service in California might not someday be in jeopardy of going extinct.

To passengers, Uber is essentially synonymous with taxis, except for some major differences—we know when and where, there is no need to exchange money, and the drivers are always nice.

The phone app that connects riders with a car service using GPS capabilities lets both the passenger and the driver know one another's location. This, in turn, removes the question of when the ride will actually arrive, how much it will cost, and who is picking you up.

Crazy brilliant.

If I owned a car, I would consider applying for a job, since I might soon be unemployed.

"Less than five minutes," Brooklyn tells me, tapping his phone.

In the distance thunder rumbles, but it's still not raining here.

The wind has picked up, though, and my guess would be the storm is moving this way quickly.

I nod, and wrap my arms around myself to keep warm. The buzz and the high of the vodka are slowly breaking down in the cool California night air.

Once Brooklyn slides his phone in his pants pocket, he shrugs out of his jacket and offers it to me. "Here, you're shivering."

"No, I'm fine. Besides, then you'll be cold."

He steps closer to me, his eyes two half moons, filled with a lustful need that I really want to satisfy. "I'll be okay," he says, and drapes the suit jacket around my shoulders.

We should talk about what just happened inside. We should talk about what is going to happen when we get home. We should . . . but instead I take his hands as he pulls the lapels of his jacket together around my front, and then get up on tiptoes to kiss him.

Just as our lips meet for the second time, the first spattering drops of rain begin to fall, and I honestly don't care.

Outside in the light rain, we move our mouths inside and outside the lines with a chemistry I'm almost afraid to admit is off-the-charts. Open-mouthed, with our tongues clashing, his hands go to my hair, mine find their way onto his face, and like this, it's impossible to deny the passion bleeding between us.

The kissing is at first soft and sweet, and then we start French kissing, which takes the kiss to a whole new level. And with this French kiss, Brooklyn is taking us all the way to the top.

Hot.

Intense.

Perfect.

Although our second kiss, it's still a lot like the first time Ross kissed Rachel on *Friends*. Rachel was so overwhelmed with emotion that she crossed the room in a rush and planted a really good French kiss on Ross's lips.

It's so romantic.

But what Brooklyn and I have isn't love, and it never will be. I might be confused about my life, but I'm not delusional. There will be no moment of realization for either of us because Brooklyn isn't Prince Charming material. He's a player, a man-whore, a bad boy, and obviously excels at being those things.

And for the first time ever in my life . . . I don't care that the man I'm kissing will never be more . . . will never be my happily ever after. There is no way I'm casting him away as a frog.

Thunder booms loudly above us, making us both jump and forcing our lips apart. We look at each other and laugh.

"I hope that's not a sign." Brooklyn grins.

I move from foot to foot, still chilled, and knowing he must be too. "I don't think Mother Nature cares what we do."

That sexy brow of his rises. "True. That job belongs to your brother."

There aren't many people outside right now. It's close to midnight, and the night is still young, so young in fact that I'd say the men inside are just getting started. And yet this man is out here with me, wanting me despite my woes, despite the fact that Cam is overprotective and will absolutely lose it if he finds out about us. "Shhh . . ." I put my fingers to his lips. "Let's forget about Cam for tonight. Okay?"

With a nod, his tongue darts out to taste my skin, and the act sends shivers down my spine.

Headlights pull up beside us, so lost in each other we never saw them coming up the drive until the window of the black Jetta lowers. "You Brooklyn?"

Brooklyn takes my hand and steps toward the car. "Yeah, you Harry?"

The guy nods and then Brooklyn opens the rear door, stepping aside for me to get in and slide across the backseat.

There's plenty of room for me to move all the way across, but

I don't. I stop in the middle, sitting on the uncomfortable hump, and not caring the way I did when I was little and my parents always put me between my brothers.

Brooklyn slides in after me, leaning back in the seat and wiping some raindrops from his face. There's glitter there too, and when I move to wipe it away, he takes my hand and bites at my thumb.

Oh, God.

The driver lowers the radio as my body convulses. "So Laguna Beach, hah? Do you live there?"

Our knees bump when the car pulls out onto the main road. Brooklyn answers the driver's question, but I'm too lost in looking at him to hear what he is saying.

Brooklyn has my hand in his and sets our intertwined fingers on my thigh. The driver is still talking, the conversation having turned to surfing. I listen intently to Brooklyn talk about the waves, his board, the thrill of the ride. The driver is just learning, so Brooklyn gives him pointers. He doesn't seem to know who Brooklyn is, and I think Brooklyn likes it that way.

With each word he speaks, he caresses his thumb over my skin. My nipples are hard, and I can feel slick wetness between my legs, especially when our hands move up and under the hem of my dress.

He's careful to be discreet. Talking, and not drawing attention to the fact that he has now let go of my hand and inched his fingers up to my panties.

I know the moment he feels how wet I am because his body stiffens and there's a low intake of breath.

You know when I told you how much I liked Uber drivers because they are so friendly? Well, right now I don't like that trait very much because this driver won't stop talking to Brooklyn.

Streetlights cast bars of silver on my lap, but the jacket helps shield what he is doing, as much as the dark of the night.

Sweet tension curls in my belly. My breath catches and holds when he traces his fingers along the lacy edge of my panties. Teasing me over and over with light strokes until I feel like I might lose my mind.

Releasing a breath, I hiss out air between my parted lips and keep my eyes fixed on the front windshield, hoping my small moan of pleasure didn't draw the driver's attention.

Brooklyn is on cue, though, talking louder, as if their conversation is almost necessary to accomplish his task.

And maybe it is. This isn't a cab. It's someone's car. And spending thirty minutes in the dark with his fingers between my legs might be noticeable without the conversation between them taking place.

So I take it back. I stick with my original proclamation that Uber drivers are friendly, and I like it.

"Isn't that right, Amelia?" Brooklyn's voice is warm, like honey dripping into tea.

"Yes," I answer, with no idea what I'm agreeing to.

The conversation goes on, and I've done my part.

Lost in Brooklyn's touch, I close my eyes and lean back against the humped seat, the heat of his hand branding the sensitive skin between my thighs. Then he cups me, the heel of his hand pressing against my clit on the outside of my panties, and I have to bite my lip to stop myself from moaning.

The sensation flows through my veins like fire, but I keep my eyes closed, unable to look at him for fear I wouldn't be able to remain quiet once I see that overwhelming lustful desire in his eyes. That I will want to reach over and touch him, touch his erection that I know must be raging. That I will want to do so much more. So, instead I settle on curling my fingers around the fabric of his jacket and squeezing tightly.

My body jerks as his flesh comes in direct contact with mine, his fingers sneaking inside my skimpy panties to run gently over my folds.

There's a low groan from his throat that he covers with a cough. That makes me smile, but when his fingers stop their teasing and glide up to caress my clit, I'm no longer smiling.

His touch spears me straight to my core, and I have to let go of his jacket with the hand not beside him to lay my palm flat on the leather seat in order to steady myself on this middle hump.

With my other hand, I grasp his pant leg.

Now anchored with support, I soak in the feel of his fingers dipping inside me, and then gliding up in my wetness to circle my tight nub.

Oh, God.

Each roll of the wheels of the car along the pavement causes my pussy to swell. I turn my head to the side and look at him. His face is beautiful in the moonlight. Between words, he glances over at me. And it's there, just like I knew it would be—the full-blown desire, the promise of a wicked night, with hot sex, and orgasm after orgasm.

I can't wait.

As we drive deeper into the night, everything becomes about this man. His hands. His eyes. His lips, which he licks when his fingers dip again inside the walls of my wet pussy.

This time when he rubs them over my clit, it pulses beneath his touch.

As if surprised, his body jerks with an excitement I've never seen in a man. Another promise in the dark of what is to come.

Breathless, aching, body burning for release, unable to focus on anything but the pleasure building between my legs, I feel myself starting to tip over the edge, but try to hold back.

I want to feel more of this incredible feeling . . . longer, longer, and longer.

More words come out of his mouth. More conversation with the driver, but then the driver's phone rings. "Do you mind if I answer this? It's my wife," the driver says.

"Sure, no problem," Brooklyn answers.

With the driver explaining to his wife about why he did something, Brooklyn settles his attention on me. Magic fingers work my clit, taking me higher and higher. There is no doubt I'm going to come on his hand, around his fingers; it's just a matter of how long I can hold off.

His breath blows hot against my skin as he leans toward me to nuzzle my ear. "Let go, Amelia."

And I do. While the Uber driver argues with his wife, I tune it all out. With Brooklyn's name on my lips, I shatter beneath his touch, so hard that I have to bite my lip to stifle the cry that tears from my throat.

His fingers keep moving, and my clit continues to spasm over and over, each surge of climax stronger than the last.

As bolts of pure bliss radiate through my entire body, I shudder and jerk and find myself spiraling into a darkness filled with an endless amount of glitter. Losing control, my nails scratch thin lines on both Brooklyn's pants and the leather beside me, to keep from shouting out. In silence, I ride out this wave of pleasure and find myself never wanting it to end.

Perhaps knowing I am having trouble remaining quiet, Brooklyn pulls his hand from my panties and wraps his arm around me, pulling me close. In the dark, he kisses my jaw and the side of the neck.

This close to him, I try to catch my breath. My body is limp and sated, but with his fresh, clean scent so close, I have to force the air in and out of my lungs.

If the driver is aware of what is taking place, he shows no sign of it. He's too busy still apologizing to his wife over and over.

Brooklyn uses the hand that was just in my pussy to rub his fingers over my lips. It shouldn't be sexy to say I can taste myself on him, but it is, and I can.

My pulse pounds in my throat.

Electrified.

Lost in the erotic moment, I find my own hand sliding up his pants.

"Hey, sorry about that," the driver says to us.

Brooklyn stops me with his other hand. "Later," he murmurs, and then replies to the driver, "No problem, man."

And that promise of a night I'll never forget is what I hear ringing in that word *later*. So while the Uber driver explains his situation to Brooklyn, I spend the rest of the ride thinking about what is to come.

And how I can't wait!

CHAPTER 17

True Romance

Brooklyn

Nothing, and I mean *nothing*, in my life ever goes as planned. And as soon as we pull onto my street and I look out the window . . . I know our night is fucked, and so am I.

Wistful for what I haven't even had yet, I unwrap myself from Amelia and try not to sound overly alarmed. "Move over," I whisper to her, and rush to get the packet out of my pocket in order to rub the stamp off my hand, and then hers.

She looks at me with a confused expression on her face, as I wipe the word *Elite* from the back of her hand. She won't be confused for long. "Why?" she asks.

"Trust me. Slide over, and fast."

With ease, she sits on the seat behind the driver. I can tell she still has no idea why I'm pushing her away, and honestly I don't have time to explain.

Placing my hand across my mouth, I mentally prepare myself as the car comes to a stop.

As if the universe wants to torture me, I can smell her on me. It's then that something inside me says this will be all I'll ever have of her.

The car pulls into the driveway, and without a glance at her, I open the door, and all I can think is . . .

Fuck!

CHAPTER 18
Wild at Heart

Amelia

The word *wait* sits on my tongue, but I can't force it out of my mouth.

Sometimes in the dark of the night we see what we want, wish for things that can never be, have hope we shouldn't.

And I fear this is one of those times.

There is not even a second thought for hurt feelings or regrets because whether I fully comprehend it or not, I'm about to face the reason I came to California.

The BMW SUV beside the Uber car is running. Even in the rain I know this, because the headlights are on and the glass is slightly fogged up. I look back and see that Cam's car is parked behind it.

Then, when I turn and look a little harder, I can make out the movement of people through my window. Cam is coming out of the front door of the house with his phone to his ear. My phone, which is tucked away in my purse, starts to ring. Cam looks up, and then spotting the car, ends the call.

It's then my gaze shifts to the movement outside my door. Keen is loading the trunk with suitcases and other things. Maggie is in the backseat, with the baby all wrapped up in a blue blanket. She is holding him close to her chest.

"Thanks for the ride," is all Brooklyn says to the driver before closing the door and rushing over to help Keen.

They are all back from Mexico, in the middle of the night, because of me. It's then reality hits me. I won't be staying with Brooklyn any longer. It is time for me to confront the truths about my family. To come to terms with my life and the lies I've been told.

My anger is stifled by the guilt I feel about fooling around with Cam's friend.

"You okay?" The driver turns around.

"Yes. I need a minute, if that is okay?"

"Yeah, sure. It's all on the clock. No worries."

Sighing, I put my hand on the door handle. Knowing I can't stay locked inside the safe harbor of this car all night, I slowly pull on it.

However, my slow pace hastens when I see Cam yelling at Brooklyn. When I see Brooklyn point toward the car. When I see Keen rushing over as if he might need to intervene.

Before I can figure out what I'm going to say to my brother, I push my door open. "Cam," I call over the sound of the thunder and the rain.

Cam comes rushing over to me. "Are you okay?"

I swing the link chain of my small purse over my shoulder. "I'm fine."

He moves closer, as if to examine me. "Where the hell have you been?"

Blinking back the tears welling in my eyes, I answer honestly, but not fully. "I didn't know when you'd be back, so I went with Brooklyn to an engagement party."

Apparently, that is good enough and he has no reason to press for more information. "Once I got your message, I came back as fast as I could. What the hell is going on?"

Following Cam, Makayla is standing beside us with an umbrella in her hand. "Cam, can you wait until she gets inside?" she scolds.

He shakes away his frustration. "Yeah, of course. Come on, let's go in." Turning, he yells, "Brooklyn!"

I turn too.

Brooklyn looks up and Cam tosses him his keys. "Presley's car seat is still in the back—would you mind grabbing it?"

Brooklyn catches the keys with ease. "Yeah, no problem," he says, already hoisting the stroller from Cam's Jeep.

Maggie waves at me, and I wave back.

Cam says something more to Brooklyn and Keen about his car, but all I can do is watch Brooklyn's silhouette in the moonlight. The way the water rolls down his lean body. The way he moves with ease. The promise of what now may never come.

"Amelia?" Makayla prompts.

I turn to see her holding the umbrella up and I slip under it, and the three of us are now shielded from the rain.

One final time they both turn to say their goodbyes. I turn too, and this time I immediately catch Brooklyn's gaze. Three seconds, no longer—that is how long my stare remains on him. Through the raindrops, it feels like forever as both of us talk to each other in silence with just this one look.

The words *I'm sorry* are all I can make out on his lips, but in his eyes, I can see so much more, and the promise of that is enough . . . for now.

This is wrong.

This is right.

This is us.

CHAPTER 19
Badlands

Amelia

The huge diamond on Makayla's left hand is like a very large pink elephant in the doorway.

After seeing it, I can't help but feel a little hurt, even though I know I shouldn't.

At Christmas, when Makayla and Cam visited New York City for a short three-day stay, Cam and I had stolen away on Christmas Eve under the guise of holiday shopping to go ring shopping on Fifth Avenue.

We'd gone from store to store to store, and in the end, we decided on a classic round stone with a band of much smaller diamonds surrounding it, allowing the high-set stone to be the center of attention.

I fell in love with it instantly, and knew Makayla would too.

With that being said, I had no idea he was proposing so soon. He'd spoken of Valentine's Day, or her birthday, or the second anniversary of when they'd met, which isn't until May. Not once had he mentioned it would be within a week of his return to California.

The door closes behind us, and I look around at all the

remodeling that has been done in Cam and Makayla's home since I was here last. With its red sofas, beige walls, and modern art, it looks so much more like a home than the bachelor pad it had once been. I know Cam has discussed buying this house, but last I heard, the landlord wanted way too much for it. I wonder if something has changed and he forgot to mention that as well.

Just like with the engagement, I don't ask. Not now. Not with all the unanswered questions on my lips, and the hostility they bring along with them as they sit there, begging to be asked, while I dread the answers that will come at the same time.

Slipping out of my shoes, I turn around, and shaking, I draw Brooklyn's jacket even tighter around myself.

Makayla notices right away. "We should all put some dry clothes on, and then I'll make some tea."

"All of my things are next door," I answer flatly. Aware none of this is her fault, I'm trying my best not to be rude.

"I'll go get them," Cam offers.

Fear creeps over me. Why, I don't know. I have no reason to be afraid of Cam finding out about Brooklyn and me, especially because there *is* no Brooklyn and me.

Still, for tonight, I think it is best to avoid any possible confrontation. "That's not necessary. My things are somewhat scattered everywhere. I'll get them tomorrow." I look at Makayla. "Do you mind lending me something warm?"

"Not at all." She smiles. "I'll be right back."

As soon as she heads down the hall and disappears into their room, I glare at Cam. "You got engaged and didn't bother to call me?"

Remorse flickers across his face. "It wasn't planned. It just seemed like the right time, and I did try to call, but I had no cell service."

Unable to be mad about that, I put aside my issues for this one moment and throw my arms around him. "I'm so happy for you, for the both of you."

"He told you without me?" Makayla doesn't sound any too pleased.

I let go of my brother and rush over to her, throwing my arms around her, too. "No, I saw the ring and asked him."

She hugs me tightly for a long time. A connection I know we'll share forever. I never had a sister, like my brother had a brother, but now I do. And *thankful* isn't a great enough word to describe it.

Pulling back, I take the clothes from her, and then hold up her left hand. Somehow, in the midst of the ugly going on in my head, the three of us end up huddling together and gushing over the ring that will someday soon make Makayla Alexander a part of the Waters family—whether that is a blessing or a curse is yet to be determined.

"Go change," she orders as she gracefully pulls her hand back. "I'll make some tea, and then leave you two to talk." She glances at Cam, and he nods.

Out of the corner of my eye, as I head toward the guest room I stayed in once before, I watch while my brother pulls his fiancée in for their own private embrace. Biting my thumbnail, I can only hope I am not about to ruin their engagement weekend too very much.

Once I'm changed and ready to talk, I scrub my face as I walk down the hall, and hope all traces of drunkenness have dissipated.

When I step into the kitchen, the light is so bright that I have to fling my hand over my eyes and blink fast so I'm not blinded.

Cam laughs. "Rough night?"

"No, not all."

And that isn't a lie.

Cam is alone in the kitchen. Two cups of tea are sitting at a beautiful round, wooden table. The kitchen, like the living room, has been remodeled in cheery reds, with beige walls and large, bold pictures of coffee cups on them.

"I thought you might be hungry," he says.

"You know me too well," I admit.

He doesn't turn around. "I know you very well."

I slump into one of the cute wrought-iron chairs and grab the flowered cup. "Mmmm . . . mint."

"Yeah, Makayla said you liked that flavor," Cam says, this time turning from his place at the stove, where he is cooking eggs, the only thing I know he can cook, and cook well.

"I do," I tell him, blowing on the tea to cool it.

He turns to the skillet. "Do you want toast with your eggs?"

I twirl the cup in front of me. "Yes, please."

Cam shovels scrambled eggs onto three plates and adds toast as it springs up from the toaster.

"You're going to make a great wife," I joke.

He turns with a plate in one hand and a glass of orange juice in the other, but says nothing. No *Shut up, Amelia*, or *Whatever*, or *Kiss mine*—you know, the terms of endearment siblings use on each other all the time, the kind I'm used to. "I'll be right back," he says instead.

That I'm not used to. "Makayla can eat with us."

His look says it all. "I think we need to talk alone."

At that I swallow, and know the time for truth has come. While he's gone, I grab the plates, some forks, and the salt and pepper, pour us each a juice, and set everything on the table.

When he comes back, he slides into the seat across from me. Without even picking up his fork, he looks over me. "What happened, Amelia, that has you all freaked out?"

I reach for the salt and sprinkle it lightly over my eggs. I'm not sure what I said on the message I left him. I'm not sure where to start. So I blurt it out. "I ran into Vanessa on New Year's Eve."

Cam snorts lightly and drinks some juice. "And what message did she have for me this time?"

Not expecting such an inconsequential question, I freeze with a forkful of eggs halfway to my mouth, but decide to chew and swallow it before answering.

It's true, in the past Vanessa would send Cam gifts, and then message me on social media when he didn't reply. Since Cam has refused to enter the modern age and use Facebook or Twitter or Instagram, it was her way of making certain he received her messages. But shortly after I went to work for my father, all of that stopped. Aside from seeing her at work, I honestly had no contact with her.

I set my fork down. "What she told me wasn't a message for you."

The crunch of his overdone toast as he bites into it is loud. "Okay, then what exactly had you running across the country and leaving me a message that I needed to get to Laguna as soon as possible?"

There is such a thing as overreacting, and now that a couple of days have passed, I feel silly that a) I came here to discuss this in person to begin with, and b) I pulled him away from his engagement weekend to come home and face something I know he'd much rather not discuss at all.

But I'm here, and so is he, so I might as well find out. "She told me Dad has been cheating on Mom for years, and that's why she left him."

I think the eggs get stuck in his throat, because he coughs and pounds his chest. "She what?"

I slide his juice glass closer to him. "You heard me."

Taking a quick gulp, he sets it down. "She has a big mouth."

Lifting my fork once again, I find myself poking the eggs, but not eating them. "Well?" I ask, swallowing the bitter taste in my mouth. "Is it true?"

"Yes."

One word. Nothing more.

Anger toward the man I considered my hero for my entire life crawls up my throat and I push my plate aside, no longer hungry. "So let me guess, then—the part Vanessa told me about her and Dad is true as well."

Blank eyes stare at me.

I force the words out. "Our father fooled around with your girlfriend when you were still together with her?"

He nods. This obviously is not at all easy for him to discuss.

"Why didn't you tell me?" I ask.

Cam's gray eyes stare at me, sincerity bright in them. "It wasn't my place, Amelia."

My hands sit idly on the tabletop. "But I blamed Mom for breaking up our family—what was left of it, anyway."

"And Mom knew you'd eventually forgive her."

My hands shake, and I try to steady them by gripping my cup. "Why? Why wouldn't she tell me it was Dad's fault?"

Cam stands and takes his plate to the sink, and then turns to lean against the counter. "She knew you idolized Dad, and after Brandon's death, she wanted you to have that one pure thing in your life."

"Pure!" I shout. "It was all a lie!"

"It was all you had left after Brandon!" he shouts.

And I freeze. He's right. After Brandon's death we were all a mess, but I was in really bad shape. Blaming myself, pleasing my father had become my world. Excelling in school, interning with him, pushing myself to be like him—it had become my life, my way of making up for not being able to save Brandon.

Cam and I share a look, one that we both know says he is right.

Drawing in a breath, I blow it out and go on. "Vanessa also told me Mom blames Dad for Brandon's addiction."

Cam's hands squeeze the counter so tightly I can see his knuckles turning white. "That's bullshit. Mom knows there is no one to blame."

My brother and I rarely talk about that time. We talk about our life before B, and our life after B, but never that time. This is, in fact, the first time we've talked about his death without me falling apart.

And it feels good.

Good to get it out.

Good to know the truth.

Sure, I get why Cam didn't want to be the one to tell me. What I don't get is why my mother would let me hate her, and allow me to continue to adore my father, who clearly has issues. Who clearly isn't the hero I thought him to be.

I think having these couple of days away from New York, spending time with Brooklyn, and reflecting on my life has lessened the burn of the shock of all of this. Although it is not over, it's not as distressing as it had it been.

Standing up and feeling much stronger than I thought I would after hearing the truth, I bring my plate over to the sink. Cam takes it and again we share a look before he turns to rinse it. One that says we are both okay. We each took a different path to grieve, and yes, we miss Brandon, but we both know he would have wanted us to let him go. To remember the good times, to never forget him, but to let him go.

Feeling an odd weight lifted from my shoulders, I open the dishwasher and glance over to Cam. "There's one more thing."

He hands me the two plates and turns the water off. "What is that?" he asks.

"Vanessa said she and Dad are still together," I tell him, closing the door to the dishwasher.

With a sigh, he grabs a towel and dries his hands. "I don't care who she is with, but I think you do, so I will tell you what I know."

We end up drinking more tea and sitting at the table. Thirty minutes later he has told me the whole sad, terrible story about the bad place he was in after Brandon died, the fact that his relationship with Vanessa had already been over before he discovered her cheating on him, and that although he will never forgive or forget what happened with our father, he has moved on. And finally, he tells me he doesn't think our father and Vanessa are together, but he isn't certain of that, either.

He goes on to tell me our father has been trying to repair their relationship, and has assured him that Vanessa is no longer in his life. For some reason, he believes him.

In turn, I tell him about my guilt. About the deep culpability I felt the morning I found Brandon dead. And how much I miss him. I tell him why I went to work for our father and that I don't think I want to work for him anymore. That it is time for me to pursue my dream of photography.

My dream.

My time.

And it feels so good.

I tell him things I never thought I'd be speaking out loud.

Cam nods. Agreeing. Encouraging. Prompting, and offering suggestions. When he suggests moving here, I laugh. When he suggests LA, I laugh harder, but my mind seems to be considering it.

When that conversation is put to rest for the night, anyway, I finally tell him how much it angers me that he feels the need to protect me.

At that, he smiles. "That, little sister, will never change."

All I can do is shake my head because sitting here now, with him, it's strange, but I'm not angry. Sure, I rushed all the way across the country to confront something I already knew must have somewhat been true, but all I feel is relief to know the truth. Relief that I am no longer living in a bubble. And relief because for the first time in a long time, I know it's time to push my own guilt aside and to put myself first.

Scrubbing his face, Cam looks over at me. "So what are you going to do?"

I glance over at the clock, which reads 4 a.m. "Go to bed." I smile at him.

He laughs. "I mean with your life."

Standing up, I look at him. "I have no idea, but do you mind if I stay here a while until I figure it out?"

Rising to his feet, he pulls me in for a hug, which is unlike him. When he kisses the top of my head, he whispers, "You never need to ask me that. My door is always open for you, Amelia, you know that."

And I do. If I didn't, I wouldn't have flown here like I did.

"Now let's go to bed," he says, pointing toward the room that will be mine.

Yawning, I manage an "I love you," and then start toward my room rather obediently, I have to admit. Again, when it comes to my brother, this is unlike me. Maybe we've both changed. Grown up. And I rather like the new us.

As I step into the guest room, which like the rest of the house is decorated in reds and beiges, I walk over to one of the two windows that sandwich the bed and stare out of it. Looking over at Maggie's house, I glance up and can see a dim glow from Brooklyn's room. Either his bedside light is on or the bathroom light.

Is he still awake?

If so, is his hand beneath the sheet, moving up and down over his hard cock?

And if it is, I wonder if he's thinking about me.

What was going to take place between us.

I hope so.

CHAPTER 20

Punch-Drunk Love

Brooklyn

A man's mind is a complex thing, especially while jerking off. With my hand on my cock, I try to push away the dirty thoughts of Amelia. You know—the ones her brother would cut my balls off for even thinking about.

Instead, I attempt to use the spank bank to relieve the morning wood issue. Nothing in my past that seems truly memorable comes to mind, though, and my thoughts wander to her.

Wander to her despite the fact that I'm freezing my ass off, and just want to go the hell back to bed. That I don't want to have to go to work. In fact, I wish I didn't have to.

In fact, the first thing I did this morning when my alarm went off at six forty-five was check the temperature—47 degrees—and then pray it was raining outside. It wasn't. Still, when I heard nothing, I got up to check for it, hoping for not just tiny droplets, but the torrential bucketfuls we've been experiencing. That was a no-go. Although the sky was filled with gray clouds, the rain was light, and I knew the beaches would be open, and that meant I had to get my ass moving.

With that, I hurried toward the bathroom in the chill of the room and cranked the water as hot as I knew I could stand it.

Before stepping in, I tried to wipe my mind clean of how wet Amelia's pussy was for me last night, of how well her body reacted to my touch, and how satisfied she looked when she came with my name on her lips.

Now, inside the small glass enclosure, I let the water flow over me, welcoming the burn that I undoubtedly deserve.

And then I think of Amelia.

So sexy.

Stroke my hand up and down.

Think of Amelia some more.

So smart and funny.

And yes, I think of Amelia.

The memory of last night is powerful enough that it makes my cock throb so much in my hand it hurts. Wrong or right, we've started something that I'm not sure we can stop.

Removing my hand from my cock, I turn the water pressure on even higher. The glass steams up, and I find myself staring at it.

The water beats on my back, pounding relentlessly, and I need it. Crave it. The punishing rhythm of the wake-up call I deserve to remind me this way of thinking about Amelia is wrong.

You say it's not.

I disagree.

If it wasn't, why didn't I tell Cam when I saw him? Why didn't I text him when I was up all night thinking about what I should do? Why don't I march over there today and ask Amelia out, right in front of him?

Not because he'll kill me, but because he'll fucking hate me—that's why. And the small semblance of family the five—no, six—of us have built here will all be blown apart.

Call me a pussy, call me whatever you want, but this is the only real family I've ever had, and I don't want to lose it.

I know we're not a traditional family by definition—Keen, Maggie, Presley, Makayla, Cam, and I—but we are a family.

Yeah, so now that I've been honest, I can jerk off to her without guilt.

This one time.

Clearing my head of the shit storm I know is bound to come, I curl my hand around my cock again. As my fingers tighten, I imagine her fingers around me because she's curious—she wants to know how hard she makes me. She wants to see how I will react. She wants to watch me come.

Up.

Down.

Slow.

It's her, doing this to me.

Her.

With my fantasy in place, I close my eyes and gently rub first around the head, and then down my shaft. With my other hand, I fist my balls. Both hands move in tandem.

Fuck, that feels good.

Because I gave myself a pass, I picture her doing this. Her in the shower with me and us free to explore each other in any way we want. God knows I want to explore her. All of her. Her pussy, her ass, her mouth. Every single inch of her.

The memory of that hot little pussy of hers has me grabbing my shaft harder and moving up toward the tip. I want her hands to be the ones gripping me, not mine, but I have to settle for this, and in my fantasy, it is her hands, not mine.

Water droplets from the shower pound my body and act as a lube, making it easier to move faster. I think of her—her face, her body, how much I want her.

Fuck!

I imagine driving my cock into her sweet pussy, and the fantasy of that makes me want to come hard and fast.

Oh, fuck yeah.

My fist pumps at a quicker pace and I lick the water from my lips. I think about slowing down, but I am already too far gone.

My forehead falls to the shower wall and I grab my balls tighter, twisting my cock to feel a little pain.

Fuck!

Pressure wells deep within me and a tingling radiates along my spine.

I am going to come.

I am going to explode.

Fuck!

As my orgasm speeds higher and higher, so does the pleasure—it feels like electricity is shooting through me. That unbelievably good feeling mounts and I can't hold on any longer.

I clutch on tight and let myself go.

As I come, my cock twitches so fast it feels like a spasm, but it's so incredibly good. I explode at the thought of her and the intensity of my orgasm shocks me. When the feeling rises again, I can't believe it.

I'm not finished.

This time I really let myself go—crossing that threshold to another world and reliving the same feeling again and again until I am spent. If just the thought of her milks me of everything I have, how will it feel when I'm actually inside her?

After the high subsides, I slouch against the glass and think—it will feel fucking fantastic.

As my breathing returns to normal, so do my senses, and I chastise myself. I shouldn't be thinking of her at all; she's Cam's little sister.

With a sudden urge to chop my dick off, I lather up with soap, rinse off, and get the fuck out of here.

I don't bother to shave.

Wrapping a towel around my waist, I wipe the steam from the

mirror and stare at my reflection.

What's it going to be . . . resist temptation or give in to it and risk everything?

Only time will tell.

CHAPTER 21

13 Going on 30

Amelia

People say that real life is nothing like it is in the movies. That's not always true. When it comes to falling in love, I think the two can sometimes resemble each other quite a lot.

You probably won't end up kissing someone in the rain for the first time, or finding the one who completes you at your place of work, but that doesn't mean the best movies aren't about love, especially the relatable ones.

Romances that feel real, make you feel like you're floating on a cloud, are the very best ones. And as I read *Fangirl*, I find myself feeling just like that.

With my red pen in my hand, I cross out some of Kate's lines and rewrite them. Taking liberties that might be unwelcome don't bother me. For some reason, I seem to be able to fall into the role of Kate with ease. And because of this, I go with it.

The hero, Kellan, is a twenty-something party guy with a big ego. He became an overnight star on a hit television show about a surfer who quits college to follow his dreams, and he thinks he is all that.

Kate is the smitten fan who has stars in her eyes when she

meets Kellan at her father's surf shop, which is being used to film an episode of Kellan's television show. After contemplating what to do for days, she finally emerges from the back room and nervously asks him for his autograph. And that is how they meet.

Not my favorite part.

Don't get me wrong—the screenplay is well written and draws me right in. It's just that Kate, who is free-spirited and lively, which is what draws Kellan to her, seems to fall under his spell way too easily. As his love interest she needs to be less nervous, more indifferent, not exactly playing hard to get, but not as awestruck, or else I don't think Kellan would be as intrigued as he is.

Other than the beginning, which is where the majority of my notes are, I think this will make a fantastic movie about finding love when you least expect it.

Technically, I'm not breaking and entering because I had to get my things anyway, and I knew where the spare key was.

Brooklyn isn't home yet, though, and it's close to four. Sadly, I have to go. Cam and Makayla had to take a ride to West Hollywood, but will be home anytime. Turns out Presley's diaper bag somehow got left behind. Maggie assured Makayla she'd be fine without it. That Makayla could send it to work with Cam on Monday, and Keen would bring it home after work. Still, Makayla insisted on returning it today. I think she has a case of babyitis.

I might have teased my brother about it this morning, and he might have given me the narrow-eyed stare he is famous for.

That was enough to tell me he's not ready for that next step. I think he feels the need to build his career first. You see, Cam is determined to be a huge success, like our father, but without our father's help. Yeah, he has daddy issues, like me. He, however, is forging ahead on his own. He owns a men's retail clothing company, and Keen works for him, and so does Maggie, but she's still on maternity leave.

It's pretty cute—this little family they have established.

Anyway, they said they'd be home by dinner, so I should probably get back and even start cooking something.

I consider leaving Brooklyn a note, just as I thought about texting him all day, but I have yet to hear from him after his abrupt departure from the car last night, so I leave his manuscript on the bed with the red pen on top of it and go.

He'll know I was here.

I take my time locking up, hoping to see him. I take my time walking around the path to my brother's house, hoping to see him. And I take my time going in, hoping to see him.

I don't.

Once inside Cam's kitchen, I force myself to stop thinking about Brooklyn, and busy myself with what to make for dinner. I find a loaf of bread in the freezer and take it out to thaw.

Just as I'm rummaging through the pantry for ingredients to make spaghetti sauce, Makayla comes in. "Hi," I say as I set the cans of crushed tomatoes on the counter.

She blows on her fingers. "Hi. I should have worn gloves. It's cold outside."

"Is it usually this cold?" I ask, opening the brand-new refrigerator and looking for some spices.

"No." Makayla sets her purse on the counter. "Or at least I don't remember it being this cold last year at this time."

There is a small container of basil and oregano on one of the neatly organized shelves that I am sure my brother had nothing to do with. I grab it, along with some fresh garlic and an onion. "I hope you don't mind, but I thought I'd make pasta and garlic bread for dinner."

Makayla rubs her stomach. "That sounds amazing. We had black bean burgers and chickpea salad for lunch at Keen and Maggie's, and I'm starving."

Opening the drawer nearest the stove, I'm not surprised to find it is the utensils drawer. "Black bean burgers? Yuck," I say, pointing my finger toward my mouth before grabbing a can opener.

"Maggie's specialty," Makayla adds, slipping her shoes off and leaving them neatly by the door. She likes things in their place. I wouldn't say she's OCD, but she's definitely organized.

Maggie's house, where Brooklyn lives, isn't so organized. I'd say I'm somewhere in the middle. Neatness is cool, but not always needed. I'm happy either way.

"How can I help?" Makayla asks, washing her hands in the sink.

I hand her a dish towel. "How about you pour us each a glass of wine and make the garlic bread, and I'll do the rest."

Once her hands are dry, she slings the dish towel over my shoulder. "Deal."

The pots and pans are all neatly hanging from the new pot rack over the island and I reach for one of each. "Where's Cam?"

She opens the wine chiller that I had not noticed and bends to study the bottles. "Oh, he saw Brooklyn when we pulled in, and he went over to talk to him."

Worried, I bite my bottom lip, and turn away from her to set the pot in the sink and the pan on the stove. "What about?" I try to keep my voice even.

After a pause, she removes a bottle of red. "I'm not sure."

The can opener is state-of-the-art, nothing like my old, hard-to-turn one, and I don't even struggle to open the can. Mid-turn, I glance over my shoulder. "Everything looks so beautiful in the house. You've done a great job."

With a smile, she opens a cabinet near the chiller and grabs two large goblets. Over her own shoulder, she tosses, "Thank you. Cam has helped."

Turning, I smirk to myself. My brother couldn't care less about how anything is decorated. "Like with what? Deciding the length of the couch to lay his ass on and watch the basketball game?"

Giggling, she pours the wine. "Well, he pretends to help. It's cute."

I fill the pot with water and set it on the stove on medium. Then I open the upper cupboard nearest the stove to find the olive oil. I pour some into the pan before stepping to the butcher block beside the stove to chop the onions and mince the garlic. "So tell me, when are you two going to get married?"

Makayla sets the glass of wine beside me and bends to grab a cookie tray from the drawer under the stove. She looks up. "I don't know, maybe this fall or even next spring. Neither one of us wants to rush it."

Turning the stove on to heat the oil, I start to chop the onions. "That's smart. It gives you time to finish remodeling the house and plan your wedding without a lot of stress."

Sipping her wine, she looks over the rim of her glass at me. "Yes. Cam has been trying to buy this house from our landlord for a while now, and I think they've finally agreed to a price. Once we actually own it, we want to finish the inside and then attack the outside. First thing Cam wants to redo is the outdoor patio."

Dropping my knife, I turn to her and clap my hands together. "Oh my God, you're actually going to get to buy this house. That is fantastic."

Her shoulders lift with excitement as she starts to cut the bread. "I think so, too, but don't tell Cam I told you. He wants to tell you himself."

"Tell Cam what?" The voice is deep, and definitely my brother's.

"I'm so busted." Makayla smiles and twists her head to kiss him.

Cam swats her on the ass, and then meets her lips. "Bad girl. I think I might need to punish you," he whispers, but not low enough.

"Stop!" I shout. The last thing I want to hear is my brother talking about sex. "She was telling me about your new house," I blurt out, dumping the tomatoes in the pan.

Cam approaches and looks over my shoulder. "Yes!" He fist-pumps. "Your spaghetti sauce is my favorite."

With a smile, I add the garlic and spices. "I know."

The wooden spoons are in the drawer on the other side of the stove, and he opens it and grabs one. Just as he hands it to me, he says, "Be sure to make enough. I asked Brooklyn to join us."

When I take the spoon, I ladle it around and try to hide my joy by bending to smell the aroma of the freshly cooking garlic. "There should be plenty."

Makayla slides the sliced bread coated with butter and garlic into the stove. "I'm going to go change, and then I'll set the table."

Just then the water boils, and I grab the box of pasta. "Don't rush."

Cam reaches for the strainer and sets it in the sink in the island. "I'll be back to help. Will you be okay?"

I shake my head. "You don't have to rush, either."

He grins. "You sure?"

Grabbing the towel over my shoulder, I swat him across the chest. "Go. I got this." I like to see my brother happy. And with his happy mood right now, I know nothing bad happened with Brooklyn.

Just as I dump the pasta in the water, my cell rings and Landon's name flashes across the screen.

Along with Carter, I talked to him earlier, so I'm surprised he's calling again. "Hello, ball boy," I answer, just to be sassy.

"It's Major League player to you, and hey," he laughs.

Putting the phone to my cheek with my shoulder, I grab the large pasta fork in the drawer. "Silly me, I forgot you received that little promotion."

His voice goes low. "You like to hit below the belt."

I know he's looking for a sexy comeback, but for some reason I don't want to go there, and I turn the conversation, just as I did earlier. "I'm just honored to get two calls in one day."

"I was worried about you. You sounded upset when you told me about your father earlier. Did you call your mother?"

The water boils a little too much, and I turn the heat down. "I did."

"And?"

My thoughts wander to what Carter told me this morning when I told him all about last night. My best friend told me not to play around with two men at once. And even though he gets that Brooklyn isn't looking for anything more than a hookup, he says that is what I am doing. Someone always gets burned, is what he told me. Seriously, I should listen to Carter. After meeting two men he really liked last summer, he secretly dated each. And what he found out was that a love triangle is never a daisy chain when both dumped him.

With that in mind, I cover the sauce and turn the heat to simmer, and then grab my wine and lean against the counter. I will keep our conversations in the friend zone until I can get over my crush on Brooklyn. "I told her what I found out, and how sorry I was. Not surprisingly, she cried, and then she asked me not to hate my father."

"But you do?"

Frowning, my brother walks back in. "Who's that?" he mouths.

I ignore his glare and swirl my wineglass. "*Hate* is a strong word. I think I'm numb right now, and disappointed."

"That's understandable," Landon comments. "Does he know you know?"

"He does. I emailed him. Told him everything, and also told him I'm taking the next two weeks off."

"And?"

"And I haven't opened his response. I'm not really ready for that. What do you say we talk about something else," I suggest.

"Sure," he says, and then asks, "So you'll be home in two weeks? I want to take you out to the field and teach you how to throw."

"Sounds fun, but I'm not sure when I'll be back," I tell him, and then catch my brother's stare. He narrows his eyes at me. I widen mine and turn my back. He knows all about our father—he sat beside me this morning when I sent the email—so his pre-occupation with my phone call has nothing to do with that.

"How about I come out there?" Landon offers. "I have next weekend off, and I really want to see you again."

The memory of Brooklyn and his fingers inside my pussy comes to mind, and the thought has my toes tingling. With Landon here, it could be messy, not to mention keeping things in the friend zone would be much harder. "No, that's probably not a good idea right now."

There's a slight pause, but he recovers quickly. "Well, if you change your mind, let me know."

With my mind still on last night, my cheeks flush a little as I remember how Brooklyn made me come, and I know I should get off the phone with another man. "Yes, I will. I promise. I'm making dinner and should probably get back to it."

"Good night, Amelia," he says, and disconnects. He's so easygoing, so smooth. I can't help but contrast that to Brooklyn, who is anything but easygoing, and much rougher around the edges.

When I turn around, I see not only my brother staring at me, but Makayla, too.

"Who was that, Carter?" Cam asks suspiciously.

"No," I reply.

"Then who?"

Makayla smiles. "Was that a boy?"

"Maybe," I admit, instantly regretting my flirty tone.

Makayla's smile grows wider. "A boy you like?"

The pasta should be done, and I turn to stir it one last time before straining it. "Maybe," I say again, this time a little softer, a little less playful.

"You have a boyfriend and haven't told me about him? What's his name?" Cam demands.

Turning with the pot in my hands, I walk toward the sink and answer with, "His name is Landon Reese, and he is not my boyfriend," just in time for the kitchen door to swing open and for Brooklyn to hear.

"Landon Reese, the Yankees' new pitcher, is your boyfriend?" Cam asks in a tone that screams he's anything but thrilled.

Dumping the noodles into the strainer, I don't look up. I really hate that Brooklyn is listening to this. "We were talking, but like I said, he is not my boyfriend. Now, drop it." My voice is stern.

Seeing the signs of a sibling fight on the horizon, Makayla busies herself taking the bread out of the oven and putting it into a basket.

Cam, on the other hand, doesn't drop it as I told him to. Instead, he presses his palms on the counter and leans forward. "Ballplayers are not the type of guy you want to get involved with, Amelia."

There he is, the overprotective big brother who can never remember I am an adult. And that I can make my own choices, and wisely, I might add.

"They're all players, just looking to get some," he adds, in case his warning wasn't enough to deter me.

I want to roll my eyes, to say something like, "You and your friends were all players once upon a time," but with Brooklyn here, I decide to tread carefully. Still flushed from the memory of last night, I look up through the steam. "We're not involved; I already told you that. So again, let's drop it."

He again ignores me. "You got off the phone with him two

minutes ago and you still look like a blushing schoolgirl."

Clearly, Cam has the wrong idea about why my cheeks are red, and now Brooklyn does, too.

Great.

"It's the steam," I tell him and then look away to Brooklyn, who is watching all of this with keen interest, a brooding disposition, and narrowed eyes. "Hi, Brooklyn," I offer, trying to change the subject. "You're just in time—dinner is almost ready."

He jerks his chin up. "What's up?" he says, as if I'm just one of the guys, and then turns to Makayla, who gets a slight hug and a kiss on the cheek.

Cam finally takes the hint, and leaving me alone, he thumps Brooklyn on the shoulder and says, "Help yourself to a beer, man," and then starts to assist Makayla, who is setting the table.

I turn around, trying not to let Brooklyn's casual greeting affect me, and open the cupboard to find a big serving bowl. There are a few of them, but they are all on the top shelf, and I have to get on tiptoes to try to reach one.

"I got it," Brooklyn hisses. My gaze shifts. He's next to me, smelling fresh-out-of-the-shower clean. Delicious. And looking very angry, with that broody look of his that for some crazy reason does strange things to my belly.

I watch, and goose bumps hump my flesh as his long, lean body stretches to grab a bowl. When he hands it to me, I allow my fingertips to graze his. "I came over today looking for you."

His mouth scrunches into an exaggerated frown and he yanks his hand away. And looks over his shoulder to find Cam invested in his own conversation with Makayla. When he discovers they are paying no attention to us, he finally answers me. "I noticed. I had to work," he says, and strides over to the refrigerator.

Making it look like there is nothing between us is difficult. It's weird how my overbearing, overprotective brother isn't bothered by Brooklyn being near me right now, yet he goes off when I talk to a guy on the phone. Then again, he trusts Brooklyn, which is the problem with all of this, isn't it?

Hating that my attraction toward Brooklyn could very well ruin his friendship with my brother, I find myself wondering if I shouldn't have just said Landon was my boyfriend, which, by the sour look on Brooklyn's face, would have ended things between us immediately.

But that would be a lie.

And I can't help how I feel about Brooklyn. The last thing I want to do is hurt him. Or push him away, no matter how selfish it sounds. He's not looking for forever, and I won't be here forever. It really is the perfect situation. And besides, my brother never has to know.

Personally, I don't think he'd hate it as much as Brooklyn thinks he would. But I do know what he'd hate. He'd hate that Brooklyn might break my heart, and that is what would drive them apart. I think Cam could get over the fact that he thinks Brooklyn overdoses on women—his words, not mine. What he wouldn't get over is Brooklyn hurting me, which is why I won't let that happen.

Don't look at me like that! I can be just another woman he has sex with. I'm fine with that.

Feeling a little flushed at the thought, I hurry over to the island and pour the strained pasta into the bowl. Once assured it isn't sticking, I head to the stove with the full bowl in my hands.

Brooklyn is back, and is now leaning against the counter next to the stove with a bottle of beer in his hand, watching me.

Feeling the heat of his brooding stare, I look into his blue eyes as I set the bowl beside him, pausing for a moment to allow him to say what's on his mind. When he says nothing, I begin ladling the sauce on top of the pasta.

Dealing with a pissed-off, brooding Brooklyn isn't how I want to spend the evening. Once I've poured enough sauce on the pasta, I start to mix it. I pause again to look up at him.

His frown has only intensified.

Obviously, he wants to know more about Landon, so I tell him in a whisper, "Landon was my blind date New Year's Eve. Things went okay. Good, even. Until I found out about my father, anyway. Landon was there when I ran into Vanessa, so I told him what happened. He helped me book my plane ticket here. I owe him."

"Owe him?"

The fury in his almost inaudible tone makes me wary. "Not like that."

"Then like how?" he demands, his voice low, but still making me flinch.

I give the pasta one last twirl with my spoon, and then reach for the pepper. "He helped me, and wants to make sure I'm okay. He's been calling me to check on me, but that's all."

Brooklyn tips his bottle back, his Adam's apple working in the sexiest of ways. With his lips still around the glass, and his eyes cold as ice, he asks, "Did you fuck him?"

He's glancing over my shoulder at my brother, who is getting a lesson on which side of the plate the fork goes, though I'm pretty certain he learned it in cotillion. I narrow my own eyes at Brooklyn and keep my lips sealed.

"Did you?" he asks, lowering his bottle.

As I lightly sprinkle the pepper over the pasta, I snap at him. "No, I didn't, but it really isn't any of your business."

In one smooth move, he takes my hand and forces the spoon up toward his mouth. To anyone looking at us, it would appear that I'm asking him to sample it. With my hand shaking, I hold it near his lips. Lips I want on me, everywhere.

As soon as the spoon meets his mouth, he whispers, "Everything about you is my business."

Game over. Right here. Right now.

The way he says those six words, the possessiveness in his tone, the hunger in his eyes—there is no way I wouldn't give him anything he asks for.

No matter how strong I want to appear to be, I'm his for the taking.

And I'm pretty certain . . . he knows that.

I nod, and lower the spoon.

"Is it time to eat?" Makayla asks, lighting the candles she's put in the middle of the table.

Cam is already sitting and is on his phone now, probably checking sales figures.

"Yes, it's time." I smile, and allow my gaze to flicker to Brooklyn. My words were meant for him, as much as for Makayla.

His chin dips, just a little, and as I step to brush past him, he whispers so low I can barely hear him, "Go to bed early tonight."

Even fully clothed, I can feel the heat of his body as I pass by him, and think . . . *you don't have to tell me twice.*

Is now too early?

CHAPTER 22

Mr. & Mrs. Smith

Brooklyn

The first scene of a film is an integral part of its storytelling. It establishes the tone and setting, and introduces the central characters. If intriguing enough, it gives viewers motivation to keep watching.

And as I slowly, quietly walk on the pathway beside the fence that separates Cam's property line from Maggie's, I can't help but compare my situation to the Alfred Hitchcock movie *Rear Window*.

The story is about a man's voyeuristic pleasures as he spies on his neighbors. In the opening scene, the camera cuts to the courtyard just outside the main character's home. Everything appears quiet and normal, each frame showing us only what the director wants us to see—a cat walking up an alleyway, a woman changing in her bedroom, and pigeons on top of a roof.

Quiet.

Normal.

However, among friendly faces, an unfathomable crime has been committed. And yes, that is how I feel right now. Like a crime is about to be committed, and even though I know this, I can't stop myself from being the one to commit it.

Amelia's window faces the street. A carport and a bank of trash cans are the only camouflage I have from the cars passing by, and from the possibility that Cam might step out to throw out the garbage, or get something from his Jeep, or worse, check on a noise he swears he might have heard.

Jack Reacher, James Bond, or Ethan Hunt I certainly am not, and yet I find myself carefully approaching her window as if I am.

The light I saw turned on before coming around the fence is hopefully her way of alerting me that she's in there, and alone.

As a teen growing up in Beverly Hills, I didn't have to sneak around. My mother was never home, so I came and went right through the front door at all hours of the night. And the girls I went to see, they just let me inside the same way, their parents oblivious to what was going on. If it had been like this, I think I might have kept my dick in my pants more often.

Nerves a wreck.

Adrenaline pumping hard.

All I know is that if I didn't need to be with her, to have her so goddamn much, I wouldn't be doing this.

Like a spy right out of a movie, I inch along the side of the house and then turn the corner. At the window I pause, and then quickly jerk my head in front of the glass to look in, before pulling it back.

Relieved she's in there, alone, I step in front of the window and hope to fuck I don't scare the ever-living shit out of her when I open it.

I know it's unlocked because I unlocked it when I used the bathroom outside the bedroom to wash my hands before dinner.

Dinner that felt like nothing but pure torture. Stealing glances with Amelia. Talking to Makayla about the wedding. Telling her about my buddy Chase's plans for his impending nuptials. Listening to Cam tell me about their weekend in Mexico with my brother, his wife, and their baby, and with each laugh ignoring my attraction to his sister. Hiding the fact that I had every intention of fucking her the minute it got dark.

If that doesn't already classify me as an asshole, this move right here certainly will. And the fact that I don't intend for this to be a one-time thing certifies it.

I wanted to tell Cam, but I couldn't. What exactly would I tell him? *Your sister is into me because she craves some of my bad, and I intend to wipe it all over her.*

Right!

That would go over really well.

Wouldn't it?

No, not at all, and so instead, I'm here sneaking around in the dark. It's my only choice.

I have to.

I can't explain why.

I just can't walk away from her, and I can't tell Cam about us either, not until I know where her head is. What does she want from me? Is this is just a fling that will end when she leaves?

As I slide the window up, Amelia jumps off her bed and rushes toward me. Her hair is up in a high ponytail and she's changed into a pair of black yoga pants and a white oversized T-shirt that hangs off her shoulder, the straps of her black lacy bra all I can focus on.

"What are you doing?" she whispers, obviously not expecting me to come and get her this way. She doesn't get it, get that I really want her, and I'll do things I've never done to get her.

"*Shhh* . . . go put some shoes on," I tell her, tearing my eyes from the paleness of her soft skin to hurry her along.

In a rush, she dashes over to her suitcase and pulls out a pair of battered Chucks. I watch her. The excitement in each move she makes. The flush on her face. And I wonder why, if she's into me, she's talking to another guy on the phone.

Well, if she wants me, wants some of my bad, she'll have to understand that I don't share. Never have. Never will.

There's this girl that Maggie calls my *go-to* girl. It's her way of saying my fuck buddy. Her name is Sasha, and we were on the network at the same time. We'd been fucking around for almost ten years, until I finally ended it for good two months ago.

The rule between us had always been when we were on, there was no one else. And it worked. One of us always calling it off sooner rather than later, we were off more than on. But two months ago we were on, and everything was cool.

Then Keen and Maggie had Presley, and I was spending a lot of time driving to West Hollywood. One night, on my way back, I decided to stop by and see Sasha, and found her with another guy.

When we were off, I never cared who she was with, but we weren't off, and there was no way I was going to fuck her when she was letting some other guy fuck her too. I told her that and walked away. I have yet to answer a single one of her calls or text messages. As far as I'm concerned, we are over.

Sharing is a hard limit.

Like I said, I don't share.

Once Amelia has her shoes on, she crosses the room once again. "Now what?"

I'm still outside the window, and I reach my hand out for her. "Come on, we're going to my place."

Unabashed, she turns back. "Should I turn my light off?"

"Yeah."

She scurries over to the door and flicks the light off.

Again at the window, she sits on the ledge. It's not high, yet I take hold of her and assist her down.

After that I close the window and take her hand. "Follow me, and stay quiet."

She nods.

I can't help but smile at her—she's the perfect accomplice.

The night is dark, the air cold. And we walk close to the house like two robbers casing out their next job. When we get to the corner, I jerk my head around it to make sure the coast is clear.

It is.

Then I look at Amelia. "We're going to run straight across, and then around the fence. We'll go in my front door."

She looks back. "You don't have to worry. I think Cam and Makayla went to bed. They weren't in the living room when I went to check."

"Okay, that's good," I whisper, hating this, hating the deceit.

This is so not a good idea.

Not in the least.

And yet, with her hand in mind, I don't turn around and bring her back to her room. Instead, I jet across the grass to Maggie's property and don't plan on stopping until I have Amelia inside my front door and up the stairs into my room.

Where we can be alone.

Unseen.

To do what her brother will ultimately hate me for.

I'm so going to hell.

CHAPTER 23

Before Sunrise

Amelia

Through the ages, women have been drawn to men who wear that dark, brooding look that suggests they are mad, bad, or dangerous to get to know.

From Heathcliff in *Wuthering Heights* to the ever-dangerous James Bond, a woman is attracted to the narcissistic features of this kind of man because they make him appear mentally stronger, more capable.

Yes, I know this.

I learned it in my psychology class.

And no, I have never been attracted to a man who fits this mold—until now.

Brooklyn's bedroom door is open, and we cross the threshold quickly. As soon as I'm in his room, I rush toward the window and look down. Cam and Makayla's room is dark, except for a faint glow. I hope that means they're in bed sleeping after their long weekend, and not watching television, wanting to say good night before bed.

"Amelia," Brooklyn commands in a husky voice.

Not surprisingly nervous, I turn around, my hands behind me

clutching the windowsill. Butterflies take flight in my belly. All of a sudden, his good looks have me wanting to fangirl all over him. No worries, though; like his character Kate, I know better.

In well-worn jeans that are slung low on his hips and a faded Lakers T-shirt that molds to his muscled chest and is snug around his upper arms, he screams sex on a stick.

I silently devour the sight of him, since I was unable to earlier, and then finally remember how to speak. "Yes," I answer.

Brooklyn stands looking larger than life, leaning against the door. His hand is still on the knob, as if deciding whether to stay or to go. Yet his gaze isn't focused on the window in worry, but rather on me. And me alone. "We have to talk about something before going any further."

Determined not to be nervous about this, I slowly start to close the distance between us. "Sure, anything."

His lazy gaze drifts over me with each step I take. And suddenly I wish I'd dressed nicer, something more put together. When his eyes reach mine, there is a look of dominance there that I find utterly appealing. "If we do this," he starts, and then raises his hand, the one not still on the doorknob, and uses his finger to point back and forth between us. "If we go behind your brother's back to be together," he says, making me aware that he has a lot at stake, "I only have one rule."

"What is it?" My voice is shaky, uncertain.

He bites at his bottom lip, that lip that is so full and lush, I want to be the one biting it. "You can't be carrying on with another man while you're fucking me," he proclaims so matter-of-factly that it takes me a moment to comprehend his demand.

Still a little shocked, I speak the truth. "I'm not carrying on with anyone else, Brooklyn."

He looks at me with doubt.

"I'm not."

"Let me clarify, then: no contact with any other male who isn't simply a friend. None."

I stare at him slightly bewildered, because no one has ever been jealous when it came to me before. No one.

There is no hesitation on his part. "Are you willing to let the other man go, Amelia?"

Stunned, I stop in the middle of his very familiar room feeling oddly thrilled.

The other man?

That makes me want to laugh a little. Landon is not "the other man." I mean, I just met him. Although I suppose in Brooklyn's eyes, after what happened before dinner, it might appear that he is.

And then there's the "do this." *Do this?* I guess as in fuck, and not just once. Even more thrilled by this thought, my pulse starts to race.

We haven't really discussed what would come after sex; we both just intuitively knew we would end up here. With the days of looks, the flirting, and the sexual tension, it was inevitable.

This ultimatum of sorts, though, I was not expecting. He is referring to Landon, of course. And no, what he's asking for isn't unfair.

The answer is more difficult. Am I willing to give up someone who could be my Mr. Right for Mr. Oh-So-Wrong?

"Amelia," he prompts, still unmoving, still acting as if he is halfway in and halfway out of the room, as if my answer will jump-start this or end it.

Realizing my gaze has fallen, I lift my eyes to meet his once again. He is gorgeous in a way a man wouldn't normally be. Hot, sexy, and dare I say, pretty. Yet beneath the pretty, beneath the guy uncertain of how to become what he wants to be, is a man. Confident and sure of who he is, in this situation, anyway.

The choice should be easy. I've been searching for my Mr. Right for what seems like forever. So why am I leaning the other way? Why is Mr. Oh-So-Wrong so appealing?

Is considering a short relationship where I know the sex will be off-the-charts hot, instead of one that might be for a lifetime, certifiably insane?

Isn't it?

Like I said, the choice should be easy. I should say no, and allow Brooklyn to become one giant ball of pissed-off alpha male and usher me right out the door.

I mean, not to be rude, but whereas Landon seems to be the boy next door, Brooklyn is the sinful bad boy. He is the one all the women go wild over for completely different reasons than they would go wild over Landon. The truth is it's in the way he looks at you, at me—with eyes that promise pleasure like I've never known.

And there it is—the reason why. The reason my decision might not be what it should be. My mouth goes dry at the thought, and I lick my lips.

I've always made practical decisions based on what my father might think. Held back from what I wanted because I was the good girl, who did good things and made good choices.

Look at my job, for goodness sake. Every day since I started I've tried to convince myself I like it, but if I want to be honest with myself, I hate it.

And then look at my love life. I've only ever gone out with guys my father would approve of. I've let them wine and dine me. And after the appropriate amount of dates, I've had boring sex with them, where I've pretended to orgasm so their egos wouldn't be damaged. And then I'd keep it going until we were both so bored out of our minds that one of us ended things.

Pathetic.

But no more.

Choosing Landon or Brooklyn will be for me.

And only me.

CHAPTER 24

Like Crazy

Brooklyn

Guilt is a goddamn hard thing to swallow.

With my hand on the doorknob, I wait for her answer. A *no* makes this whole thing go away.

No hurt feelings.

No betrayal.

In a way, it would be the easiest answer—for both of us.

She can run off into the sunset with that Prince Charming she's dreamed about since she was ten, and I would be left to carry on the way I always have.

A rebel.

A manwhore.

A player.

A pantydropper.

A Hollywood Prince with a tarnished crown.

But fuck if that lifestyle no longer interests me. The thought of my dead-end job and the endless parade of pussy makes me want to blow my brains out right now.

Amelia looks at me, contemplating my demand.

Everything about her turns me on. Her perceived naïveté, and the sex kitten beneath it that I want desperately to explore. Her vibrancy and how contagious it is. Her beauty that makes every other woman dim in comparison. Even her smile knocks me off balance.

Without even knowing it, she's changing my life.

Yeah, so even though a *no* would be easier, I don't want easier anymore. I want her, any way she'll have me.

Consequences be damned.

This isn't about Cam. It's about her and me, and this burning attraction that can't be denied.

I raise a brow, letting her know time is running out.

Tick.

Tock.

Finally, she opens her mouth, and all I can think is . . . *please say yes*.

CHAPTER 25

9½ Weeks

Amelia

A word is just a word, until it changes everything.

"Yes," I answer huskily.

Something primal enters his eyes. It makes me feel extremely vulnerable, but the sensation isn't scary in the least; it's exhilarating, sinful, delicious.

His hand drops from the doorknob, the gatekeeper between us, but I raise my own hand to let him know it hasn't been fully decided yet.

He frowns, yet says nothing; he does, however, place his hand back on the doorknob, a sign to let me know for certain that he will walk away.

I push that aside and focus on moving forward. Even with the decision made, the "not sharing" rule has to be mutual. "Yes, I can," I repeat, my voice quivering in a way I hate, "but that means you can't be with other women either."

Brooklyn is my age, and yet the look he gives me makes him more of a man than any guy I've ever been with. "That's implied, Amelia. For as long as we fuck, we only fuck each other. If you want out, or I do, either one of us just says the word."

I take a tentative step toward him. "And when I leave, this ends. It won't be messy or emotional. And we don't tell my brother, so you don't have to worry about your relationship with him. I don't want anything to come between the two of you, especially me."

Perhaps agreeing, or perhaps simply deciding to stay, he lets go of the doorknob and strides toward me. Before I can say another word, he hauls me into his arms and crashes his mouth to mine.

The moan that escapes my throat isn't on purpose. It's just the way he runs his hands possessively up my arms to clasp my shoulders, and then upward again, to my throat, and finally to cradle my face, is so unlike any way any man has ever touched me that I lose control immediately.

The way he kisses me—as though he is starved for me, as if we've been forced apart by some exterior circumstances and suddenly brought back together—it's enough to make me whimper.

I've been kissed by dozens of frogs, toads, and would-be princes, but never like this. Never where my toes curl and the room seems to shift sideways. Never, even in my wildest fantasies, could I have dreamed of anything like this.

It's over the top.

Explosive.

All-consuming.

The tiniest of glimpses of what is to come.

One of his hands moves from my face to curl an arm around me, drawing me closer, anchoring me tightly against him. I can feel his hardness against my belly, his straining erection more than prominent, another promise of what is about to come.

His lips move.

His tongue strokes.

His cock pulses between us.

And we kiss and kiss and kiss, until finally he breaks our

connection, his breath exploding all over me, and leaving me gasping for air.

I look up.

His blue eyes glitter. "I can't believe we're doing this."

I nod, tongue-tied.

His mouth moves close to mine again but doesn't touch it. Instead, he skims my jawline, his lips just brushing my skin. "Cat got your tongue, Amelia?" he asks, nipping at my earlobe.

"No," I manage, more hyperaware of his presence than ever.

"Talk to me. Tell me you want me as badly as I want you," he commands in a husky voice that elicits a full-body shiver.

"Yes, I want you," I tell him as that shiver races across every inch of my flesh.

"Tell me you aren't going to regret this." This time the calm authority in his voice reassures me that I am making the right choice.

"I won't," I mouth, but that is not enough to ease his mind. It's evident on his face when I pull back to look at him. Perhaps what he wants to know isn't that I won't be the only one who won't regret anything. I run my hands up his chest. "You, Brooklyn, are not going to regret this," I reassure him.

The blaze in his eyes is like an inferno. "I don't doubt it," he murmurs, and then he tugs on my ponytail, lifting my chin, and lowers his mouth to mine.

This time, he sips at my lips, grazing them with his teeth, nipping with just enough force that they tingle from his touch.

Somehow our hands find each other and our fingers intertwine.

My mouth remains closed as his lips work hard to coax it open. And coax it open he does when he licks between my lips in the most delicious way, leaving me desperate for his tongue. And not just in my mouth.

As if he could hear my thoughts, he breaks the kiss and looks at me. "Your mouth tastes so good. Can I taste the rest of you, too?"

I nod, incapable of words. I find my voice just enough to sigh when he slides slowly to his knees in front of me.

With his fingers hooked in the waistband of my yoga pants, he slowly slides them down inch by inch, revealing the wild zebra-print panties I bought yesterday when I went shopping. Wild, bold prints were all the store had. So unlike me, but I kind of fell in love with them and went a little crazy. I bought seven pairs with equally crazy prints.

His eyes flare as soon he sees them. There is a raw hunger in his features that appears almost primal.

An uncontrolled shiver works up my spine. My nipples harden, pressing against the lacy fabric of my new bra.

Once he gets me out of my sneakers and pants, his palms slide up the back of my calves and up higher to the back of my thighs.

My heart thumps as I try to breathe.

Again, he looks up at me; this time, though, his mouth quirks to the side. "Take your shirt off."

Swallowing and then sucking in a deep breath, I pull my T-shirt over my head, not for a moment even considering denying him his command. "My bra, too?" I ask huskily.

His gaze is fiery as it rakes over my chest, and then he gives me a slight nod. "I want to see those nipples you've been teasing me with for days."

Slowly, I reach back and unclasp my bra. The cups loosen, baring the bottoms of my breasts.

Brooklyn draws in a ragged breath. "All of it."

Carefully, I lower my bra, allowing the straps to slide down my arms in a seductive fashion, and then let it fall to my feet, his feet.

"Beautiful." His voice is a low growl of appreciation.

After a few moments, he closes his eyes and turns his face to kiss my bare thigh just below the lacy edge of my panties. He kisses me there the way he last kissed my mouth—teasing.

Oh, God, the feeling of his lips so close to my pussy is enough to drive me out of my mind. He's on his knees in front of me, and still he's the lethal one.

Sucking gently on the soft flesh of my inner thigh for only a few more seconds, soon his mouth is lifting and I feel his breath and the wetness of his mouth through the scant material of my panties.

I swallow the murmur of his name, not sure I should allow the intimacy I'm feeling to show so soon.

Brooklyn's palms caress upward, over my ass, fingers hooking into my panties at my hips to pull them down my legs.

Breathless, I step out of them, looking down at him.

Raw heat emanates from him, and he keeps his eyes on mine as he spreads my legs wider, baring my pussy. Slowly, his gaze lowers and he seems to be devouring me with his eyes. "Fuck, you're bare," he growls.

Before I lose my nerve, I blurt out what I thought about texting him all day. "I haven't been with anyone in over a year."

His eyes are still on my private parts.

I feel the need to explain. "I wax for my own masturbation purposes. I come faster like this."

There—my confession might be too much information, but at least it is out of the way. I haven't had sex with a man in over a year. I hope he reads through the lines that that means I might be a bit rusty.

His eyes gleam as he looks at me. "Your pussy is going to be so tight."

Okay, not the pity party that I was expecting.

Without another word, he runs a single finger down the center of my pussy, and then using both hands, he spreads me open, baring my most intimate flesh to the cool air in his room.

I can't help but watch as he goes between my thighs, putting his mouth right over my clit and blowing on it.

Oh my God!

It's like a jolt of electricity so strong I have to bite back a cry, one hand going to his head as my hips pump forward.

His tongue sweeps over my clit and he toys with it repeatedly, swirling his tongue around and then sucking at it with gentle tugs.

I rest both hands on his head and thread my fingers through his beautiful hair. Hair that is not quite brown, but not light enough to be blond, either.

The quick movement of his mouth has me gasping for breath.

For some reason, I find my eyelashes fluttering, unable to watch and feel at the same time. I fear I might topple over.

When he switches from the tip of his tongue to the flat of it, the sensation is even greater, causing desire to pool deep in my belly, spreading like fire to every part of my body with each swipe of his wet tongue.

"Sit on the edge of the bed," he tells me.

And I gladly do.

Now I'm spreading my legs wider and I'm tilting my pussy toward him so he can have access to every part of me.

Using his hands, he holds onto my thighs and drags me even farther to the edge of the bed, exposing me even more.

I look down.

His eyes are wicked as he stares at me.

I stare back, lustful, yearning, wanting.

Lowering his mouth, this time he starts to nuzzle, licking his tongue right down to the center of my pussy.

Gasping for breath, I pop up onto my elbows to watch.

His hands are on my ass now, drawing my core to his mouth in every way.

With my body his for the taking, Brooklyn mouths my entrance, flicking his tongue expertly and then delving inside me, fucking me with his tongue.

Everything about this is new. Men have gone down on me, sure. Licked around my clit, used their fingers to fuck me and bring me to orgasm quickly. It felt good.

This is nothing like that.

This is so much more than good.

This is incredible.

This is the work of a man who knows how to bring pleasure to a woman. This is for me. To make me feel consumed, devoured, wanted. Which I really like. His mouth owns me, and it feels hot, wet, and wild.

I'm on the edge, my orgasm building quickly. As if he knows this, he slows his mouth, brushing his tongue lightly from my center back to my clit and then kissing his way back down to my center.

The sensation forces swirling heat all through me, and I gasp in delight.

For the briefest of seconds, Brooklyn looks up, his eyes burning brightly with lust, enough to make me want to come more than I ever have.

"Brooklyn, please," I whisper.

"Yes." He pauses again.

"Don't stop."

He chuckles, the sound vibrating over my clit and sending me even closer to that magical place I can practically picture. "I don't plan on it. You taste so goddamn good, Amelia, I just might eat your sweet pussy all night."

My hands find the sheets and I hold on to them tightly, thinking I really don't know if I can survive another five minutes, let alone five hours. Although the thought of a man at my pussy licking and kissing it for that long is tempting, the reality is my body is burning to the point of pain.

"Oh, God," I call out.

"Do you want something else, Amelia?" he asks, knowing that he is driving me wild. By the tone of his voice, it is on purpose.

"Yes, I want to come," I blurt out, more direct with him, in his room, and naked, then I have ever been.

Slowly he licks around my clit, already teasing me to the edge again, but not letting me jump over it. "Beg me, Amelia. Call out my name, and I'll make you come like no one ever has."

The second part is a given; I already know that is going to happen. The first part, well, I already know that Brooklyn is an alpha male, and as such, control seems to be a driving need. Honestly, I don't mind submitting, but like Kate, I know I have to be careful about how often and when. The chase is what makes a man come back.

In this case, though, begging is the right choice. "Please, Brooklyn, please. Make me come."

Within moments of my second plea, he's inserting a finger inside me, licking his tongue around my clit, placing his other hand on my ass and circling the puckered skin there.

That swirling heat I felt earlier flares out of control, fierce enough to spin my world a little, and then I'm in a place where unicorns and rainbows are everywhere. A colorful sea of hopes and dreams made possible by the orgasm rocketing through me.

I don't have to tell him it is the best orgasm I've ever had; I'm sure he can see it on my face and hear it in the tone of my voice as I cry out.

Before I'm even fully recovered, Brooklyn is on his feet, ripping his shirt right over his head. Scooting back, I rise to my elbows and watch him. The in-control alpha male seems to be a little out of sorts; perhaps *hurried* is the best word.

As he toes off his scuffed work boots, I watch him. He's so

freaking hot, standing at the foot of the bed. Stripping. Almost naked.

I lie here dizzy with exhilaration, and somehow manage to smile at him.

Beautiful and brooding in that way he has about him, he can't hide his desire for me. It's there, all over every inch of his coiled body. And I can't stop looking at it.

The hum of my body has yet to stop; in fact, rather than stop it seems to have morphed into an ache that only he can satisfy.

His eyes burn over me with blazing heat as he unfastens his jeans and yanks those and his boxers down his hips at the same time.

I make a small noise of pleasure when I see his straining cock. It's big and beautiful. Perfect.

Stepping around the bed, he's close to the headboard in two small strides. His muscles bunch when he reaches for me, taking hold of my thighs and pulling me to him.

Sucking in a breath, my hands start shaking and I clutch the sheets to steady them. I don't want to appear as nervous as I am.

Those blue eyes practically simmer when he says, "I can't wait another second to be inside you, Amelia."

Meeting his intense gaze, I don't hold back, and answer him in the only way I can. "I'm more than ready, Brooklyn. I feel like I've been waiting forever."

With that, he reaches for a condom in the bedside table and tears open the foil packet. Once he's rolled it on, he positions himself between my legs.

Up on my elbows, I throw my head back and feel his cock push into my already swollen pussy before I see it. Instantly, I feel crazy for him. All of him.

Need.

Want.

Desire.

The slow build of something magical starts to take root.

Watching me, he slowly pushes in. Just a little, just his head. Then, just as slowly he withdraws, dragging his cock through the flesh of my soaking wet pussy. And then returning to my entrance, the condom wet with my desire, he surges fully inside me. Deep. Hard. Fast.

My gasps mingle with his.

"Oh, God!" I scream.

"Christ, you're so tight," he growls.

The shock of his first full thrust nearly sends me over the edge. "Oh, God!" I scream again.

The sensation of him inside me is so overwhelming, I can't stop from crying out in pleasure over and over. He's filling me so utterly and completely. He moves again, and I'm so tight around his cock, I have no idea how he is going to move faster. This time I moan without words.

He stops. "Did I hurt you?" he asks, his voice raspy, sexy as hell.

I shake my head. "No. Not at all. Please. Don't stop."

His fingers dig into my hips, and he begins to move again. Harder. Faster. Yet, still in control. "You're greedy, Amelia," he says, and the caution in his voice is something I want him to shed. I want him to be wild with me. Wild for me. Crazy.

"Brooklyn, please," I beg, looking into his eyes. Telling him it's okay to move faster and let go.

His movements quicken at the same time his hands begin to explore my body, sliding from my belly up to my breasts. He palms them and tugs at my nipples. I watch him, mesmerized by his touch.

His cock so deep inside me moves at a steady pace, and my entire body begins to hum again, so much so, I give up trying to remain on my elbows and allow myself to fall to the mattress and let him consume me.

"Your nipples are cherry red. Beautiful," he says, staring at them.

Saying nothing in return, my hands find his, wanting to feel his skin like he is feeling mine. I start at his wrists and slide my palms up his arms, reveling in his strength beneath my fingertips.

While moving inside me with a steady pace, he finds my hands and has them over my head before I can blink. My eyes widen in surprise, but I leave them there. My palms are flat on the mattress; he holds them in place. After a moment, I try to pull them back, but he holds them tighter. When I acquiesce, he makes a low noise deep in his throat. The way he commands my body with a power I can't explain sends a deep thrill through me.

He withdraws and thrusts again, jolting my body with the force of reentry in a way that makes me dizzy with anticipation.

His gaze sears me as he buries his cock deep, deep inside me.

I'm underneath him, pinned beneath his body, and he now moves at a punishing pace. I find myself getting higher and higher. He is a drug. I'm high on him. And I can't get enough.

In.

Out.

Up.

Down.

Hard and fast he moves.

Deep.

Deeper.

Breathless, he lets go of my wrists to slide his hands under my ass and draw me even closer to him.

He must be close to coming, and I know I am.

Wanting to connect in an even closer way, I find myself wrapping my legs around his waist.

The sexy look he gives me tells me I made the right move, and sends me so close to the edge that I don't even dare breathe or I know I'll be going over it.

He pounds into me, and the feeling has my breath exploding in a violent rush. As he withdraws and surges forward again, his hands tighten around my ass and spread me wide open.

It's unlike anything I have experienced before. I find myself on a cloud. I clamp my lips together to stop from crying out, not ready to come because this feels way too good, but so wanting to.

I look up, lost to him.

Satisfaction beams in his eyes. "Let go," he demands.

And I do; louder than before, I cry out, my arousal like a fever. My orgasm, hot and wild, explodes so intensely, it's even harder than before.

He's deep inside me.

So tight.

So tight and so deep that I swear I can feel the pulsing of his cock against my walls. His skin slaps mine, and as if wanting more from me, he keeps up the punishing pace.

My orgasm doesn't stop. I call out his name, over and over. He stills, his cock still pulsing inside me.

And only when I close my eyes, limp and sated, does his body go taut against me. He groans and rasps my name. I open my eyes to watch him come. His lips press together and every muscle in his arms and chest coils tight.

He continues to thrust until every ounce of his orgasm is milked. "Fuck, you're incredible," he grits out.

And then he goes deep and stays there, slowly lowering himself on top of me until he covers me with every inch of his body.

God, he feels so good.

Seconds later, he rolls us, and then stands. "I'll be right back."

And he is. Without the condom on his cock, he's back beside me. I rest my head on his chest and stare at his body. In this postcoital moment of bliss, I allow my fingers to roam over his smooth skin.

With a hand flung over his head, he lies still and lets me do whatever I want. Look, touch, pinch, rub, palm, feel, and revel.

Finally, I break the silence. "I knew sex with you was going to be incredible."

Moving his arm away from his face, he smiles at me then, not the brooding badass look I usually got. "Oh, yeah, how so?"

I circle one of his nipples. "I don't know. I just did."

"There has to be a reason."

"I guess I know you've been with a lot of women."

"That doesn't mean anything."

"No, I guess you're right. To be honest, the way you look at me sends a vibe I can't explain. I don't know, have you ever fantasized about something, but never acted on it?"

Brooklyn pulls me right on top of his body and I use my elbows to push up. "Sure, a lot of things."

"Like?"

"Quitting my lifeguard job. Getting my screenplay produced. Making something of my life."

His hair is over his eyes and I push it away.

He looks at me. "What in particular do you fantasize about?"

I shrug because it seems so far out of my reach anymore. "Photographing important moments for a living," I say.

"And?"

"And?"

"Yes, and what else?"

I smile. "I don't know."

"Come on, there has to be something else."

I blurt it out. "Finding the person I want to spend my life with, and great sex."

Normally, something like that might send a guy running for shelter, but Brooklyn takes a moment to think about it. "As in two separate things?"

I bite my lip. "Yeah, I guess. When I think about exploring sex, it's not necessarily with the man I see as my husband."

"Ahhh . . ." he says, "the sex part is with someone like me. Someone you see as a player who will never settle down." There's a sadness in his voice I'm surprised to hear.

Not wanting to say yes, even though that might be true, I offer, "It's with someone my father or brother would never approve of, and that is why I never have pursued anyone like that."

"Before," he adds.

My brows quirks in question.

"Before me."

"No, that's not what I mean," I insist, but I know he doesn't believe me. I wish he did.

Brooklyn pushes it aside, though, and smoothes his hands over my ass, where he rubs slow, lazy circles around my cheeks, and then his lips curve into a sexy grin. "Since I am willing to allow you to objectify my body, tell me some things you've never tried that you fantasize about."

I can feel the pink painting my cheeks. "I'm . . . not sure. Just wild, unabashed sex. The kind people talk about."

"Come on, you have to specific."

"I can't."

"They're your fantasies. You must be able to name at least one thing."

My head begins to explode with a montage of images—sexy lingerie, being tied up, toys, steamy hot sex, and endless fucking.

Curiosity seems to pique Brooklyn's interest and he rolls me off him to get up on one elbow, and then stares at me. "Are your fantasies as kinky as a threesome?"

Heat suffuses my cheeks. "God, no, I'm way too jealous for something like that."

"Anal sex?"

I wrinkle my nose. "I don't think so. I'm not sure."

He lifts an eyebrow and amusement glitters in his eyes. "Okay, moving on. How about bondage?"

I hesitate and then sigh. "Nothing hardcore, no whips and chains, but I liked when you held my hands over my head."

His knee moves between my legs, and he looks at my pussy. "Okay, good to know. Spanking?"

I shake my head. "No way."

That gets a chuckle out him. "So no kink."

Feeling a little ridiculous for bringing it up, I blow out a breath. "I'm hopeless," I tell him. "Never mind. Let's talk about something else."

Gently, and very unexpectedly, he caresses my cheek. "Nah, I'm not giving up. You like to masturbate, right?"

Dropping my head to the pillow in embarrassment, I can't even answer.

"Show me," he says, his voice thick and hot, not an ounce of humor in it.

I peek up, and my embarrassment fades immediately when I see the hot lust in his eyes. "But I don't have to—you're here, and you're much better than my own hand."

His finger swipes across my pussy, and then he brings it to my mouth. "I want to watch you. Start by tasting yourself, Amelia. Taste how sweet you are."

Incredibly turned on right now, I can't believe it, but I do. I suck on his finger, practically licking it clean.

Brooklyn sits up and eases me onto my back with a gentle nudge. "Now, touch yourself," he says in a strained voice. "I'll tell you what to do to make it feel so much better."

I place my hand on my pussy.

He gets on his knees now, towering over me, giving himself a bird's-eye view of my body. "No. Start by pinching your tight little nipples and slide your hands down your body, slowly."

Unsure, I look at him.

He nods. "And then when you reach your pussy, I want you to run your fingers up and down your center, all the way to your sweet ass, over and over, until I tell you to stop."

For some strange reason, I find myself doing as he has in-structed. My eyes flitting from him to me and back, over and over as I begin to play with myself. I gasp when he takes his cock in his hand and gives it a little stroke.

"What do you think?" he asks, the tone in his voice oozing with something almost feral.

I think a lot . . .

I think I really like him even though I shouldn't.

I think that was the best sex of my life, and by the looks of things to come, it's about to get even better, hotter.

I think I'm in a whole lot of trouble when it comes to this man.

I think I know better.

And then I look into his intense blue eyes and the way he is stroking his cock, and think . . . *I'm so screwed.*

CHAPTER 26

Eternal Sunshine of the Spotless Mind

Brooklyn

Perhaps a contract would be appropriate in a situation like this.

A signed piece of paper that dictates the terms of the relationship Amelia and I are embarking on.

It could define the means by which we are allowed to interact, so whatever this is between us doesn't turn messy. And no one gets hurt.

No one.

Her, or me.

One of the clauses could limit the amount of time we spend looking at each other when we are not in bed. Another could dictate the tone of voice we use with each other when we are not engaging in sexual relations. And most important, there should be a clause that prohibits body language as a way of communicating outside of fucking.

Because this is just about sex.

Sex.

Or it is supposed to be, anyway.

But you know as well as I do that there is a fine line between just sex and more. And that embarking on such an arrangement can lead to unfamiliar territory. Just like you and I both know someone is going to get hurt.

Someone.

Her, or me.

Putting all those issues aside because a contract to define our interaction when we are together is just ridiculous, I know I have to tread lightly and remember this thing between us is short-term. Her plans aren't set in stone, but she's talked about going back to New York in just over a week.

And that is when we agreed our story would end.

Therefore, you can see why treading lightly is the best course of action.

Sure, we like being together.

We have fun.

But I know it won't lead to anything more.

It can't.

We don't want the same things—in the long run, that is. She wants to get married and have a family. I don't see myself doing that. Can't see myself doing that with the job I have now, anyway.

In the short run, we are on exactly the same page. With the sexual tension alleviated, we get along pretty well. She's up for anything. Turns out, it's not kink she's looking for in a sexual relationship. She just wants hot, wild, unabashed sex. And that, I can give her. She's never been with anyone who has bothered to get to know what it is she likes or needs in the sack. Hard to believe, but no one has helped her discover more than the basics of missionary-style sex, with some occasional oral thrown in for good measure, I suppose.

That is something I figured out the first night we were together. Every day since, I've taken things a little farther, drawing her out of her comfort zone and helping her explore what she has been missing. Like I said, she's pretty much up for anything.

Monday I took her riding on the back of my bike up to Mulholland Drive in LA. She brought her camera and took pictures while I sat at Dead Man Overlook to rewrite some of the scenes in my manuscript. I saw what Amelia meant about Kate acting way too spineless, and made some tweaks. Afterward, we went to Mulholland Tennis Club, where my mother is a member, and fucked in one of the private bathrooms. I bent her over the wooden bench and took her from behind. It was smoking hot.

Tuesday it rained all day, so we went to the old movie theater in town and watched a flick from the sixties. When the movie ended, we snuck into the old viewing room that is now only used for special occasions, and fucked in there. She rode me on one of the big leather chairs. Her tits moved up and down, and I sucked on them while she came all over my cock. It was fanfuckingtastic.

Wednesday I had to work in the morning, and we spent the afternoon at The Cliff drinking mojitos and role-playing my screenplay. It was a huge help. And yes, we fucked in the bathroom. I spread her legs wide and with her palms flat against the cool metal, I took her against the stall door.

Today is Thursday, and this morning I took her to LA to tour the Chinese Theatre and see the Hollywood sign. We didn't fuck anywhere; there was nowhere we could. But she blew me on the drive back, and she is coming over as soon as Cam crashes for the night.

Luckily for us, Makayla, who works from home, has been in San Francisco since Monday afternoon. She runs her own jewelry line and uses a company there to help her produce orders. She won't be here until late tomorrow. About the same time Keen, Maggie, and Presley will also be arriving.

That's when the fun and games will end for the two of us, until Monday anyway. The weekend is going to suck. Too many people around and the risk of being caught will be too great.

Getting caught means explaining. And explaining that we both agreed we'd have a sex-only relationship to the people we both care about, who have significant others now, seems ridiculous. Even if it is hot, off-the-charts, mind-blowing, no-holds-barred sex.

Of course, Amelia's reasons for embarking on this type of relationship are different from mine, or now that I think about it, maybe they are the same.

She's looking to end up with a man who will be her Prince Charming. She can deny it all she wants, but I was there when she was ten and tried to turn me into him. And I was there on the porch that night she showed up and voiced, in so many words, that what happened to her made her doubt what she'd always dreamed of.

She shouldn't doubt that.

For her, I'm certain he does exist.

And for that reason, I am also certain I cannot be him. I am not husband material. In fact, I'm far from it. I've been with countless women. I don't have a steady job. I don't own a home. And I've never been good at being responsible.

I glance at my manuscript, and think that doesn't mean I don't want those things. I do. It's just getting there. Succeeding. It scares me.

Will I be like my mother if I do? Motivated. Driven. Successful.

Or more like my father? Always wanting more than I have and willing to risk it all to get to the top.

Rewriting another of Kate's lines, I wonder if with the changes I'm making, my mother will think it's better.

Not to sound full of myself, I know it's on trend.

It's a story about an irresponsible guy finding love when he least expects it. A boy-meets-girl kind of story where the boy falls in love with the girl, but the girl is a hopeless romantic and doesn't think the boy is for real. Through a number of twists and turns, rights and wrongs, and countless mistakes, the boy proves the girl is for him.

Fangirl is the kind of modern love story that although on trend, isn't what people might expect, and that is what I love about it.

My thoughts begin to wander to how to make this screenplay stand out even more, make the viewer feel an entire range of emotions, when my phone rings.

"Hello," I answer, looking at the page and not paying attention to the caller ID.

"Brooklyn, it's Ryan Gerhardt from next door."

I tuck my pencil behind my ear to pay better attention. "Hey, Mr. Gerhardt, how are you?"

"Listen, that's why I'm calling. Not so well. My mother took a fall, and Pam and I need to go to Florida tomorrow."

Leaving my manuscript on the coffee table, I walk into the kitchen and decide I should probably eat something. "I'm sorry to hear that. Is there something I can do to help?"

"Actually, yes. Pam and I were hoping you might be able to stay at our house for the weekend and take care of Romeo and Juliet."

Looking out the kitchen window, I glance next door at Mr. Gerhardt's giant, ultramodern beach house. "You want me to dog-sit your Yorkies?"

He laughs. "I know it's last minute and definitely not the most glamorous request you'll receive, but our normal dog sitter is out of town, and Pam doesn't trust anyone else. Would you be able to spend the weekend over here and take care of them? We'll return on Monday."

"Sure, I can do that." Stepping over to the refrigerator, I open it and sigh. It is practically bare, except for Maggie's vegan items, which seem to have an unnaturally long shelf life. I really need to get my shit together and go grocery shopping on a weekly basis, and maybe even start cooking.

"That's great," he says. "Pam and I would really appreciate it. By the way, how's that screenplay coming along?"

I grab the container of pasta Makayla sent home with me on Sunday. "Much better than it was last time we talked."

"When you think it's ready, I'd like to read it."

A smile cracks across my face as I close the refrigerator door. "Are you serious?"

The dogs bark in the background like someone just got home, probably Mrs. Gerhardt. "Yes, I am," he tells me. "You've been writing that story of yours for over two years. In a way I feel like it's a part of me, the way I've watched you slaving over it on the beach day after day."

"I just might hold you to it," I answer, and then pop the lid off the container to stick it in the microwave.

"You'd better," he says. "Now, about this weekend, do you have time to come over tonight so I can show you where I keep the booze and how to use the hot tub?"

Before I can answer, I hear Mrs. Gerhardt talking in the background. I give him a second to respond to her, and hit the reheat button in the meantime.

"Yes, dear," he says. "Yes, of course I'll give Brooklyn instructions on how to care for Romeo and Juliet. I'll ask him to come over right now. No, my love, that shouldn't be a problem," he adds. "Did you hear all that, Brooklyn?" he asks.

With a laugh, I pull the leftovers out and set them on the counter. They can wait. Besides, if I know Mrs. Gerhardt, she'll have something much better than leftovers on the stove. "Yes, sir, I did. And I'm on my way."

Fist-pumping the air, I look over at his house through the kitchen window.

Hot tub.

Booze.

And a secret getaway for Amelia and me.

Looks like my weekend just got a whole lot sweeter.

CHAPTER 27

Annie Hall

Amelia

Paris and Helen, Dante and Beatrice, and yes, even Han Solo and Princess Leia—these are romances that have become legends.

And for the most part television shows aren't shy about recreating romances that walk similar paths, ranging from harmonious to downright rocky.

I think I learned the most about love from watching Ross and Rachel on *Friends* when I was younger. Their back-and-forth love interest in each other proved a powerful pull, one I couldn't step away from. The angst sometimes was enough to drive me over the edge, but through the comedy I persevered and always rooted for them to come together and stay together.

Yes, I'm a romance buff through and through.

And no, *The Walking Dead* is definitely not my kind of television show. I think I might even prefer one of those obstacle-course game shows to it, and that isn't saying much at all, considering I think they are boring.

My brother, though, he loves that show, and of course wants to start Season Two, since he made me watch Season One over the past three nights. "So that's a no to watching it?" he asks, stretching his long arms and linking his hands behind his head as he tips the chair back.

"Help me clear the table, and we can discuss it."

Cam looks around at the mess in the kitchen, and then groans. "You are still the messiest cook I know."

"Thanks." I wipe my mouth with a napkin and contemplate another forkful of lasagna.

"It wasn't meant as a compliment," he smirks, setting the chair on all fours.

Rising to my feet, I grab the casserole dish, which is still more than half full. "Haven't you heard—all the best chefs are messy? It's what makes the food so good."

"Right, whatever makes you sleep better," he laughs.

I shrug. There is no rebuttal. It's just simply true.

"You should have let me invite Brooklyn over." He points to the dish in my hand. "He would have polished that off."

The slight blush that creeps up my neck at the sound of Brooklyn's name is one I want to conceal, so I quickly turn and step toward the island. "I wanted to spend some time alone with my brother, is that a crime? But I'll bring the leftovers over to him later, if that makes you feel better."

It's not a lie, but not exactly the truth. Having Brooklyn over with just Cam at home would make it almost impossible to hide the insane connection that seems to be growing between us with each passing day. Brooklyn and I are so in tune with each other in the oddest way. I say, "I'm thirsty," and he says, "How about we grab a hot chocolate?" and it is exactly what I'm craving. Or he says, "Let's watch television," and I put on the Me TV channel just in time to catch an episode of *Batman* with Adam West and Burt Ward, and he makes a playful comment, something like, "Pow! Bam! Zonk! I love this show."

"Did you hear me?" Cam says, setting both of our dirty dishes near the sink.

Blinking away my thoughts, I look up from wrapping foil over the glass dish. "No, I'm sorry. What did you say?"

He turns the faucet on, and then looks over at me. "You cook like Mom."

Sealing the edges tightly, I meet his gaze, and smile. "I know."

Grabbing one of the pans I used to make the creamy red sauce, he starts to rinse it. "I spoke to her today. She told me you and she have been talking almost every day."

Circling the island, I open the refrigerator and shove the dish inside. "We have, and things are going really well. When I get home, we're going to go away for a weekend, just us, and work on trying to fix what I broke."

Cam squeezes some soap into the pot and starts to wash it. "And what about Dad? Have you decided anything yet?"

He and I talked endlessly about this every night this week, but each time I have been left more and more confused. I walk over to the table. "I actually made a decision today while I was taking some pictures."

"Oh yeah, I saw you were in Hollywood. I assume Brooklyn took you. I'll have to thank him for that."

While gathering the grated cheese, salt and pepper, and our empty water glasses, I look at him in shock, my heart going tickety-tock that he saw my Instagram post. "Since when are you on social media?"

With a shrug, he sets the clean pot on the counter and picks up one of the dirty dishes. "Since I decided to venture into online sales. Not only do I have an Instagram account, but I reopened my Facebook page and am thinking of joining Twitter."

"Wow," I tell him, setting the things in my hand on the island. "I'm impressed."

After rinsing the first plate, he opens the dishwasher. "Don't be. You still won't see me posting anything personal. I think it's odd people want the whole world to know their business. Anyways, you were saying."

Reaching across the counter, I grab the sponge from the sink and wipe the table. "That I'm going to quit my job and look into doing something with photography."

The sound of a slap on the granite has me whirling around.

Cam is grinning at me.

"What?" I ask.

He's back to the dishes, but his smile is still there. "I've been waiting so long for you to decide to do something you like. Not that I'm encouraging you to leave The Waters Group; I just think working as a photographer has been your dream for so long, and I hated that you weren't pursuing it."

Touched, I toss the sponge in the sink and slide the glasses his way. "Why didn't you ever say anything?"

He looks at me, assessing. "I know you want to be independent. To show everyone that you are grown and can make your own decisions. Besides, you didn't need another thing on your plate to make you feel like a failure."

To most people that comment might have been offensive. To me it is anything but. To me it proves just how well Cam knows me. There are times my brother and I argue, there are times we get along better than most siblings, and there are times we are brutally honest with each other. This is the latter, and darn it if it doesn't make me teary-eyed, because he is right. Before, I might not have been able to handle him judging me. Now, though, I don't see it that way.

Closing up the dishwasher, he hits the start button, then walks around to where I'm standing getting ready to return the salt and pepper to the spice cupboard. Taking them from me, he sets them down and puts his hands on my shoulders. "It's okay for you to be happy. Brandon would have wanted that for you, and for me."

His comment surprises me. He doesn't bring up Brandon

often. Aside from the night he returned from Mexico, he hasn't mentioned his name once. I look up at him. "I agree. He would want that for both of us."

"Come on," Cam suggests, "let's collapse on the couch in a food coma and watch mindless television. I'll even let you pick the show."

I look around. There are a few more things that need attending in the kitchen. "Sounds like a plan. Go on in, and I'm right behind you."

When he has gone, I finish cleaning up and just as I'm about to go join him, my phone buzzes. I pull it from my pocket. There is a text from Landon asking me if I am okay. I have not answered a single one of his texts since Monday, but I can't just ignore him. That is rude. So I send him a text. A short one that says I am fine. And leave it at that.

Carter has been very vocal about my decision to accept Brooklyn's ultimatum, as he calls it. In his words, "If you were a guy I'd say you are thinking with your dick and not your brain, but since you're a girl, use your own words."

That's Carter for you.

Telling me to pick one, and then when I do, wondering why I picked the one I did.

In the living room, Cam is stretched out on the couch watching a rerun of *Where's My Latte?* I flop on one of the chairs and look over at him. "I met Gigi Bennett the other night when Brooklyn took me to her and Chase Parker's engagement party."

And yes, I'm testing the waters, or I'm testing Waters, the second case meant to have a capital *W*.

With mild interest, he appears to give the flat-screen slightly more attention. "Yeah, I've met her too."

"What did you think?"

He shrugs in that way of his when he's not really interested in the conversation.

I glance at the scene on the screen and watch how bubbly and perky she is. "Honestly, I felt a little cheated."

That gets me a laugh. "Why?"

"She was nothing like her character on the show. And I don't know, I just thought she would be."

"That's Hollywood for you," he says.

I guess he's right, but still, something about Chase and her just seemed off. Their wedding is next weekend, though, and so far it's still on. This is the perfect time to bring up Brooklyn's invitation for me to attend the wedding with him. Casually, I throw out, "Brooklyn said I could go to the wedding with him, if I want." He hadn't been quite so nonchalant about it. He'd requested that I join him when he had his face in my pussy. When I seemed reluctant, like it was too much like a date, he told me to dress fuck-hot and skip the panties; he'd make it a night I'd never forget. How could I turn that down?

"Oh, yeah," Cam says, now doing something on his phone. "You should go. It's not every day you get to attend an up-and-coming actress's wedding."

Looking at the return text from Landon on my phone, I quickly respond with an "I'm sure," to his question, "Are you sure you are okay?" and then move past it to the one from Carter, before answering Cam with, "Yes, maybe I will." My response is offered lightly, as a second thought, but on the inside I'm screaming in delight.

Cam, not in the least bit suspicious, sets his own phone beside him on the couch and stares steadfastly at the sitcom. By the time it comes to an end, I notice his lids appear to be closing. It's only eight thirty, but he looks tired. I know he got up really early this morning. I wonder if he'll fall asleep out here, and if he does, if I'll have to sneak out the window again.

God, I hope not.

"Here," he says, tossing me the remote. "You can watch

anything you want."

Quickly setting my phone on the chair, I catch the remote and hold it in my hands. "Do you mind if we skip TV watching tonight? I think I might read for a bit," I tell him, giving him the option to bow out.

Cam sits up and runs his hands over his face. "No, not all. I'm pretty wiped out, and I have to call Makayla anyway. Will you be okay by yourself?"

At the question, I feel that guilt come tumbling back. I hate keeping what is going on between Brooklyn and me from him. I can't do it for much longer. I swear I'm about to break. The answer is simple. If I can't tell him, then I need to leave. "I'll be fine," I say.

Walking toward the hallway that leads to his bedroom, he stops at the entranceway and turns around. "You know, Simon Warren could use a photographer. Right now we're subcontracting out the work for the fall line and it's costing us a bundle."

I shift a little in my chair to fold my legs up under me. "Cam, stop trying to take care of me. I'll be fine."

His expression changes. "I'm serious, Amelia. Keen and I have been discussing bringing a photographer in-house for the past couple of months. You'd be doing us a favor."

Unable to stop myself, I roll my eyes.

He laughs, but not quite his usual hearty chortle. "If you don't believe me, ask him."

Laying the remote next to my phone, I reach for the book I've been reading on the side table. I can't say I haven't thought about moving out here. "I think I need to quit my current job and settle things with Dad before I figure out what comes next, but I appreciate the offer."

Although I know there is no way he is giving up, it is so not his nature, he shrugs nonchalantly as if he is. "Well, if you change your mind and decide being close to your brother is where you want to be, the offer stands," he pauses, "until I hire someone, that is."

"Playing the brother card. That's not fair."

With a raised brow, he laughs, and this time it sounds better. "Had to give it a try."

I wave my hand at him. "Good night, Cam. Tell Makayla I said hi, and if I don't see you in the morning, have a good day."

"You too." Turning around, he starts down the hall and pulls out his phone before he even makes it to his bedroom.

The coast should be clear.

I'm so out of here.

CHAPTER 28
Good Will Hunting

Brooklyn

We are officially in the Age of the Bromance.

Celebrating the deep, platonic love between two or more male characters is what viewers are gravitating toward these days.

The men involved in the bromance often have nicknames for each other, share a history, and have a seemingly infinite capacity for ball-busting humor.

Nevertheless, they're always there for each other with a commendable loyalty. Even when things aren't going well, you can usually count on them to find their way back to each other.

Adding the bromance element to *Fangirl* will likely broaden my audience and, at the same time, give this screenplay the jolt of humor it needs.

Giving Kellan's male friend, Colton, more screen time is easy enough. Like my buddy Chase and me, Kellan and Colton grew up together deep in the trenches of the 90210 zip code, which is established early on in my manuscript.

Carrying their interactions through on the page comes naturally. I even assign Colton the nickname my brother has given me,

Pantydropper.

Leaning back in my chair at my desk, I take the pencil from behind my ear and begin to tap my pencil on the piece of paper in front of me. My imagination starts to soar as I immerse myself in their lines of dialogue. I mix in some wit and zingers with fuck yous and other insults. It's more than a little fun. I'm careful to put a more sophisticated gloss on their relationship than my real one has.

Time passes as I busy myself with my manuscript, but soon enough I find that I'm keeping an eye on the time on my phone. Close to nine. Each minute that ticks by is another minute sooner that she'll be arriving.

Way too eager to see her, I find my mind drifting from my task at hand to visions of bending her over this desk, or taking her up against the door before she even crosses the threshold. Or perhaps . . . there is so much more.

Anticipation licks up my spine, my entire body growing heavy with lust as I imagine her tied to my bed, and spread for me. Being balls deep inside her. Thrusting so deep, so hard, until she calls out my name over and over and comes around my cock.

Somehow, she's become a drug, and like any good addict, I am hooked. The withdrawal is going to suck.

"Hey. I made it."

Twirling around in my chair, I almost fall off it as my body leaps to life. Amelia is standing in the doorway to my bedroom, naked, except for the scant material of a leopard thong covering her sweet pussy. "Take it off," I command in a quiet voice. No hello, no greeting of any kind is in me right now, just an urgency to see her bare body and to get inside her as soon as humanly possible.

"In a hurry?" she says, her pulse visibly pounding with excitement in her throat.

"I feel like I've been waiting all day," I tell her, my voice tight with need.

Amelia obeys, her hair tumbling around her face as she bends, and slowly, very slowly, lowers the material over her hips, and then kicks it out the door. Her eyes are on me the entire time, that body language of hers one that can't be denied. This particular one conveys that sleepy look, which glows with a burning desire.

Does she even know what that does to me? "I can't wait another minute to be inside you," I tell her, staring at her and catching the wanton look she's giving me.

Everything about us is dangerous. The way we need to connect, the way neither of us can wait, the forbidden fruit all we can think about. Adam and Eve. Layla and Majnun. Cleopatra and Mark Antony. Guinevere and Lancelot. And we know how those stories ended. Still, none of that matters as I find myself unable to wait another second to have her.

Opening my desk drawer, I pull out a condom from my latest stash and realize I need to stock up because for all the shit I take for whoring around, I've never had this much sex.

Now completely naked, she steps toward me. "Good thing, then, that you don't have to."

More than ready for this, I unfasten my fly and pull out my dick. A small noise escapes her throat and I quickly roll the condom on. When she's standing between my legs, now spread wide in the chair, I smile at her. "Turn around to face away from me."

And she does. No questions asked, just anticipation more than evident in that gaze of hers.

The large, thick leather chair doesn't even creak when I scoot to the edge of it. Once there, I reach up to put my hands on Amelia's waist, and within moments I'm guiding her onto my waiting cock.

She gasps when I sink into her wet pussy and I groan when her ass comes to rest on my lap. *Oh hell yes.* She is tight, so tight, and her body is so responsive to mine. So much so that she's already quivering around me with only a few shallow thrusts upward.

I lick my fingers and use them to wet those always cherry-red nipples of hers, and then I pinch and roll them into tight peaks.

Amelia turns her head and kisses me. Our tongues meet and dance, slowly at first, then faster. When my hands slide down her belly to find her clit, she breaks the kiss with a small gasp.

The chair starts to creak beneath us and I jerk my hips up to push inside her deeper, stroking into her wetness and taking everything I can.

The possibilities of pleasure are endless. I can play with her clit so easily in this position while she rides my cock, or I can return to palming her breasts and take her to the edge over and over.

But fuck if her pussy isn't like liquid heat surrounding my cock, seducing me to take her deeper and deeper into the depths of hell, and therefore making playing with her nearly impossible.

Amelia gets the rhythm of this position fairly quickly, and I have to stop playing with her clit and just hold on. I've learned quickly that I don't have to teach her what to do. I haven't had to all week. And in this case, I don't have to guide her hips to rise and slam down on my rock-hard cock. She has figured it all out on her own. And fuck if it doesn't feel so goddamn good.

Within seconds, I am on fire, my arousal sharp and rising higher with every single lift and slam of her body. This is going to be quick for the both of us, no lazy climb to the top right now. My body buzzing with adrenaline, I thrust hard and fast, my hips slapping loudly against her ass. Her response is to push harder on my cock until I'm balls deep and losing my mind.

"Fuck, that's it," I tell her, and nuzzle her neck to nip her earlobe.

I watch as chill bumps dance across her skin and she moans, already close to her own orgasm.

"That's it, baby, ride me, get us both there."

"Oh God, oh God," she chants.

The guttural moan she makes fuels my own impending orgasm into a full-fledged inferno.

This is down and dirty. I fuck into her deep and hard, she riding me in the same relentless, forceful rhythm that has me gasping for each and every breath.

"Touch yourself," I tell her in a strained voice. "Use your fingers, Amelia. I don't want to leave you behind, but I'm not going to last much longer."

She hurries to finger her clit.

"That's it, baby. That's it. Touch yourself faster. Ride me harder. Fuck, that's it. I'm going to come so hard inside that sweet little pussy of yours."

Those dirty, illicit words send her hurtling right over the edge. Her back bows and her hands find mine, pressing down on them with the same ferocity she is using to slam her ass down on my hips.

If I could have filmed this, I would have. I want so much to watch her face as she explodes around my cock in a wet rush.

I fuck her until her last scream, and then I let myself go into the blinding light. Finding that place where nothing exists, I still, and then give one last thrust, draining myself dry.

Sweat beads my brow and the exertion must be more than evident on my face because when she turns, she looks the same. Her gray eyes glow with a primal heat that bears the evidence of satisfaction. And I assume my blue eyes reflect hers.

"You're fucking beautiful," I growl, when she falls back against me.

"I doubt that right now," she laughs.

"Don't," I tell her, my fingers dancing across her clit and sliding up and down her wetness.

She shudders as my touch triggers a tiny aftershock. And then so do I when her swollen pussy squeezes my cock tight. After a long moment, she whispers, "I love it when you talk dirty."

I kiss her neck, nipping at her sensitive flesh. "I know you do," I tell her, and then find myself saying, "I want to film us." It just comes out.

Not saying no, she simply asks, "Why?"

"I want you to see what I see. To see how beautiful you are when you come."

She turns then to look at me, wetting that lovely mouth with her tongue. "Okay, you can. But only for you and me."

With not an ounce of humor, I assure her, "I'd never let another man watch the way you come when you're with me, baby."

I nip at her shoulder. "How about Saturday night?"

"What about Maggie and Keen?"

"Turns out Mr. Gerhardt needs a dog sitter, and guess who he asked."

Her laughter is out of control. "You," she manages, trying to run her fingers through my hair in her twisted position.

I push her upward to her feet and lightly tap her bottom. "Go clean up," I tell her, and then rise behind her to remove the condom.

She heads for my bathroom, but quickly looks over her shoulder. "So Saturday night, then?"

I nod, disposing of the rubber, and then opening my desk drawer to pull out a sheet of paper. "Yes. We have that whole big house, hot tub and all, to ourselves. And I want to fuck you bare."

Stopping in the doorway to the bathroom, her fingers grip the door frame. She's on the pill. We've already discussed that. I know she's never had unprotected sex; we've discussed that as well. I never have either. When your mother gets accidentally pregnant twice in her life within two years by two different men, you never want to chance it. Until now. Until the craving to take her bare, feel all of her, and in a way make my mark on her before this ends, becomes way too much to withstand.

I flick the paper with my finger. The noise has her head turning again, this time slower, eyes flashing with heat.

My heart pounds in my chest. "I went to the clinic. I'm clean. Here are my results."

Now wide-eyed, she looks at me. Is she going to shoot me down? And then she smiles that thousand-watt smile of hers that I don't think I'll ever forget. "Good," she says. "Those condoms are a pain in the ass."

Relief flashes in my own eyes and I cast her a smile filled with enough enthusiasm to make me hard again.

"Hey, Pantydropper." Cam's voice is coming from the bottom of the stairs. "I think your latest conquest left something behind."

Panic fills the distance between Amelia and me. I motion for her to close the bathroom door and then quickly do up my fly before rushing toward the door that I stupidly left open.

Just outside it, at the top of the stairs, I come face to face with the guy who has become my best friend over the past couple of years, the guy whose little sister I just banged, and instantly I know I'm going to rot in hell.

Guilt plagues me as I try to find my voice. "Hey, what are you doing here?" I manage.

"I brought my sister's lasagna. She said she'd bring it over, but I think she hit the sack early."

"Fantastic," I tell him.

"Why do you ask? Are you not happy to see me?"

I step past him and head down the stairs. "You know I always love to see your ugly mug, but isn't it past your bedtime?"

He chuckles, following me, and completely unaware that his sister is hiding in my bathroom. "Yeah, I have been kind of lame lately," he says, "but nothing beats your brother."

"Hold that thought," I tell him, racing past Amelia's underwear and through the living room in case she left her clothes anywhere in sight. Unlike Cam's house, this house has a galley kitchen. Long and narrow, and luckily with little space to leave anything, or noticeably leave anything anyway, with all the baby stuff everywhere. Opening the refrigerator, I grab two beers and hand him one. "Now, do tell."

Popping the top, he tosses it in the sink and then hikes up on the counter. "Okay," he says, "so we're at one of the hotel's finer restaurants and the service is slow, on purpose, you know?"

I nod, popping my own top and taking a quick swig.

"Keen, who I guess was on baby duty the night before, has one fucking drink, and then, right in the middle of the restaurant, while we're waiting for our meals to arrive, he starts snoring."

Eyeing the wrapped dish on the stove, I set my bottle down and head toward it. "Are you fucking kidding me?"

"Serious as fuck," he laughs. "Right there in the middle of the restaurant, while Maggie and Makayla are talking wedding plans."

The scent of the food makes my stomach growl as I pull the tinfoil aside, and I grab a fork. "Yeah, that little guy hates to sleep. I think both Keen and Maggie might keel over from exhaustion before he gets a two-hour stretch in."

Cam runs a hand through his hair, his own exhaustion clear. "Don't say that, man," he says. "Makayla offered to keep Presley Saturday night at our house so Keen and Maggie can go out on a date and have some time alone."

When I offer Cam a piece of lasagna, he shakes his head no, and I resume my position across from him to dig in. Around a mouthful of food, I say, "Good thing I won't be around then."

He gives me a wicked smirk.

I take another sip of my beer and then ask, "What?"

He hops off the counter and sets the empty in the sink. "After you took my sister to that engagement party, and then seeing you home all week, I thought maybe you were back on that celibacy kick. Guess I was wrong."

Hell.

Before I can even answer, he steps closer to me and puts his hand on my shoulder. "She's planning on going to that wedding with you next Saturday. Don't—" He pauses.

Guilt floods me, and my heart fucking flies out of my chest.

"Don't forget you invited her to tag along. She's counting on it," he says.

"I wouldn't do that to her," I tell him, swallowing the surge of anger I feel that he thinks so little of me.

"I didn't think so," he offers as a way of making peace I guess, and then heads for the door. "Oh, and one more thing," he says before he opens the kitchen door. "Makayla wants everyone to have dinner at our house tomorrow. Seven. Okay?"

"Yeah, sounds great. I'll be there."

The door closes and I sag in relief. My pulse beating a mile a minute, I make my way to the stairs and drop onto one and sigh.

Putting my face in hands, I can't help but wonder . . . *what the fuck am I doing?*

CHAPTER 29

Wonderland

Amelia

Visions of a porn studio and Johnny Wadd are all I have been thinking about.

Yes, bright lights, huge barrels of lube, racks of bathrobes, and Johnny's thirteen-and-a-half-inch cyclopean trouser snake are what have been filling my dreams, or rather my nightmares.

Hey, don't look at me like that. I only watch that stuff when Carter makes me. He's into porn, big time, mostly gay, but depending on the actor, sometimes straight as well. But really, what I know about porn studios isn't from watching porn.

Last year Carter flew to Kink.com in San Francisco to tour the studio, under the guise of doing a magazine shoot for work, but really, he solicited the spread.

Good for him.

Right?

Anyway, when he got back, he told me all about it, and the giant barrels of lube are true. He took a picture and showed it to me. There are two of them, both blue. One kind of lube is water based, the other silicone, and both barrels have huge pumps attached to the top.

Right now there are lights all right—not huge spotlights, though, but rather twinkling ones above the hot tub. The night is gorgeous, a little chilly, but warm inside the confines of the bubbling water.

Brooklyn's laughter is out of control, so much so he's holding his stomach. "You really thought that?" he asks.

Taking a sip of the champagne he bought for us to drink, I narrow my eyes at him across the small expanse. "You could have been more specific."

"Baby," he laughs, tears practically streaming down his face. "I didn't think I had to tell you I would use my iPhone. I mean, I'm not Ron Jeremy."

Overhead the moon is full and the stars twinkle just like the lights. I sigh, looking up at them, and rest my head against the tile of the hot tub. Today, Brooklyn took me hiking in Crystal Cove State Park. And Cam was aware. As with the wedding, he didn't even think twice when I told him.

The lying is getting to me, though, and I don't know how much longer I can do this.

Brooklyn reaches through the water and props my feet on his lap. When he begins to massage them, I moan in sheer pleasure. When he presses into my arches and rubs my soles, I groan out load.

"Was it too much hiking for you?" he asks me.

"No," I laugh, "I live in New York. I walk everywhere. The boots, though—they were Makayla's and didn't fit right."

His gaze turns serious. "You should have told me. I would have stopped and got you a pair that fit."

There is a softness in his voice that makes my heart squeeze. Most of the time it is easy to pretend this thing between us is only sex, but then he shows me a side of him I don't expect, and I wonder if it could be more.

A dangerous thought. One I shut down immediately. I heard

my brother the other night. Geez . . . he called him a pantydropper, again. This time it stung deep in my chest, like a knife to the heart. But isn't that what he is? After all, I'd dropped my panties for him without him even asking. I'm sure I wasn't the first, and I'm certain I won't be the last.

I pull my legs back. "It's all good. I'm fine, but I think I'm ready to go inside. If that is okay with you?"

"Sure. Are you cold?"

I nod. "A little."

As if worried about me, he stands and hauls me into his arms. "Come on, I have just the thing to warm you up."

With his hands on my naked body, and the touch of him branding me, it really does seem like we could go beyond the short time we've designated to be together, except we haven't told anyone about us, and even if I didn't know he's not my Mr. Right, I don't live in California. A long-distance relationship could never work. Ever.

When Brooklyn hands me a big, white fluffy robe, I laugh. "See, this is just like a porn stage, after all," I say.

Before I'd arrived, Brooklyn had started a fire in three fireplaces. The one in the kitchen, which is wood, and the ones in the family room and bedroom, which are gas. With the fire now blazing, the smell of burning wood is decadent as he opens the door from outside.

The Gerhardts' kitchen is any cook's dream. White marble counters that glisten under pendant lights hanging from the tall ceiling. A huge eight-burner stove. Two ovens. And three sinks. The house I grew up in was nice, but it was a brownstone with limited space. In this house, I think I could get lost.

As soon as Brooklyn sets the empty champagne bottle on the counter, he looks at me. "Tell me what's going on?" he asks.

I glance away. "Nothing."

He takes my chin in his hands and forces me to look at him.

"Amelia, tell me."

Another wave of emotion swirls through me. I move closer. When I try to kiss his mouth, Brooklyn turns his head. Our bodies are touching, but he doesn't let me touch his lips with mine. We stay this way, unmoving, for a moment or two—so long I think I might have aged fifty years.

Finally, he gives me his gaze, and when he does, he settles his hands sternly on my hips. "Talk to me."

Talk. We've talked about this. It doesn't change anything. But this time I'll put it a different way. This time I'll be clearer. I get up on toes to be closer to him. "Promise me this isn't going to end messy."

That's when his mouth takes mine, and the kiss I wanted just a minute ago to ease his mind turns into something else. Something stronger, harder. Something that I hope is reassurance, but have a strange feeling is not. When he breaks the kiss, he presses his forehead to mine and says, "This isn't going to end messy as long as neither of us let our emotions get in the way."

I didn't love that. Not at all. Emotions are already in the way. I wanted reassurance. That was not what I got. What I got was reality. And I know I have to live with that because it's true.

The loud sound of the wood crackling has the Yorkies, Romeo and Juliet, lifting their heads for a moment from their beds and yelping, but then they resume their sleeping position, obviously tired from the long walk Brooklyn took them on before I arrived.

Slowly, Brooklyn pushes my robe from my shoulders. And slowly I untie his and push it from his shoulders as well. Before he lets it fall, he removes his phone and sets it on the counter beside us.

When we are both naked in the kitchen in front of the fireplace, I get up on my toes again and kiss him. This time he lets me. He kisses me back. This kiss is different from the last. It is beautiful. Passionate and sweet. He breaks it first to laugh into my ear when one of the dogs starts to snore. I put my arms around his neck and jump up.

With no hesitation, no struggle, he catches me, and I wrap my legs around him. He rests my ass on the edge of the counter, not far from his phone, and looks at me. I nod, letting him know it is okay. I want him to video us. I want to be able to watch what this was between us when it is over. He taps the screen, and then leans his phone against the champagne bottle.

We hadn't planned to fuck in the kitchen. It isn't where I thought I would make my first sex tape. It just starts to happen. His cock is hard between us, and I pull his ass closer with the heels of my feet so I can stroke him.

With his warm skin against my palms, I rub him up and down. In a sudden swooping movement, he captures my mouth with a force that had he not been holding me in place might have sent me reeling backward on the counter.

Again, I have this feeling that seems like so much more than it is, and I really wish it didn't.

Forcing my mind to let go of that stuff that might suffocate me, I switch from my palms to my fingers and allow them to drift over his heat and hardness. He makes a small, soft noise into my mouth when I circle his head, once, twice, three times.

As if on its own, our kiss pauses, our mouths still touching, but unmoving. Too lost in the moment to do anything else.

Breathing heavily and feeling unusually needy, words fall from my mouth that normally wouldn't. "Tell me you want me," I breathe against his lips.

"I want you, Amelia." Brooklyn presses his face into the side of my neck, where his hot breath caresses me, and a shiver races along my spine.

I tilt my head so he can mouth my skin as my hand works along his length. "Say you want to be inside me."

"I want to be inside you."

"How much?" I give my palm a twist around the base of his cock.

His voice breaks a little when he answers. "So much I can't even tell you how much."

I find his gaze then, and heat flares vibrantly in it. As if unable to wait another second, he grabs my hips and drags me closer to the edge. Like this, his cock nudges my pussy. It is more than evident that I am wet for him, and so ready.

And then he moves just a little more. I moan when he pushes inside me, balls deep, the counter at just the perfect height for us to connect.

"Fuck, you feel incredible," he mutters.

"Oh, God."

Moving slowly, he buries his face against my neck as he fills me. His teeth press my skin, and I arch to get him even deeper inside me. When he bites me lightly, I moan, this time whispering, "Fuck me," into his ear.

He bites harder as he increases his pace, fucking into me, bare and impossibly deep.

I put one hand on the back of his neck while my other grips the counter. His hands are on me, holding me in place, keeping me safe. Unable to otherwise move, I use my heels to hook around his ass, urging him on.

As we begin to hit our stride, he pulls away just a little, and I drop my hand that was then tugging on his beautiful hair.

When he grabs his phone, I become oddly intrigued as he somehow manages to put it between us, and starts to capture the connection of his bare cock inside my pussy.

We both watch as his cock disappears into my pussy, and then as he withdraws, how slick he is with my juices coating him.

It's so hot to watch, but he doesn't keep the phone close for very long before he sets it back to capture us from a distance.

I know why.

This isn't going to last much longer. It can't. He's bare inside me, and I am surging on the way to orgasm, and the shudder of Brooklyn's breathing tells me he's close too.

"Kiss me," he hisses, regaining total control of my body.

And I do, so hard our teeth clash. His tongue twists with mine as he fucks into me harder. When he shifts us just a little, it applies just the right amount of pressure to my clit, and that's when I light up like a Christmas tree. Coming so hard, I scream out his name, and he swallows my gasp as my pussy clenches all around his bare cock.

Not five seconds later, he goes taut against me, every muscle in his arms and chest straining, coiling tight. Words spill from his mouth, but I can't make out what they are. He thrusts again, jetting deep inside me. His release is well under way. Soon I can feel the dampness between us, can hear the wet sounds as he sinks into me one final time.

Brooklyn presses a kiss to my neck, just below my ear, and whispers something that I can't hear.

Pleasure consuming me, I don't even notice when he reaches to turn the video off until the sound of him setting his phone on the counter alerts me to it.

Soon he is slipping out of me. "Let me grab a towel to clean up."

I grab hold of him before he disappears into the bathroom. "I want to sleep with you tonight."

From under thick lashes, he looks at me. "I think you just did."

I tug on his hand to draw him to me. "I mean fall asleep in bed together."

With the gentlest of touches, he pushes a piece of hair from my eyes. "Do you think that is a good idea?"

I nod. "Cam and Makayla have Presley. They will be so busy with him, they won't have time to think about me. I'll sneak back before the sun rises. It will be fine."

Brooklyn smiles at me. "Sure, as long you think it will be fine."

As of late, I am not sure anything will be fine . . . but I am certain Cam and Makayla won't notice where I sleep.

You see, I have this need to sleep in Brooklyn's arms.

To embed myself even further into his life . . . and I have no idea why, since I know the end is nearing.

And there is nothing I want less.

CHAPTER 30

Less Than Zero

Brooklyn

Francis Ford Coppola is one of the greatest screenwriters of all time. And if you ask me, Cameron Crowe runs a close second.

Billy Wilder, though—he was the one with the brass balls. Pushing taboo topics into mainstream America when everybody else was afraid to do it. Shit, he introduced cross-dressing in *Some Like It Hot* and alcoholism in *The Lost Weekend* before those topics were even spoken about out loud in the forties and fifties.

Today, though, things are different. Pushing the limit is almost expected. In fact, it is almost needed to succeed.

As I type the words *Fade in* across the top of my page, and then the words *Scene Heading* below it, I wonder what else is out there that hasn't already been brought to the big screen.

The truth is that screenwriting is a skill that requires a vivid imagination and a job where such skill is very much underappreciated in the film industry.

As students, we were told this very simple and real fact the first day of class.

We were also told that creating a script that is fresh, flowing, and translates off the page is exceeding hard, but very satisfying.

And that wasn't a lie.

Fangirl is well on its way to being one of those scripts, I hope. In fact, it's almost ready for another pass from my mother, and perhaps a first read-through by Mr. Gerhardt as well. And still I'm sitting here, adjusting the headings, the actions, and the transitions, worrying that the simplest of errors will make it unreadable. Unlikable. Unacceptable.

Amelia resurrected this manuscript and whatever happens, I owe her a lot for having faith in me and for reminding me that this is what I want to do for the rest of my life. Not lifeguarding. Not living off my royalties from *Chasing the Sun*. Not starring in a new reality television show. Screenwriting is my passion, and because of her I am actively pursuing it. Pushing my fears aside and going for it, I'm finally ready to jump.

Once I finish *Fangirl*, I have so many other ideas I've started and set aside, but now I'm ready to pick them back up.

The other day after I ate her pussy while she rode my tongue, she joked that she owes me for not making her sleep on the street the night she came into town. God only knows where she might have ended up. I joked that she saved me from a life of the blinding sun and endless days on the beach. She was kidding. I was not.

Closing the Word document, the one that mimics the marked-up pages of the manuscript beside it, I look out the window at the surf.

The week flew by. I can't believe it is Thursday already. I didn't see as much of Amelia this week as last. A, I worked more. B, Makayla was home during the days. And C, I didn't try hard to be available when she was.

Amelia told me she would be headed to New York this Sunday to talk to her father and clear out her desk. When I asked her what was next, she told me she didn't know. She did tell me that

Cam offered her a job, but she wants to settle her life in New York before she decides.

Makes sense.

I get it.

I'm sure I'd be the same way. Close-one-door-before-you-open-another kind of thinking. Makes the unknown a little less scary. Fuck, haven't I been doing that for the last three years? Lifeguarding to avoid putting myself out there? Shit, maybe it's time to quit. Maybe, just maybe it's time to move back to LA. What I hate about it is exactly why I need to be there—to conquer my fear of failure.

Coming to this conclusion, I start to feel a little guilty about blowing Amelia off today to work on my manuscript. It was more about me trying to protect myself than anything else. Looks like I have more fears to conquer. Perhaps I should lay it all out there for her. Tell her I want more. Tell her I want to try to be that guy she dreams about.

Yes, with only three days left, I probably should.

Just as I pick up my phone, it starts to ring in my hand. The name *Natalie James* flashes across the screen. I take a moment to regard the phone, and all I can do is feel my pulse quickening with each terrible ring.

Natalie is my father's wife. Wife number five. She calls herself a dancer, but really she's a stripper. Not the ideal stepmother. Luckily, or not so luckily, she calls me only when she needs help dragging my father out of some bar he crawled into after an audition bombed or his agent told him he didn't get the role.

If you've ever watched *Entourage*, my father is the equivalent of Johnny Drama. If you haven't watched that show, then think Gary Busey.

Rather than answer my phone, I simply cock my head to the side and stare at it with contempt. Sounds like I'm a shitty son, but the truth is he's a shitty father. When I was a kid, he was never around. When I landed my gig on *Chasing the Sun*, he was always around. Looking to party with the producers, score drugs from the cast, or ask me for money.

On the third ring, I wait . . . no, pray . . . she hangs up. Not in the mood for her stories, which are dramatic and go on and on.

On the fourth menacing ring, I pause for a brief moment to gather my thoughts, and then begrudgingly answer. "Hey, Natalie, what's going on? Is everything all right?"

"Oh, shit—thank God, I got you! Brooklyn, Todd is in the hospital and—"

Experiencing an odd feeling that I have never felt before, I cut her off immediately. "Natalie, what happened?"

She immediately plunges into every detail of how my old man ended up in a hospital bed. "It was past two a.m.," she tells me, "and Todd and I were at a busy intersection in a dirty corner of Hollywood, just blocks away from the Chinese Theatre. People were spilling out of bars and heading home. The place was crowded. It seemed safe. Sure, the Strip was emptying out quickly, but it was clear prime time was just beginning. Hookers were pouring out onto the sidewalk, circling the block slowly in packs of twos and threes, and causing a traffic jam as cars slowed to a crawl to check out the selection and ask how much."

I draw in a breath.

She continues. "Your father and I were there to score some good, old-fashioned heroin in order to celebrate his being cast on an ABC prime-time network show."

I wait for her to continue.

"We drove farther to another corner on a tip from a dancer friend of mine who lives in the area. And we knew we were in the right place when we started seeing transvestites and gigolos."

I say nothing.

"We parked our car in a side alley and approached the corner on foot. A pack of about a dozen thugs loitered in the shadows of a brightly lit donut shop. Inside, two pimp-looking guys decked out in gold chains and with teeth grills, surrounded by a couple of haggard, masculine-looking prostitutes, were eating donut holes, laughing and boasting."

"And then what?" I urge.

"I wanted to leave, but your old man bought a pack of smokes and lit up, trying to look as nonchalant as possible while he surveyed the scene."

"And then what happened?" I ask.

"When he finished his smoke and edged a little closer to a dude leaning up against the shop's exit, he asked if the guy had any smack. I hung back. The guy stared hard at him for a few seconds, just long enough to make Todd nervous, and then shook his head. Then, all of sudden, he swung his head to the right and walked away without a word. That's when we saw a patrol car had turned the corner and was slowly creeping by. The people hovering in the shadows dispersed without a sound."

"And?"

She sighs. "We both walked away. With no buy, your old man wouldn't give up. He baited a homeless drunk down the street with a couple of bucks and a cigarette in the hopes of getting some information. He was told he had to go to the Valley to get smack."

"Don't tell me you did?"

"No! But we should have left then. A group of what we thought were young punks farther up the street were laughing, and when your father asked them if they had any H, they smacked him on the shoulder and said sure thing."

I start to get impatient, but continue to listen.

"Amid a patch of shuttered shops, your old man whipped out his money, and got the shit beat out him. I ran. I had to. When I came back, he was lying on the sidewalk down the alley. With the help of some guy I promised a thousand bucks to, we got Todd to the car, and to the hospital."

Christ Almighty! This is an awful lot to take in. And who knows what the truth is, and what is made up. For all I know, they were trying to score a hooker or a gigolo. That's how crazy the two of them are together.

Fuck.

Fuck.

Fuck.

"Is he okay?" I ask.

Her voice is low. "The doctors said he'll be fine. Just a couple of broken ribs, some minor cuts, and heavy bruising. He should be able to go home tomorrow."

"That's good," I offer, and look out to the calm surf of Laguna Beach, and remember why the fuck I'm here and not there in LA. Because of him and the stupid shit he does.

"Can you come," she asks, "and bring a thousand bucks? The guy who helped me is in the waiting area, waiting for me to pay him."

"Shit, Natalie, really? That's why you're calling me?"

"Don't judge me, Brooklyn. I'm doing the best I can. And that's not the only reason why. I need you to help me get him home tomorrow. I kind of drove into a light pole when I was parking the car at the hospital, and it's not drivable."

Running a hand through my hair, I want to say no. To cut him out of my life for good, but I can't. "Yeah, Natalie, I'm on my way."

"Don't forget the money. I have no idea what this guy will do if I don't pay him."

Gritting my teeth, I answer, "I'll stop and get the cash. And I'll stay at my brother's in West Hollywood tonight to help you get my father home tomorrow, but after that, please don't call me again."

She hems and haws, but says nothing more.

Hanging up, I call my mother to warn her the press and paparazzi will probably be hounding her once the story is leaked, but as usual, I get her voicemail. I leave her a message, and then call my brother.

Keen answers right away.

He always does.

Sometimes I think he and Cam are the only two people I have in this world I can count on.

And look what I'm doing to Cam. Going behind his back and fucking his sister. That makes me just as despicable as my old man.

Without rethinking anymore, I decide Amelia has made the right decision, and I need to leave it alone.

Forget the talk.

Forget the idea that I could be her Mr. Right.

Obviously, I couldn't be farther from it.

CHAPTER 31
The Wedding Date

Amelia

The wedding invitation stated black-tie affair.

Although I was surprised long dresses were required, I was happy to shop for the perfect one.

And with Makayla's help, I found it—a vintage black sleeveless column dress with a fun cutout in the back.

Accompanied with bold jewelry including a big cocktail ring, I look in the mirror and know I am rocking my look. Think Audrey Hepburn in *Breakfast at Tiffany's* without the gloves . . . and the cigarette holder.

That is me.

I wish I had time to find a cigarette holder, just for the fun of it, but in Laguna, there was no chance of that.

I kind of miss the big city. I'm not sure I could be happy in a town like this. I like the beach, but I love the hustle and bustle of the city more.

With my hair up, sexy shoes on, and pearls hanging down my back, I feel like old Hollywood. Edit that. With no panties on, I feel like *slutty* old Hollywood, which I find appealing for some reason.

Brooklyn and I haven't seen each other since Wednesday. He had to help take care of his father. The thought of seeing him soon has butterfly wings fluttering in my stomach.

Trying to ignore my nerves, I roll some lip gloss on and then spritz myself with perfume.

Tonight is our last night together, and I want it to be perfect.

The doorbell rings, and although normally Brooklyn just struts in, I know it's him. Rushing to reach the door before Cam, suddenly this feels like prom all over again. And with my big brother watching over us, it will be until we leave. *Crap*, I won't even be able to kiss Brooklyn unless I get there first and sneak one. Thank God we don't have to exchange corsages. That was always the worst part of everyone staring.

Much to my dismay, Cam gets to the door first. I stay in the shadows while he opens it, and right here in the hallway my knees go utterly weak. Suddenly, I'm glad it was Cam that arrived at the door before me.

Remember John F. Kennedy Jr.?

Just picture him in any of the dozens of black-tie affairs he'd been photographed at with his tuxedo and bow tie and hair slicked back. That's exactly what Brooklyn looks like as he stands in the doorway.

His hair appears darker because he's had it cut shorter. It's no longer wild and messy, but instead very tamed and very polished. He has traded his board shorts for a tuxedo that looks like a million dollars on him. And that bow tie, it's delectable.

I greedily take in the sight of the guy who normally dons the "I don't give a fuck" attitude. Not tonight, though. Tonight he is conforming.

Unable to stop myself, I allow my eyes to linger on him. And like an addict getting my last high, I fear it is going to be far too long until I can get my next fix.

Trying not to be that fangirl type that he dislikes, I draw in a breath and turn the corner.

"Amelia," Brooklyn says in a low voice.

Cam turns to look at me, and his eyes nearly bug out of his head. I ignore him. "Hi, Brooklyn." I wave, and I feel like the schoolgirl I once was.

Keen and Maggie didn't come down this weekend. Maggie's mother came to visit, and Makayla drove up to West Hollywood to meet them and do girl things. Which leaves Cam here, alone, to hover. Perhaps I could just stride past him, and right out the door? Ha, I guess not.

"You look beautiful," they both say at the same time.

"Thank you," I awkwardly reply to both of them, as I walk toward the still open door.

The sun is bright and both men appear to have halos around their head. Angels they are not. The wedding is at sunset and I'm sure the air will be cool. With that in mind, I grab the wrap I bought and continue toward my brother and the man I've been sleeping with, the one who isn't my boyfriend. The word *lover* seems more appropriate, and for some reason I hate that. I hate the way we've shaped this relationship into something secret, something dirty, because it is anything but.

My brother's low whistle jolts me out of my thoughts, and thank God, it has nothing to do with me. "Nice car," he comments to Brooklyn.

Outside is an old-fashioned shiny black Rolls-Royce limousine. Brooklyn shrugs like it is no big deal, but I know it is; I know he hired it for me, because he knows I'm obsessed with everything from the forties, fifties, and sixties.

Cam and Brooklyn exchange insults, Cam accusing Brooklyn of looking to regain his movie-star status by wearing that monkey suit. And then Brooklyn hits Cam with how he's just warming up to get ready for the day Cam gets that ball and chain attached. In the end, they smile at each other, and both call each other variations of the word *fucker*.

My eyes are on Brooklyn, though, and not the gestures he is making or what he is saying, but rather on his mouth.

That mouth.

And God, that smile.

That slow, lazy smile that promises hours of pleasure. I can't even imagine how many legs that smile has spread because I want to spread mine the minute we get in the car.

Keeping things casual between us in front of my brother, Brooklyn says, "You ready to go to this circus?"

His tone is so casual, in fact, I swear if my hair wasn't up, he might rub his hand over the top of my head like I was a kid going to a ball game.

Finding it hard to pretend, I laugh anyway. I need to get away from this sham, though, and fast, so I kiss my brother on the cheek and say, "Goodbye," and then take a step out the door.

Cam watches from the doorway. "Have fun."

"As much as we can at a circus," Brooklyn comments over his shoulder, and follows in step beside me.

I look over at him. "Will there be monkeys and elephants?"

With a laugh, he looks over at me through the fringe of his lashes, smiling. Devastating. Charming. "Paparazzi and press, so yeah, I guess there will be."

"As long as there aren't any clowns. I hate clowns," I say.

"You hate clowns?" he asks, surprised.

"Yes, they're just creepy."

His gaze slides lazily over me, making me feel like he's stripping me naked. "I guess they can be," he responds, his eyes now simmering as he meets mine. "That's a really nice dress."

"Thank you," I tell him, and stop just before getting to the car door that the driver has already opened for me.

"I got this," Brooklyn tells the driver, and the driver promptly resumes his place behind the wheel.

Not exactly alone, but close enough, I look up at him. "I bought it with you in mind," I remark as I tuck my body into the plush leather and allow the thigh-high slit to reveal itself.

The move is casual. Cam, who is still in the doorway with his hands in his pockets, would never know the slit is an invitation to sneak under my dress, but Brooklyn does.

With his back to Cam, his teeth graze over his bottom lip and then his tongue sneaks out as if he just wants a taste. And oh, how I really want to give him one.

"Naughty girl," he murmurs, just before he closes my door to strut around the car to the other side.

The chilly night air might not have presented itself yet, but goose bumps are already humping my flesh.

The other door opens and Brooklyn slides in. With the partition already up, there is no need to watch what we say, yet Brooklyn remains quiet until well after the car turns off their street.

For the longest of moments he simply stares at me from across the backseat, and I wonder if he really is going to make this evening platonic.

But then he reaches across the seat and slides me into his strong hold.

I look at him. "I missed you." Words I shouldn't say, I know, but words that are true and need to be said.

"It was only three days." Casual words. True words. Words that still sting. Words that aren't "I missed you, too."

Before I can respond, and ask him to please not put a wall up on our last night together, he crashes his mouth over mine, hard, heated, demanding.

God, I love this about him. The way his need for me is so great, it overpowers everything else.

His tongue pushes into my mouth. Hot and sensual, it glides over mine as he licks playfully at the roof of my mouth. Teasing me. Taunting me.

Enveloped in his heat, I can smell him, his cologne that is as tantalizing as his own natural scent, and I swirl my tongue around his to get a little taste of his deliciousness.

After a few moments of fighting for control, I relinquish it and allow myself to melt into his embrace.

Our kisses are rarely simply kisses, and this one definitely is not. And I want more. More of him. More of his heat. More of his touch. More of his sinful mouth. I want to tell him he can write anywhere. I want to ask him to come to New York City with me. I want to tell him he's everything my fantasies were ever made of. That I want him—forever.

The realization paralyzes me.

Is Mr. Oh-So-Wrong my Mr. Right?

As his teeth graze over my bottom lip, he nips at it, and I ponder my thoughts. But then he gentles his assault on my mouth, lapping his tongue over the spot that he nipped, and then he pulls away. His eyes are dark, filled with heavy lust, but his words are darker. "Thank fuck tonight is the last night we're doing this, because I honestly can't handle the lying to your brother anymore."

Stunned that he is glad we are ending, I suddenly feel wrecked. With my legs wobbly and my voice shaky, all I can do is put my fingers to my tingling lips.

Brooklyn rubs his palms down his thighs. "We should probably avoid any kind of PDA at the wedding. Gigi has given the press open access, so there will be a lot of photographers and the photos will be plastered all over every news publication."

I swallow. Hard. And nod. "Yes, that is probably a good idea."

And then, as if combating some inner turmoil, his jaw goes tight and he turns to look out the window.

As the car speeds toward our destination, my mind becomes a flurry of upheaval. The past two weeks play over and over like the loop of a movie.

Why is he shutting me out?

But I know why. Because this really is the end. And we said this wouldn't end messy. I'm the one who had insisted on it, after all. And wouldn't me bringing up his hot-and-cold behavior do just that?

Before I can even gather my thoughts, the car comes to a stop at a small helicopter-pad landing in Newport Beach.

I look out the window. Beautiful, leggy women and tall, handsome men are being ushered into waiting helicopters to be brought to Catalina Island.

Paparazzi are, just as Brooklyn had said, off in the distance, snapping picture after picture. There is also press parked right beside the helicopter pads, happily snapping away. I think all of young Hollywood has come to watch what is being touted as the wedding of the decade. Gigi Bennett made sure of it, posting endless photos on social media of the wedding preparations over the past two weeks. Pictures ranging from the typical cake testing and dress shopping to more private things like her undergarment selections and their honeymoon destination.

If Brooklyn called this a circus, it's because Gigi has turned it into one. There isn't a person in the entire United States, I bet, who doesn't know who is invited to this event and where it is taking place. So much for secrecy. And because Gigi accidently let the cat out of the bag during an interview, she has altered a couple of things. One being reducing the number of press allowed. The other being nixing the wedding party from participating in the ceremony. She announced she wants to walk down the aisle alone, and gave no reason. There are rumors that her bridezilla tantrums caused discord between the wedding party and fueled this decision. Brooklyn has no clue. All he knows is the former attendants are still to come, just that they will be seated in the audience.

The door opens and Brooklyn offers me his hand. I hadn't

even noticed that he'd gotten out of the car; my mind was whirling so much from all of this craziness.

The sun is blinding and I shade my eyes as I look around at all the sunglassed faces, which I'm sure I could name if their shades were removed. Some I can name anyway. Luckily, I don't get stars in my eyes very easily. Being a New Yorker, I'm used to running into celebrities.

Brooklyn ushers me toward the crowd, and I suddenly feel exhilarated and wish I had my camera. I might not have stars in my eyes, but this is Hollywood's elite, and I wouldn't mind capturing the moment.

A woman wearing big Chanel sunglasses is staring at us. She's standing next to a man in a black three-piece suit and straw hat. I think the man is Tommy Riggins, star of last year's hit movie *Dreamworld*. The plot was straightforward, though the movie anything but. The setting was on a remote island and Tommy was the owner, who opened his home to his guests and ensured all of their dirtiest dreams would come true. I read the other day that the sequel, *Eroticworld*, is currently in production.

The woman removes her sunglasses and waves to Brooklyn. That's when I recognize her. She's Sasha Gomez and like Chase Parker, starred on the MTV network with him. Although I've never asked Brooklyn about her, I know that they have been an on-again, off-again item for years.

Because Sasha is still in the limelight, they've appeared photographed together many times. Carter is the one who is always keeping up with those things, and I really wish I had now.

Brooklyn gives her a smile, a real smile. I'm not jealous, or I don't want to be; it's just I thought he'd give her that classic badass nod of his and walk right past her. Instead, he smiles at her, and he hardly ever smiles at anyone.

Moving past her, he shakes a few hands, kisses a few cheeks, introduces me to many television stars whose shows I have never seen, and many that I have, and I let it go.

As the crowd thins, and another helicopter lands, he bends down to whisper something in my ear, but I can't really hear him.

The *thwump-thwump* of the helicopter's rotors is way too loud.

Rather than shout, I just nod and smile at him, and then I take a moment to admire him. How calm and cool he is in this environment. How amazing he looks with his trousers perfectly creased, his white shirt crisply pressed, and his cuff links gleaming in the sunlight.

How he looks like he's right where he belongs . . . in Hollywood.

A true Hollywood Prince.

CHAPTER 32

Reality Bites

Brooklyn

I wish I could tell you this place is crass.

That it is Hollywood overkill like everything I've ever known Hollywood to be, but I can't.

I wish I could say this is the circus I thought it would be, but in fact, it is anything but. And it makes me wonder if my perception has been off all these years—if I haven't been blinded by the lights of my parents, and somehow unable to see past them.

Sure, there are tents at the bottom of the acres and acres of green-sloped grass, but there are no elephants or peanuts anywhere, just a white sand beach and pristine surroundings that make this the event it has been touted to be.

The wind blows cool over us.

And as I glance at my phone and read the text on it, I close my eyes and sniff the salty air because it is ripe with possibility.

Feeling on top of the world, I look over at Amelia sitting beside me. And even though I know in a matter of hours we said we would be over, I can't help but take her hand and squeeze it.

I want to ask her to stay.

In fact, I'm going to ask her to stay as soon as we leave.

Don't look at me like that.

We'll talk to Cam together; he'll understand.

I hope.

I'll explain to him that I'm a changed man.

I'm going to quit my job as a lifeguard, and finally be what I want to be. Finally put one foot in front of the other, and jump.

In fact, I'd say that today is the beginning of the new me. And she's the first person I want to share my news with. I want to tell her Mr. Gerhardt loved my manuscript. And that Blake Johnson, who is Mr. Gerhardt's nephew, and one of the biggest indie movie backers in Hollywood, wants to talk to me tomorrow about the possibility of moving forward to production.

I want to thank her for not doubting me.

Tell her that I wish I hadn't doubted myself.

That being born into Hollywood royalty and growing up in the shadows of famous Hollywood parents wasn't easy.

That it took me this long to realize I can be my own person.

And that even though my father is washed up now, there was a time he was all anyone wanted to talk about. And even though my mother is behind the camera now, there was a time people went out of their way to snap her picture and sell it to the highest bidder.

It was a time in my life when I was either Brooklyn James, Todd James's son, or Brooklyn James, Emma Fairchild's son.

That was even the case when I starred in *Chasing the Sun*.

But, I can honestly say right now, that time is gone.

As I breathe in the cool air and feel the heat lamps on my skin, I know it to be true. This generation of Hollywood knows me—Brooklyn James, the guy writing a screenplay they can't wait for me to share.

And it feels so fucking good.

Just as the traditional wedding march starts to play, I move our hands to her leg and slip my fingers under the slit of her dress to feel her silky, smooth skin.

I've been an asshole to her, and I intend to make it up to her.

Reluctantly tugging my gaze away from her to Chase, who is standing up front in a white tux, black tie, and white pocket square, I can't help but envy him.

Always the guy the girls called *heartbreaker*, he found the right one and decided to settle down like it is the most natural thing in the world.

We all turn our heads to catch a glimpse of the bride, but the archway remains vacant.

"What's going on?" Amelia whispers in my ear.

With her body so close to mine, it's easy for my fingers to inch a little higher inside the slit of her dress. "Probably just a timing issue," I whisper.

She looks over at me, and then down. Her lips twist in scorn and her eyes narrow.

I don't like it that she's upset with me.

She looks like a pissed-off kitten whose claws want to come out. And yeah, my dick gets a little hard at the thought of her scratching my back.

Among the chatter of people, I lean even closer, and take her wrap and purse and set them on her lap.

She casts me another frown and firmly puts her hands on top of the items to stop my movement.

"Don't be that way," I whisper. "I'm sorry for being an ass."

"An *arrogant* ass," she whispers to me.

I smirk at her. "Yes, that."

Her hands remain where they are, but they are no longer pushing down and blocking me from her pussy. Nobody is paying any attention to us, and I quickly discover she did just what I told her to do—came pantyless.

Fuck me. She's so hot and silky smooth.

The music continues to play and as my fingers ever so gently caress the wet folds of her pussy, I let my mind wander to visions of just us sitting here. And if we were alone, how I'd grasp her firmly by her hips and hoist her right onto my lap. Unzip my fly and set her right on top of me and tell her to ride me. How it would be quick, hot, and out of control because my need for her is that fierce.

"Gigi is not anywhere on the island," someone calls from the archway.

The hushed whispers turn louder and I quickly remove my hand. People are standing now, and the music stops.

"It's because of the video," the woman behind us remarks rather loudly.

Curious, I turn, the delicious scent of Amelia's pussy still on my hand and wafting toward my noise. "What video?" I ask.

Gigi's costar is the one sitting behind me, and her lips are pursed in disgust. "The one TMZ just released of Chase at some strip club."

"Oh, my God," Amelia gasps under her breath.

Knowing he didn't do anything wrong, and it seems ridiculous for the bride to run off because of that night, I say nothing and turn back around. Amelia is on her phone searching for the video, and when she pulls it up, the headline reads, "Chase Parker is a sex addict."

My blood boils with rage. This is the Hollywood I remember. The one that lives and breathes fabricated lies and ridiculous accusations.

And then my blood is boiling for an entirely different reason because a text scrolls across Amelia's screen with the name Landon Reese attached to it and the question "How's the wedding?" beside it.

My entire body tenses.

Fuck me, I'm such an idiot.

The whole time I've thought this was real, all I have been is the bad she'd been craving. And I fucking knew it. And still I let it happen. All the while she has been fucking me, she's been in contact with the good.

The one who is her Mr. Right.

Furious, my entire body starts to shake.

Fear flashes in her eyes when she notices my brooding stare. "It's not what you think."

I brush my lips against her ear. "Yeah, it is. You broke my one rule."

And my heart . . . but that she'll never know.

CHAPTER 33
The Goodbye Girl

Amelia

We all want to find that perfect guy. We're all looking for love—the big kind, the kind that will change the world as we know it.

We spend so much of our time waiting, searching, and going through the motions of dating until we find what we're looking for.

Or maybe it's not like that. Maybe there is never a first or second date. Maybe it starts with sex. Yet still, a relationship blossoms.

But we know it can't last. It's not meant to. Still, we have hope.

And I had hope.

I have hope.

Yes, I have been texting Landon, but only on a platonic level, and I gave myself the excuse that since I wasn't "carrying on" or fucking I wasn't breaking Brooklyn's rule, but I was, and I knew it.

I can't explain why I didn't just let Landon go. Not even now as I sneak out of my brother's house and over to Brooklyn's, where I have to explain it to him.

He's finally home.

I saw him being dropped off an hour ago.

I've been home much longer.

Once the wedding was officially canceled, all the guests were helicoptered off the island. Brooklyn put me on one of those choppers and arranged for his driver to take me to Cam's. He told me he was going to hang back to be with Chase, and although I believe that was probably true, I also know he wanted me out of his sight. Gone.

And he was just way too polite about it. The way he huskily uttered that one single word, "Goodbye," it practically broke me. When he walked away, I waited for him to look back. He never did.

Finding the hidden key near the rear door, I unlock it and step inside. The house is dark. Really dark, and there is not a light on anywhere.

Familiar enough with the layout, I sidestep Gracie's dog dish—Gracie is Maggie and Keen's dog that they bring with them on the weekends—and make it through the galley kitchen without a sound.

"What are you doing here?" The words come out of the dark of the living room and are directed toward me.

I have to stifle my scream. I hadn't seen Brooklyn sitting on the couch. "I want to explain," I tell him, switching on the light on the side table just outside the kitchen.

It is dim, but I'm able to see him. "Nothing to talk about, Amelia. Go to your brother's until it's time for you to go home."

"Those texts are not what you think."

A half-empty bottle of whiskey and an ashtray filled with cigarette butts sit on the coffee table in front of him. Brooklyn holds up a near-empty glass. "It's exactly like what I think. I was the bad you were craving, and he is the good, the guy you see as the one." He grits the words *the one* through his teeth, like it's painful.

Feeling ashamed, empty, and heartsick, I sit beside him, not touching him. "Brooklyn, that's not true and you know it. That's the way you see it, the way you always have, which has been the problem all along, hasn't it?"

His hair is rumpled, his shirt unbuttoned, his bow tie hanging loose around his neck. "The problem," he says fiercely, "is that you've been sneaking around like I'm a dirty little secret, and I let you."

Nausea curls in my stomach. "Bullshit!" I scream. "You didn't want my brother to know and I went along with it. So face the real reason, Brooklyn. You knew you wouldn't be staying with me and didn't want to deal with the aftermath. That's the truth."

His face twists into a snarl. "That, Amelia, is bullshit."

"No! No, it's not. You never stay with anyone. It's like no one person is enough for you, and you knew I wouldn't be either."

He runs a hand down his face and draws in a long, ragged breath. When he blows it out to look at me. I can smell booze and cigarettes when he talks. "Is that really what you think of me? That I'm just that pantydropper our brothers call me? Because if that is true, you don't know me at all."

I am looking at a wounded man. All I want to do is make this right. And because of this, I act before I think. I move toward him. I'm very close to his lips when I say, "I do know you, Brooklyn, I do."

Doubt lingers.

I move closer still.

Then even closer.

I'm a breath away.

And then with that aggression he harbors so well, he takes my mouth for a bruising kiss. His lips move relentlessly over mine, his hands wander, firm and punishing, down my body, and then he pushes me back on the couch cushion.

And God help me, but I want this. Need this. As much as he does.

Frantic, he pushes down my yoga pants and then opens my thighs to dive between them.

His mouth is on me in an instant, and I cry out when he licks me. It feels so good, and I feel like it's been forever, when it's only been a matter of days. Those soft lips of his move against my clit, and I cry out some more. When he pushes his fingers inside me, and he groans against my pussy, I find myself unable to hold back my orgasm and I scream out his name in pleasure.

Within seconds, his fingers are fumbling with his belt, and then his cock is pressing against me right before he pushes into me.

Unable to remain quiet, I cry out again in pleasure when he fills me.

Hot.

Wild.

Crazy.

Unabashed.

Brooklyn buries his face against my neck and I throw my head back. His teeth press my skin, then bite. A burning strike that is more pleasure than pain.

We move together in the most feral way. Animalistic, our need for each other is all that matters.

To get deeper, his hands move under my ass, pushing me against him, and I tilt my pelvis to allow him that pleasure, and myself, too.

The couch protests as we rock it.

Normally, we would have both laughed.

There is no laughter now.

Brooklyn fucks me hard and fast, and I rake my fingers over his back, giving myself up to him.

This is his final goodbye to me, and all I can do is say it back in the same way.

He says my name when he comes. Then again, lower. Softer. He slows the pace, thrusting once more. Then again. That last press of his pelvis to mine pushes me over the edge into orgasm, but this time there are no rainbows or unicorns.

Breathing hard, Brooklyn presses his forehead to mine. Whiskey breath caresses me. When he pushes himself off me, I feel the loss instantly.

He doesn't look at me as he slides to the other end of the couch. My feet still so very close to him, yet the small space between us now seems like a giant divide.

Within moments, he pulls his pants up, and then waits for me to drag my yoga pants up.

Pulling my legs closer to me, I do just that.

I want him to stop me. To crawl on top of me and look at me. I want him to tell me I'm his. That he wants me more than the earth and the sun. That I'm his everything. That we'll tell my brother together and everything will be okay. This isn't where we end. This is where we begin.

Of course, he doesn't.

Instead of looking at me, he looks down, pours himself another drink, and sips it. Then he sets the glass on the coffee table and stands up.

I stand, too.

He starts for the kitchen. "You should go."

His back is to me, and as I follow him, I wipe the tears from my eyes with the heels of my palms. Rubbing them on my pants, I watch him as he opens the door. Watch the strong, confident man that I didn't make mine, and have to stifle my cry.

The cool breeze hits me, and I shiver.

Brooklyn does too, although I doubt he knows it as he stands there, waiting for me to leave. To get out of his life.

I push up on my toes and kiss him softly on the mouth. "I'm sorry, Brooklyn," I say in a low, hoarse voice. "I wish you could see that."

He shakes his head, just a little. "Don't be. We both knew how this was going to end."

End.

There it is.

Yes, we did know all along that when we ended . . . it would be messy.

And messy, it is.

CHAPTER 34
A Walk to Remember

Amelia

The John Wayne Airport is only nineteen minutes from Laguna Beach, but there is no direct flight to LaGuardia.

At the time I booked the flight, I hated the idea that Cam had to drive me fifty-nine minutes to LA International and drive fifty-nine minutes back to Laguna.

Right now, I'm thankful for the extra time.

Cam's hands tighten on the wheel. "I'm going to fucking kill him, Amelia."

I draw in a ragged breath. "You can't. You promised me you'd hear me out and understand."

He sighs and runs a hand through his hair. "I have heard you out. And what I've heard is that he took advantage of you at a time in your life when you were confused."

I shake my head. "Then you haven't been listening to me, Cam. I pursued him. I wanted him. I wanted something I'd never had before, a taste of bad, and he gave me what I wanted. Just like you do, like Dad does, and shit, just like Mom did when she hid the truth from me. To you, and everyone around me, I'm a princess. Well, I have news for you: I don't want to be that girl anymore."

He looks over at me, and then out the window, as if pondering my words.

I reach over and squeeze his arm gently. "I'm telling you this so he doesn't have to, Cam. I know how guilty he feels, and I know it's only a matter of time before he would have told you. I'm trusting that you understand how much I care about him, and I want you to promise you won't let it come between you."

His nostrils flare, and his hands curl even tighter around the wheel. "I don't know, Amelia; that's not something I can promise right now."

"Then don't promise, just make sure it happens. I love him, and I don't want his life to change because of me."

With a softer stare than the one he gave me moments ago, he glances over me. "You love him?"

Feeling like such a silly girl, I cover my eyes at the realization. "Yes, I think I do. I don't know. Everything is such a mess between us anyway, so it doesn't really matter."

Moments of silence pass until Cam speaks again. "If you care about him so much, and he cares about you the way you say he does, then why are you leaving?"

Dropping my hands, I glance over at him. "I just am."

There is so much more to it. The secrecy that ate us up. The way we started. The way we ended. My refusal to see that what was right in front of me was what I had been looking for the whole time.

Toads.

Frogs.

Princes.

Sometimes it's not easy to tell the difference.

And sometimes it just should be.

Shame on me.

CHAPTER 35
Fight Club

Brooklyn

On sitcoms, after a split the man typically finds some new girl to fuck around with while the girl sits around sobbing into her Häagen-Dazs ice cream. But in real life, men don't move on so quickly or get over it so easily, either.

Regardless of the reason for the break, and mine is pretty damn good—he is the better man for her, he has his shit together—straight and simple.

Even knowing this, I still feel like shit.

That doesn't matter. We needed to end. I could see she was waffling, knew she was second-guessing our decision, and when the text presented itself, I pounced.

I mean if Chase and Gigi couldn't make it, how the hell could Amelia and I?

Yeah, I knew Amelia wasn't carrying on with him. She was in this thing we had going on together all the way. A guy can tell. But we had to end, and there it was—the perfect reason.

The way to let her go.

A clean break.

The end.

The truth is, though, there is no *good* way to break up. It's always messy. Always. Amelia and I were fooling ourselves into thinking our end wouldn't be.

Breakups suck. No ifs, ands, or buts. The only breakup I remember being amicable was my first. It happened the summer before college. I had graduated; she hadn't. I was going off to college and leaving the show; she wasn't. For months, we knew it would be ending. When it did, we enjoyed a candlelit dinner and swapped breakup gifts, complete with wrapping paper. As breakups go, it was flawless. But the niceties can account for only so much—in the end, it did nothing to dull the hurt.

Since then, besides Sasha, I haven't let a girl in, other than Amelia. Seeing Sasha last night was strange. I felt nothing but a fondness for all the years we shared. And later, when we talked, she told me she felt the same. It felt good to put her in my past once and for all.

Setting my coffee mug on the counter, I wonder when I will be able to say the same about Amelia because right now, it fucking hurts.

I grab my pencil and take these feelings and pour them into this intimate exchange between Kellan and Kate.

It's the only thing I can do with them.

Suddenly, the kitchen door swings open.

My head jerks up from my manuscript to see Cam staring at me with a murderous look on his face. Fury blazes in his eyes, and I know. I know she's told him. And fuck, I should have been more ready for this, but I'm not.

Stomping toward me, he grabs me by the neck of my shirt and hauls me off the kitchen stool I've been sitting on since Amelia left hours and hours ago.

"What the fuck is wrong with you?" Cam roars as his fist connects with my jaw in an explosive punch.

Stumbling back against the counter, I just stare at him. I won't fight back. I can't. I deserve this. And besides, it's not like I didn't know this day would come. I knew it all along, didn't I?

Taking the three steps that separate us in a matter of seconds, Cam takes hold of me again, but this time pushes me backward and looms over me. "I trusted you with my sister. Trusted you to do the right thing. And I just put her on a plane in tears. So tell me, friend, how is that the right thing?"

Shit, I can't even look him in the eye. Guilt racks me, and I have no answer for him. How do I tell him it was the only way? That I did it for her. He would never see it that way. She's his baby sister. The one he adores. The last thing he wants is for her to get hurt.

Fuck, I did this all wrong.

Did her and me all wrong.

Shoving me back one more time, he gives me a look of disgust. "You can be an asshole, you know that?" he says hoarsely, and then pounds across the wooden floor until he reaches the kitchen door. With his hand on the knob, he pauses. "I thought you were better than that."

When the door slams, and I'm alone in his wake, all I can think is . . . I am.

I am.

All I need is time to prove it.

And I will.

CHAPTER 36
Stand by Me

Amelia

Two men with six-pack abs passionately embrace and begin kissing. Soon, they tear each other's clothes off. The camera zooms in as the pair writhes against each other's naked bodies. Eventually, one of them gets on top and a full-on anal scene ensues.

Normally, I don't watch porn.

But since Carter had it on when I came over, I told him not to bother to turn it off. At least he wasn't jerking off to it.

He was actually working on image edits, and had it on as "background noise." It was I who sat down to watch.

"Change the channel," he offers, fixated on his computer screen. "I know that isn't your thing. I'll be done in five minutes."

Flicking the remote, I move through almost a dozen stations. There's a girl dressed as a nurse, administering a shot in the form of a dildo. Two men in leather suits with assless pants on. And a threesome making a daisy chain. None of which grabs my attention and screams "watch me."

Carter doesn't discriminate between gay and straight porn. As long as the men are good-looking, he's down with whatever is on. He actually likes to watch porn, and not just for jerking-off material. He finds the skits amusing and the storylines intriguing.

That's why he has all the porn stations. Clicking to another, and another still, I end up stopping on Playboy TV when I see a couple fucking on a kitchen counter.

As the guy thrusts violently into the girl, I can't help but think how different this is from the sex tape Brooklyn and I made. The one where Brooklyn is actually making love to me, not fucking me.

I figured out what he said to me that night, what he whispered into my ear. It took me hours of watching us together, but he said, "I love making love to you."

Swoon.

I wish I had heard it then, because figuring it out after our forbidden affair ended has only put me in the hopeless romantic category.

Sighing, I click the television off and look over at Carter. He is fiddling with his mouse. "What are you doing?" I ask.

"Editing," he says with another click and drag.

"I know that." Getting to my feet, I walk over and stand behind him. On the screen is an image of a woman in a wedding dress. He's blowing it up. I watch as it grows larger and larger on the screen. Tapping the paint can icon, he adds vibrant red to the bouquet of flowers that is held in her hands, along with yellow, green, and orange. When he zooms out, I can see that she is sitting on the ground with a pair of Chucks on.

Leaning even closer, I ask, "Who is that?"

He changes the specs in the adjacent window and I watch the photo zoom out some more. "Just a girl I hired to be a jilted bride."

"Really? Why would you do that?"

"Because I'm not a wanker. These images are hot right now, and I wasn't shooting any weddings in the next couple of weeks, and I wanted to add to my stock photos. I already uploaded the jilted groom prints. I thought I showed them to you?"

I pull my mouth to the side. "I don't think you did."

"Well, they're selling like bloody mad with the whole Parker/Bennett debacle."

I thump his shoulder. "Yes, I bet they are."

He twirls around in his chair and puts his hands behind his head. "By the way, did you see the news yesterday? I can't believe Gigi Bennett leaked the tape as a publicity ploy."

"Me either! And did you see where it got her? A nomination for an Emmy."

"No shit—I missed that."

"Yep. I swear it was all a publicity stunt, but what do I know?"

Carter turns back around in his chair and taps his keyboard. "You should have taken some pictures yourself. Of that night and the wedding debacle."

"Carter!" I scold.

He raises his palms. "I'm just saying, you would have made a fortune."

I shake my head. "Has anyone ever told you what an ass you are?"

Standing up, he heads toward the kitchen. "All the time, especially when I make them come, and then tell them it's time to leave."

I follow behind him. "That's enough talking shit. Tell me about Eli. How are things?" I raise a suggestive brow.

Reaching for the wineglasses, he glances over at me. "Nothing has changed since last week. We still haven't shagged. If that's what you are asking?"

"Still?" I laugh.

"Why do you think I'm watching porn?"

Grabbing an opened wine bottle from the refrigerator, I set it down and stare at him. "What's going on? Why wait this long?"

"Grab the cheese, will you?" He sidesteps me to reach for a box of crackers in the upper cabinet.

"Carter."

"Because," he says, "we both want to take things slow."

I put the cheese on the table and uncork the wine. "Any slower and—"

He cuts me off. "Don't say it." Reaching, he grabs the block of cheese to slice it on the butcher block. "I already know what you're going to say, and that is why I invited him to come with me to Niagara Falls next weekend."

I giggle as I pour the wine into our glasses. "Separate rooms?"

"Fuck no. This is a romantic getaway, and if it doesn't move things along, nothing is going to."

"Carter Kincaid in a sexless relationship?" I tease. "It's unheard of."

The plastic sleeve of crackers is loud when he dumps it on the plate. When he looks up, he makes a face at me. "Speaking of slow moving, did you call Landon back yet?"

I've been back in the city for four weeks. And it has been a productive four weeks. I've spoken to my father on countless occasions. It's good I took that time to cool off. It helped. When we met, I told him how disappointed in him I was. What happened wasn't really my business, but that man I put on a pedestal is gone. Still, he is my father, and I can't cut him out of my life. He isn't seeing Vanessa, at least. It wasn't my father she was with that night, thank God. And he did fire her when he found out what she'd said to me. The things she said about Brandon I think hurt him the most.

I also quit my job in the grown-up way, giving two weeks' notice.

In addition, I've been spending most of my days in Brooklyn, the place where my mother lives with her new husband. She and Josh got married over a year ago, and although I attended the small affair, it was begrudgingly. And I never took the time to get to know Josh. He is really sweet, and funny, and a talented artist who loves my mother.

My mother, father, and I went to Brandon's grave together yesterday. Slowly, our family is healing from his loss, and although things will never be the same, I think we have all made peace with our feelings, in our own way, Cam included.

So yeah, a month, and no, I haven't heard from Brooklyn, the person. I've called him and left him messages. The first one before I got on the plane to let him know I'd told Cam about us. The second one when I landed to tell him I missed him. The third one that night when I got in bed all alone and hated the mess I'd left behind. Countless messages later, he has yet to answer a single one.

And yes, it's time I let him go.

I sip my wine. "I did call Landon," I tell Carter. "We're going out tomorrow night."

He raises a brow. "Do you think that's a good idea?"

Popping a piece of cheese in my mouth, I shrug. "It's just dinner."

"Hmmm . . ."

"What?" I ask tartly.

"Are you sure you're ready to move on?"

I take another small sip of wine. "Yes, I am."

"I'm not so sure about that, Amelia."

Narrowing my eyes at him, I say, "I don't have a choice. And technically I met him first, so I'm moving back." I try to laugh, but for some reason I can't.

"Just don't hurt him."

His words sting. I don't think I've ever hurt a man, and I don't want to now. But Landon has been pursuing me, so I think I owe him this date. Unable to talk about it any longer, I twirl around and head toward the living room with my glass in hand. "Come on, let's watch TV."

Watching porn has to be easier than facing the truth . . .

That I messed my life up and it is never going to be the same.

CHAPTER 37

The Prince of Tides

Amelia

L andon is a patient man.

In fact, I bet if you looked up the word *patient*, his handsome profile would be beside it. Never have I met someone as understanding as him. That in itself should be a sign that he is the Prince Charming I've been looking for.

I'm not sure what he sees in me. When I asked him, he said there is just something between us that he feels compelled to explore further.

Romantic.

Right?

We've been dating for the past two weeks and he hasn't pressured me for so much as a kiss. I'm glad, because I am nowhere near ready to embark on a new physical relationship. An intellectual one is about as far as I've been able to manage.

Such a huge difference from the initial impression he made on New Year's Eve, when he was all hands, and tongue.

He really is a gentleman.

Dashing.

Charming.

Kind.

Understanding.

Very understanding.

Even though I'm moving to California to take the job my brother offered me, he says we can make things work. He's a ballplayer after all, and on the road half the time, so he can spend his off-season anywhere he wants.

And yes, there it is. I made a decision. I'm moving to California. I felt amazing when I was there. Almost like a different person. Being back in the city has felt a bit stifling, and the day I couldn't breathe any longer was the day I decided to move.

But I'm not moving back for him.

He doesn't live next door to Cam anymore.

He is Brooklyn, of course.

There, I said his name.

I know you wanted to know.

But that's all I know about him. I got that small bit of information from Makayla. And even then, she was pretty closemouthed about anything else. Not that it matters; he's already long forgotten me, I'm sure.

And besides, it wouldn't have mattered if he did still live next door because I don't want to live with my brother. I'm going to get my own place as soon as I get there and get settled. Probably somewhere in Los Angeles. Maybe close to Keen and Maggie; that way my brother won't worry about me so much.

As for the job with Simon Warren, it isn't exactly my dream job, but it is a stepping-stone to the world of photography, and I am very appreciative to have this opportunity.

Funny how things work out, but I met this actor at the Parker/Bennett wedding debacle. His name is Jagger Kennedy. He plays Gigi's brother on *Where's My Latte?* He also has starred on the big screen, and is most famous for playing the role of Ian Daniels in *No Led Zeppelin* a couple of years ago.

Anyway, his wife is Aerie Daniels. She wasn't there, but she's the senior editor for *Sound Music*, a magazine owned by Plan B that I really admire. Jagger told me to look them up if I moved to LA. That his wife has photographers on staff, and you never know when she'll be hiring another.

I think in due time I will do just that.

It's my dream job, after all.

Music playing and snow falling outside, I'm inside the warmth of my apartment and packing the last of my boxes when my cell buzzes. I glance at it casually by my side on the counter, and nearly drop the wineglasses in my hands when I see the message is from Brooklyn. It says two words: *I'm sorry.*

Two words that make my world turn upside down.

Just then, I happen to notice that the song on the radio changes. I try to distract myself by listening to it. Singing along to the lyrics, I wrap the glasses in brown paper and grab another. The last. The very last thing to be packed.

Then, I sneak another look, as if those two words might have disappeared or changed into something else, another two, something more like *fuck you*. After all, I did tell my brother about us, and even though I did it for Brooklyn, I'm not sure he saw it that way.

Suddenly, I'm not sure about anything.

Moving.

Leaving the city.

Being so far away from Carter, and my mother, and even my father.

Teary-eyed, I glance around my small apartment. Boxes that Carter neatly labeled are ready to be moved into storage until I secure my own place. Furniture that Landon insisted be wrapped in heavy plastic are also awaiting storage pickup in the morning. I look at the bare walls. The emptiness of it all.

And for the first time, I find myself second-guessing my

decision to move across the country.

With sweaty palms, I set the glass down and pick up my phone. Holding it tightly, I allow myself to contemplate what to text back.

Then I start to wonder if I should even text anything at all. Minutes pass as I stand here paralyzed, singing along to a song I'm not sure I could tell you the name of. And then like a sign from above, one that wants me to focus on my life, the song changes again, but this time I know the title.

I'm listening to this song by the Spin Doctors called "Two Princes."

The lyrics are similar to my story. Two princes. One princess. A choice to make. And perhaps even a happily ever after.

Unlike a fairy tale, though, my story doesn't start with "Once upon a time." Oh, how I wish it did, though. The thing is, a lot has happened in my life that has made me who I am. And because of this, I have a lot of issues to resolve before I can get to the end. Yet, rest assured, in its true form—this will be a love story.

It has to be.

Like the song, it's about me and . . .

This one.

And that one.

You'd think choosing Mr. Right over Mr. Oh-So-Wrong would be easy, but it isn't.

In the light of day, it all seems so clear, but now, in the dark of the night, Mr. Right doesn't seem so right, and Mr. Oh-So-Wrong doesn't seem that wrong.

I met one before the other. Spent more time with one than the other. Now one is ready for the next step, but I'm not sure about the other.

None of that matters.

What matters is in my heart, and I have to dig deep enough inside to figure out what it is telling me. Move forward or go back.

God, I wish I knew.

The doorbell rings.

Rushing over to the door, I swing it open wide, expecting my mother, my father, my best friend—anyone but him.

There he stands with a smile on his face and a bouquet of flowers in his hand. Before I can even take the flowers, I look at the cell clutched tight in my fingers. At the two words I don't know what to do with. They're from him. The other man.

This isn't a love triangle; it never was. It's simply about choices.

This one.

Or that one.

Mr. Right, or Mr. Oh-So-Wrong.

With the text still unanswered, I stare into this man's face, and then at my screen.

Who should I choose?

I stand here, reeling, my mind wandering back to how it all began. How I went from searching for the right one to finding two men within twenty-four hours.

Two princes, but only one that is meant to be mine.

And I know which one.

"Hi," he says.

"Landon, what are you doing here?" I ask, taking the flowers he's handing me.

His smile is wide. "My flight to Tampa got canceled, and I figured with all the packing you probably hadn't eaten dinner yet. Am I right?"

I nod, staring at my phone. Glad he will be here longer. Glad he is still in the city, but not exactly over the moon.

"Then come on, let me take you out."

I look around. "I don't know. I have so much to do."

"I insist," he says.

"Okay." I smile.

Setting the flowers down, I grab my coat, hat, and gloves, and we venture into the Village.

The walk is spent with Landon telling me about his day. I listen. Or I try to, the entire time my heart beating faster and my palms a little sweaty in my gloves as I think about those two words, *I'm sorry*, and what they mean.

We end up at a new place called Soup and Noodles because Landon has been there, and he says the chicken noodle soup is out of this world.

There's live music. Some indie band I don't know. The restaurant is tucked neatly off a side street, and I didn't even know it was here, but it's nice inside, and I like it.

Landon grabs my hand as the hostess leads us to our table.

He helps take my coat off.

Sits beside me rather than across from me.

Smiling at him, I pull my gloves off and am grateful to be out of the cold.

Landon orders for us, two soups and a loaf of French bread. He's easy to be with. And he always makes me laugh.

"See?" he says, when he finishes telling me about his schedule. "It's insane."

"It is," I tell him, my mind on Brooklyn and why he bothered to text me at all.

"It's the insanity, though, that's makes it all worth it."

I laugh. "Maybe that's because you're a little bit insane."

He moves a little closer. "Is that a bad thing?"

I drag my spoon through the noodles left in my bowl. "No, not at all."

"Good," he says, pushing his empty bowl away.

I wipe my mouth with my napkin and look over at him. "I should probably get home. I have to finish packing."

"Yeah. Thanks for joining me on such short notice."

Outside, we walk in silence, our breath fogging the air and our boots leaving slush marks on the sidewalk. Somewhere between our soups arriving and now, his attention seems to have drifted, and mine is where it has been all night—on my phone. Still deciding if I should answer the text, and looking for a sign that *I'm sorry* isn't the absolute end, although I'm certain it is.

Back at my place, Landon pauses in the doorway. When he leans to kiss me, I turn my head.

"Amelia," he says, his voice soft. "I'm not going to call you anymore. Whoever is on your mind isn't me. But if things don't work out, give me a call. Who knows, maybe it just isn't our time yet."

Tears dip down my cheeks, and I get on my toes and softly kiss his cheek. "Thank you, Landon. Thank you for noticing what I didn't."

At that he laughs. "I wish I could say I didn't, but the guy on your mind is the one you should be with."

When I close the door, I lean against it and pull out my phone. I read the message again, and this time I type out the message, "Why did you let me go?" but I never send it.

And then I close my eyes and whisper into the darkness . . ."*My Prince.*"

CHAPTER 38

Everybody Wants Some

Brooklyn

The standing joke in Hollywood is that using a standard-required screenplay format will help get the screenplay read.

Twelve-point Courier font is a necessity.

Two brass brads in white, three-hole-punch paper.

With approximately 90 to 120 pages.

Title is important, although not always.

Yes, to play it safe, I delivered my manuscript to Blake Johnson in that format the day Amelia left. And he said yes.

Yes.

Fangirl got the green light!

The yes came almost six weeks ago, five days after Amelia left, to be exact.

And I've spent every single one of those days working my ass off to prove to myself I am the right man for her.

That I can be responsible.

Grown up.

Mature.

I moved out of Maggie's house to be closer to the studio. And truth be told, to be on my own. I rented a condo in West

Hollywood, which I have the option to purchase if I want.

Blake is independently producing *Fangirl*. That means we are moving at lightning speed. Stars have already been attached, and at my request, Chase Parker is playing Kellan. My mother is directing, and Scott Edwards is producing it.

Preproduction is well under way. Location scouting, storyboards, production schedules, permits, budgets, and more are done.

Production design, art direction, costume designs, rewrites, and more rewrites are almost done.

Purchasing film stock, getting a film crew together, hiring a caterer, renting sound stages and equipment—all almost done.

Shooting—about to begin.

And then there is postproduction, which will be minimized to get the movie out by November.

With so much to do, I can't believe I agreed to meet Keen for lunch today. I stride down the hallway of the Simon Warren offices on Melrose and open my brother's office door to see if he is ready to go.

He is not the one in there, though.

Imagine my surprise when I see Cam sitting behind Keen's desk. I've been avoiding him since the day we came to blows. Skipping family meals and cutting his calls short.

Truth is—I feel like a shit for what I did.

I don't regret what happened with Amelia, but I should have been a man about it and told her brother from the start. Proved I wasn't the asshole everyone thinks I am.

I stumble over my words. "What is this?"

"We need to talk," Cam tells me, standing up and placing his palms on the desk.

"Yeah, we do," I respond, leaning against the wall and crossing my arms. Not at all liking the ambush, but knowing it is time to put all the cards on the table.

"Then talk," Cam says tersely.

Uncrossing my arms, I walk toward him, then stop on the other side of the desk and flop in the chair. "I'm sorry."

He nods, saying nothing.

"I fucked up. I should have told you about what was going on between your sister and me."

His eyes narrow. "And what exactly *was* going on?" There's a challenge in his voice. Something like, *say she was your plaything and I might cut your balls off.*

With a huge intake of breath, I rub my jaw with my hands. "We . . ." I pause, pulling my hands down my face. "We started out just having fun."

His entire body goes live wire.

I quickly add, "Or that is what I told myself. It was never just fun, though. She is a very special woman, and I knew that from the minute I saw her on your porch."

"Yet, you kept her at a distance?" His tone is angry.

"I did. I was a coward. I said it was because of you, but it was all me. I knew I wasn't right for her."

"And you know this how?"

"Because I'm in love with her." I tell him bluntly, surprising even myself, but knowing it's true.

His eyes narrow. "And so let her go?"

"Yes, she deserved more." It's why I've worked my ass off. It's why I can't get her out of my mind. It's why I texted her.

Sitting down, he steeples his hands, and the corners of his mouth quirk down even farther. "That's really fucked up."

I narrow my eyes at him. "Fuck you, you don't get to judge. I love her, and want what is best for her. I thought you of all people would understand that."

"I'm not judging. It's just if you love her, you have a funny way of showing it."

His laugh is dry, and I consider my next move carefully. I can tell him to fuck off, that his sister or not, I want her, or I can be calm and act like a man.

Almost instinctively my eyes dart to the wall and the collage of photos Maggie hung. They are of everyone in our happy, little unconventional family. All of us sitting around a bonfire at the beach. On Christmas morning when Maggie gave us all socks she had attempted to knit while she was pregnant that looked more like ass warmers, if there were such things. Of the life we'd all built because we had no one else. Of the life I want desperately to remain a part of. Sure, I'd always have my brother, but I want Cam and Makayla, too. And Amelia. I clear my throat, emotion taking hold of me, and then set my gaze on Cam.

Those gray eyes so much like his sister's narrow on me. "Ignoring her for the past six weeks isn't any way to win her back."

Shock tears through me. "You're okay with this? I mean with her and me together?"

Cam shakes his head at me. "She's my sister, for Christ's sake. All I care about is that she is happy, and if you make her happy, what do I have to complain about?"

I stare at him, my mouth open.

Cam stares right back. "You don't have a lot of faith in our friendship, Brooklyn, or in yourself for that matter."

I slam my hand on the desk. "That's bullshit. The last thing I wanted was to do anything to separate this family we've built. It's the only fucking one I've ever had."

Cam circles the desk and comes to stand beside me, offering his hand. "Then don't. I think you're a great man, Brooklyn. I'd be happy for my sister to end up with you. And I think she would, too. If you ask me, you're the only one who thinks it isn't possible. That thinks she's out of your league."

"Everything okay in here?" Keen is standing in the door.

I look at him, and then at Cam. "Yeah, I think it is."

"Does that mean you'll start coming to Sunday dinners in Laguna again? Because I'm sick and tired of cleaning up all by myself."

"Fuck you, fucker," Cam says. "I help."

Keen leans against the wall and props a foot up. "Yeah, right—you help by laying your ass on the couch and warming up the television."

"That's bullshit," Cam remarks, and looks at me. "Tell him, Brooklyn—tell him how much I help."

I make a face. "Keen has a point. You do end up watching football most of the time."

"Fuck you," he says with a smile. "And just so you know, my sister arrives in a few hours."

"She does?" I ask.

He lifts a brow. "Yeah, she's moving here. And what are you going to do about it?"

I start pacing a tight line in front of my brother and my best friend. "I don't know. Do you think she'll talk to me?"

"Not sure," Cam breathes out. "She told me you texted her yesterday, but she wasn't sure what to make of it."

I pause and ease into one of the two chairs beside him. "Yeah, I did, but when she didn't answer I just assumed it was her way of telling me to go to hell."

"You know what they say about assuming." Cam smirks.

In a surprise move, Keen picks me up from under my arms. "Stop being a pussy and go get the girl. Shit, you write movies for a living—don't you want to know how this ends?"

Standing on my feet, I shrug out of his hold, and then grin at him. "Yeah, motherfucker, I do."

"Then tell me," Keen demands, with amusement in his tone.

"The only way it can. With me getting the girl," I answer, and head out the door to LAX.

To get my girl.

CHAPTER 39
Sleepless in Seattle

Amelia

The airport looks more like a shopping mall than a place people come to travel to and from their destinations.

The tiles gleam white under my feet as I walk toward the main gate. Everywhere there are people milling around. Looking to my right, I see two glass elevators leading to an upper floor, which is a food court. To my left is a large open area with blue fabric-covered seats that are completely occupied by people on their phones, laptops, and tablets.

The air is cool, and only the faint aroma wafting from the food area gives this large space any scent.

I keep walking, following the signs for baggage claim. This airport is so different from LaGuardia; nicer, I guess, is the best way to put it.

Some stairs lead up to an open viewing deck where eager children watch the airplanes take off and land. There are mounted telescopes for them to look through and the back wall is one large window. Behind the telescopes is a scale model of the airport with the runways marked on it.

In front of me is a group of little old ladies in Las Vegas

T-shirts hugging their grandkids.

In my flats and skinny pants, I move fast, eager to get to baggage claim, and more eager to start this new chapter in my life.

My phone pings with a text, and I stop to pull it from my pocket. Assuming it's Cam telling me he is running behind, I'm shocked to see the text is from Brooklyn, and even more shocked to see that it directs me to look to my left.

My heart starts to pound frantically.

I draw in a breath.

When I finally turn my head, I see him coming down the escalator. As I exhale, my breath stutters raggedly over my lips, and for a brief second, I simply forget how to breathe.

Frozen in place, I stand in the middle of the busy airport as heat infuses my entire body. Unmoving for moments, I don't know what to do.

With my mouth dry, I lick my lips and wait with uncertainty. What does this mean? What is he doing here? How did he know I was coming?

Once Brooklyn is off the escalator, his gaze catches mine and holds it, all the while striding toward me with an odd determination. There's something different about him. Like that brooding stare of his has morphed into something different. Something softer, and yet those blue eyes still simmer with that confidence I have grown to admire.

Seeing him, seeing his gorgeous face and pretty mouth, something snaps inside me, and exhilaration takes over.

Suddenly I'm on a roller coaster with the wind in my face, and all I want is for it to go higher, move faster, and never stop.

With my heart beating a mile a minute, I start to run toward him as fast as I can. Now I'm off the roller coaster. Instead, I'm on the ledge of the tallest of building and I'm about jump. If he doesn't catch me, at least I tried.

Like a scene from a movie, we meet in the middle of the busy airport and when I throw myself at him, he catches me and twirls me around.

He doesn't let me fall.

It really is like a cheesy movie, and we're starring in it as the romantic couple.

Brooklyn buries his face in my neck and nibbles. And in turn, I squeeze him as tight as I can. Then he sets me down and pulls a bag from his pocket. He laughs when he looks inside. "I got you a cookie, but it's squished now."

I grab the bag from him, and then throw my arms around him again. "What are you doing here?"

This time when he pulls back, he keeps his hands anchored on my hips. "I came to tell you how fucking sorry I am, and get on my knees if it means that you'll forgive me."

When I don't answer, because I can't, because my words are stuck in my throat, slowly, he starts to lower himself. I stop him. Joy floods my heart and tears well in my eyes. "Brooklyn, of course I forgive you. What went wrong between us wasn't just your fault. It was mine, too. But you have to believe me, those texts were innocent—"

He shushes me with a finger over my lips. "No more about it. No more rules. No more pretending this isn't real, and absolutely no more sneaking around."

The crowd thickens around us—another flight having landed, or maybe another one taking off. Still, we don't move. We stand in the middle of LAX, with our hands on each other and our eyes only for each other, and then he takes my mouth in a swooping kiss that makes me weak in the knees. Pulling me closer, his mouth is hard and fierce over mine. I cling to him just as fiercely as he kisses me.

This is not the homecoming I expected. It is so much better. But then I realize we have things to settle before can get to our happy ever after. "Sir Towhead," I say, around his lips.

"Yes, Princess Amelia," he mutters with a laugh.

"You are my Mr. Right and I want you to be my Prince Charming. Can you do that?" I ask.

Brooklyn smiles. A genuine smile meant only for me. "I think I can, but first I have one thing to ask you."

Tears leak from my eyes as I stare at the man who once upon a time at ten years old had married me. "What is it?" I ask, breaking our embrace to wipe the tears from my cheeks.

Taking my hands in his, he places them over my tears of joy, and then those blue eyes find mine. "I love you, Amelia, and I want you to be mine. Can you do that?"

This time when I launch myself at him, I nearly topple him over. "Yes, I can do that. And I love you, too."

And that is how my prince, turned toad, turned frog, turned prince again came to be mine.

It might not top Cinderella's story, but it comes pretty darn close.

Don't you think?

I know I do.

EPILOGUE
Spotlight

Amelia

L ove comes in many different shades. Sometimes it's consuming and violent, other times it's goofy and messy, and sometimes it's sweet and perfect.

Hollywood, of course, loves every single gradient—from love triangles, to long-distance romance, to a teenage lust you could only hope for. And sometimes they even love a quirky, finding-love-when-you-least-expect-it kind of romance, as in the case of *Fangirl*.

The limo picks us up at 3 p.m., and we drive for what seems like a million miles. As soon as we get to LA, the drive becomes even slower because streets are closed off everywhere.

A block before our destination, we are brought to a stop and the car is searched, and then we're in the home stretch. Excitement flutters like pinwheels all around me. I can't believe we're here. All I can do is squeeze Brooklyn's hand and look out the window in wonder.

Giant, twenty-four-foot-high twin golden Oscar statues loom large outside the Dolby Theatre, and suddenly I can't feel my hand because Brooklyn is squeezing it so tightly. It's hard to believe we're here. Here where all the eyes of the world are focusing on those statues with the most anticipated ceremony of the year just minutes away from commencing.

My heart feels like it's pumping out of my chest. I glance over at him and smile. He looks so nervous. Covering our connected hands with my free one, I mouth, "I love you." His free hand covers mine and he mouths it back, and he finally gives me a small smile.

Before I know it, we're exiting the car. Someone pushes a ticket into Brooklyn's hand to get the car back later, and he shoves it into his pocket. I shade my eyes and look toward my right. It's so unreal. The sea of black limousines can be seen for miles and miles. Photographers, too. Flashes going off like mad as they attempt to capture every step each star takes. And stars are everywhere. All stopping to pose, with their hair done perfectly, their fancy clothes, and their designer shades, every woman looks like a princess and every man a prince.

Glamor and sophistication are everywhere. I feel like I want to blow glitter—that's how happy I am.

I look over toward Brooklyn, my brother, and Keen, and realize none of us has any idea what to do now.

Within moments, a woman wearing a headset and a black pantsuit asks, "Brooklyn?"

He nods, and the woman introduces herself, adding, "I just came back from walking Emma through. What a nice coincidence. Would you like me to take your party through?"

"Yes, that would be fantastic," he answers.

She glances down at her clipboard. "Would you like to walk past the cameras?"

For only a moment he hesitates before responding, "Yes."

All together, we take a few steps and head into the throng. The four of us are so nervous, not a single one of us utters a word.

No jokes.

Or backslaps.

Or jabs.

Just wobbly legs that bring us closer to our destination with every single step we take. The closer we get, the more my gaze wanders, and I take in even more of my surroundings. To the left of me are large grandstands that have been set up to allow spectators a view of everyone exiting their cars curbside, and then beginning their walk toward the auditorium.

Every one of the spectators gawks and gasps as we make our way up the red carpet. I watch as the stars in front of us run the gauntlet of photographers, stopping for a pose every now and then. Some stop to give interviews to the horde of TV news crews and entertainment reporters along the way, and others pass right by to enter the tent and go through security before entering the theater.

The attentive press ravishes Brooklyn. The prince of Hollywood is on the red carpet, and this time not as a guest of either of his famous parents. This is all him, and Hollywood loves their royalty. After all, the four of us are at the Academy Awards for three very good reasons.

Number one: *Fangirl* has been nominated for Best Original Screenplay. Number two: Chase Parker has been nominated for Best Actor. And number three: Emma Fairchild has received a nomination for directing.

When *Entertainment Tonight* asks me what I am wearing, my nerves take flight. But then I look at my dress and smile. I'm wearing a red strapless dress with white embroidered scripting all over it. Jordan Cartwright, the head designer for Simon Warren, made it especially for me. The scripted lines are movie quotes from *Fangirl*. I answer, and I know this is huge for Simon Warren because my brother can't stop beaming.

At the bend in the red carpet we pause. More cameras flash. Brooklyn has his arm around me, and we pose just like those in front of us did.

Adoring fans are shouting how much they loved *Fangirl*. Press is asking if there will be a sequel. Brooklyn smiles, waves, poses, and answers every question with the confidence that attracted me to him from the moment he found me on the front porch of my brother's house.

The red carpet ends and we are escorted into the security tent, where we have to show our identification.

As we wait to move along to the next step in the security line, Brooklyn's hand cinches my waist and he leans forward. His clean scent assaults me and my head automatically turns toward him. When I do, his mouth skims over my jawline and his lips brush lightly over my skin.

Pressing his front to my back, he nips at my earlobe, eliciting a full-body shiver that sends chill bumps racing across my flesh, and whispers, "I am so fucking you in this dress when we get home."

Whoa. That sounds so . . . delicious. I twist a little more and bend my knee, allowing the slit of my dress to open and one of my super-high sandals to show. "With my shoes on?" I ask huskily, the excitement clear in my voice.

"Oh yes," he murmurs. "Definitely with your shoes on. In fact, they'll be the only thing you're wearing when you scream my name."

The line starts moving and our dirty talk is put on hold for what undoubtedly is the biggest night of Brooklyn's life.

Nervous himself, he takes my hand and escorts me through the maze of people. He looks incredibly handsome in his tux, as do Keen and Cam.

Getting the three of us inside took some major string pulling on Brooklyn's mother's part.

Sadly, Makayla and Maggie couldn't attend—not enough tickets—but they are at home with Presley, who is walking and gets into everything now. Television will have to do it for them.

The Dolby Theatre has a ground floor and, above that, three mezzanines. I look up to the never-ending ceiling. This place is huge, and so elegant. Shiny stage, lights everywhere, and seats for miles and miles.

Amid the array of dresses, tuxes, and champagne flutes is a lot of Hollywood chatter. Mostly about which commercial break is best for making a run to the bar. That makes me giggle.

There is a crush to get in, as a disembodied voice tells us urgently that the Academy Awards will start in five minutes.

Finding our row, Brooklyn squeezes my hand even tighter. He is now so visibly nervous that I wish I could sit on his lap and distract him by placing kisses all over his face. Obviously, I can't, so I squeeze his hand and whisper, "You got this."

We sit way in the back with the rest of the unknowns. Brooklyn sits to my left, Cam to my right, and Keen to Brooklyn's left. The four us are intermixed with the entire team from *Fangirl*.

Emma turns from the row in front of us and gives both her sons a warm smile. Taking Brooklyn's hands, tears glimmer in her eyes. "I'm so proud of you," she says, with genuine excitement in her voice.

He squeezes her hand back.

"I love you, Son," she says, her voice thick with emotion.

"I love you too, Mom," he says.

The gap that formed between Brooklyn and his mother over his teen years has been slowly closing. And now she, too, joins us for Sunday dinners. Brooklyn's father, on the other hand, asked for a role in the movie. And although due to Brooklyn's urging he was cast as Kellan's father, he never made it to the first rehearsal.

With the knowledge that his father has to want to help himself, Brooklyn has accepted that he can't be responsible for Todd James. And also no longer fears following in his footsteps. With that, a huge burden has been lifted from his broad shoulders.

Suddenly, the music begins, lights flash, the curtain lifts, and a voice announces, "Ladies and gentlemen, at Hollywood and Highland, it's the Oscars."

There's a slight pause, and Brooklyn wipes the hand I'm not holding down the front of his pant leg. He leans over and says, "I'm here because of you, and regardless of what happens tonight, that is what I will always remember."

As this year's host makes his appearance by running onstage in a pair of jams with sunblock below his eyes and a surfboard under his arm, everyone in the audience reacts positively and screams loudly.

The host erupts into song, a parody of all the movies being presented this year.

With my fingers crossed, I hold on tight to Brooklyn's hand when the first movie star walks out onto the stage to present the Best Supporting Actor award. Next up is Best Supporting Actress.

The host comes back out onstage, now in a tuxedo, and tells us how the nominees become winners. And then two movie stars come out to present Best Original Screenplay. They start by telling us writers are the backbone of the industry, and everyone applauds. They add, "And we also think you are all extremely hot." Everyone chuckles, but I don't laugh; instead I think, *Don't you know it*.

One of the actresses announces, "Here are this year's nominees for Best Original Screenplay."

Five typical Hollywood-type manuscripts flash across the screen and then the room goes utterly quiet.

"And the Oscar goes to . . ." the other actress says into the microphone as she pulls the paper out of the envelope. "*Fangirl*, Brooklyn James."

"Holy shit," he whispers, in a state of shock.

"Oh, my God!" I squeal, tears streaming down my face.

Applause explodes and so does my heart. Still in a state of shock, he turns to kiss me, then to his brother, who hugs him fiercely, and then back to me.

Flashes go off all around us as the music explodes, and as Brooklyn stands he slips a small velvet box from his pocket and sets it on my lap. Leaning down, his voice is raspy and charged at the same time. "This is because of you, Amelia Waters, and I want to spend the rest of our lives writing our story."

Hurrying up to the stage, he is handed the Oscar. Standing there in a daze, he looks around, humbled, and the love and support of Hollywood surrounds him.

Up at the microphone he starts, stops, then starts again. "There are so many people I need to thank for this," he says, and then goes on to thank Ryan Gerhardt, Blake Johnson, Chase Parker, his brother, his best friend, the producers, the cast, the crew. He pauses. "And I want to thank my mother, Emma Fairchild, for showing me you have to work for what you deserve."

The music starts to cue for a wrap-up and Brooklyn holds his hand up. "I have one more person I need to thank, and that's the love of my life. Without her, I wouldn't be here tonight, and I hope when she opens the box I left on her lap, she says yes, and agrees to be mine forever."

Everyone turns in my direction, and my cheeks flame. There are loud cheers and yells of congratulations, but I shut it all out and focus on the one man heading back in my direction.

Tall and handsome, beautiful and amazing, my Prince Charming approaches me, and rather than take his seat, he sets the Oscar on it, gets on one knee in the crowded theater, and opens the velvet box he had set in my lap minutes ago. "Will you marry me? Be my princess forever and ever?"

I look at the sparkling ring. "Oh, Brooklyn. Yes. Yes, I'll marry you."

The host talks to the audience, and we're no longer the focus as the ceremony moves along.

My attention, though, is on Brooklyn as he takes the ring

from the box and slips it on my shaking finger. "I promise," he says, "that we will live happily ever after."

I throw my arms around him and whisper into his ear, "I have no doubts that we will."

Some fairy tales start with you kissing a frog, and then another, and another, too. Some start with you going in search of your Prince Charming, and hoping like hell that you find him. And some fairy tales start with you stumbling upon Mr. Oh-So-Wrong, who was actually your Hollywood Prince all along.

You just didn't know it.

But you do now.

And isn't that the best ending a princess could ever ask for?

I think so.

AUTHOR NOTE

All of the chapter titles are named after movies. There are so many it was hard to come with the best ones.

My favorite movies are *The Notebook*, *27 Dresses*, *How to Lose a Guy in 10 Days*, *Sweet Home Alabama*, and *Because I Said So*.

What are yours?

ALSO BY

NEW YORK TIMES BESTSELLING AUTHOR

KIM KARR

And watch for these titles coming in 2017

Heartbreaker—this is Chase's story
Tie the Knot—this is Cam and Makayla's final chapter